Plane Jane

Robert Fischer

Martin Pearl Publishing
www.martinpearl.com

Published by
Martin Pearl Publishing
P.O. Box 1441 Dixon, CA 95620

First Edition: June 2010

ISBN: 978-0-9814822-4-8
Library of Congress Control Number: 2009941491

PRINTED IN THE UNITED STATES OF AMERICA

10 9 8 7 6 5 4 3 2 1

Acknowledgements

To my wife and best friend, Helga Fischer

Stephen R. Gospe, M.D. and Karin Kotite proofread
Jamie Blair provided editorial services

Cover design by John Hamilton Design

Prologue

THE distant groaning of an aircraft propeller, a familiar sound in an area where coca is grown, did not interrupt the card playing. Few glanced upward as the DC-6 came in for a landing. It was half past three in the afternoon, somnolent time in the tropics, with the humidity close to a downpour. The windsock hung limp on a pole. Tilting his cane chair back and rocking slowly, Juan Garcia decided to wait for the people inside the airplane to come to him. They were obviously gringos. Juan's workers adapted the same quiet insolence as their boss. Garcia could faintly make out the faded markings on the fuselage. *Looks like an Air Mexico retread,* he thought as he idly scratched his mustache.

A man with Mexican features, and a woman whose red pony tail poked out the back of a baseball cap with "Stanford" printed on the visor, descended from the plane. Both wore thin, sweat-soaked khaki pants, and their shirts stuck to their bodies. Garcia could see a gorgeous ass outlined by the woman's underpants.

"What do you want, gringo?" He addressed the man.

The woman answered.

"We tried reaching you guys on the radio. We need gas, so we thought we'd pay you a visit."

"We got gas. I'll send the truck over. You play cards?"

"No time for cards right now," the red head answered. "We've got to pick up some doctors about a hundred miles south of here. We just need fuel, but if you have any more of that beer, we'll buy some."

"Going to a doctor's convention?" Garcia said with a sneer.

The woman ignored his tone. She sensed an edge of danger in Garcia and his companions, but decided to respond with a smile.

"I'm Mary Jane," she said, "and this is Jesus Martinez, my pilot."

Garcia stared at her and continued to scratch his mustache. "Mary and Jesus—like in the Second Coming?"

He gave a little grin. "It's a good thing I've been a good boy all my life. You're a funny lady—I like that. OK, come on and sit. Have a beer. The fuel truck will be back in about half an hour."

Mary accepted the offer by leaping up on the porch and shaking the man's hand.

"Juan Garcia," he said. "I'm the foreman here."

"Foreman of what?"

He waved vaguely.

"The estate. Construction work. Airport maintenance." He shrugged. "Whatever comes up." He glanced at Jesus. "Does he talk?"

"I talk," Jesus said.

"Hey, Mr. Garcia, could you give us a guided tour of this area while we're waiting?" Mary smiled at him sweetly.

"Sure, lady." He winked, pointing to a Chrysler van with its roof and the passenger doors missing. "I'll take you for a drive in our Rolls Royce. Be my guest, huh?" He rocked back and chuckled.

EVERYTHING went as planned. Mary and Jesus got a good look at the airstrip and its perimeter. Their tour consisted of a drive by a banana grove, a scrap yard of airplane parts, and down to the end of the runway, where Mary surreptitiously dropped a small direction-finding radio beacon into the grass. Garcia told them about the presence of a paramilitary group a mile west of the radio shack. He referred to them as "banditos." Mary noted that there were no gun pits or guard facilities near the runway or along the horseshoe-shaped road that curved behind the shack. The road led to the village of Bajos two miles away. Bajos was twelve miles north of the city of Oaxaca, which had become famous as a narcotics center when the city police chief was discovered to be the head of a major crime syndicate.

Mary liked the airstrip's isolation. She also liked Garcia's stupidity.

"Mr. Garcia, do you take care of those airplanes over there?" She said, pointing toward seven aircrafts, ranging from a single engine Piper in need of a paint job, to a massive, box-shaped, heavy-lift transport. She was keenly interested in a sleek Gulfstream IV, a jet generally used to ferry around corporate executives. But, she was careful not to show it.

"Well, my men clean them up before they go out," Garcia

answered. “Fill up the tanks, help with the loading, and clean the inside, that sort of thing. Got to please the rich, you know.” When he smiled his eyes completely closed.

“We’re thinking of leaving our DC-6 here on our return trip, maybe for three or four days. We have business in Bajos. Any problem with that?”

“No, it’s OK. You call me on my cell phone for arrangements. No one uses the radio in the shack, not enough traffic. Bring some beer—Tecate if you can find it. Maybe some Mendoza cigars.” His eyes swept over her body. “We can have a party.”

They continued to talk until the fuel truck arrived. Satisfied with their recon, Martinez climbed into the DC-6 cockpit, revved up the engines and squinted at the sky. He determined that there was less than an hour’s light remaining before sunset.

“Great performance, Mary. You missed your calling.”

“What’s that?”

“Actress, you know-the eternal vamp?”

“Better take off, Jesus. Let’s not press our luck. Take a pass over those banditos and down the road toward Bajos. We don’t want any nasty surprises.”

As Jesus taxied the DC-6 down the runway he noted that, other than a tattered windsock, the landing zones had no markers—no lights and no beacon towers for navigation aids.

“I’ll be in back suiting up,” Mary said. “It will be totally dark in about ten minutes. Drop down to twenty-five hundred feet as you approach the end of the runway. I’ll unlock the rear door, but I won’t open it or jump till you slow to sixty knots. It’s okay if you stall slightly, just make sure I don’t have a hundred knot gust sending me out over bandito land, okay?”

"No problem. When you exit, I'll bank twenty-five degrees and maintain two thousand feet on automatic pilot. Remember—when you're ready to take off in the Gulfstream, don't use the radio. Just give me a bleep on your walkie-talkie. I'll have the rifle in the doorway covering the radio shack and your flight path. Not that I'll have much lock at that distance."

At exactly 8:45, in total darkness, the DC-6 slowed and Mary exited headfirst. She dropped nine hundred feet before opening her parachute, never taking her eyes off the bundle hanging thirty feet below her. From it, a powerful but invisible infrared spotlight beamed down at the ground. As she floated toward earth she used her special vision goggles to scope out the planned drop zone. She landed in the dense ferns that grew along the runway, not more than two hundred feet from the radio shack. With no wasted movements, she pulled a peasant skirt over her khaki pants, covered her head and shirt with a coarse woolen shawl, and fitted a black wig over her red hair. Slinging a potato sack containing her tools over her back, she could have been taken for a village woman walking home from work.

She walked down the runway toward the Gulfstream as though it was something she did every day of her life, and she fought the worry that nagged at her. *These keys better work. I'm not a fan of lock picks...*

No one appeared to be around any of the airplanes and she heard no unusual sounds—no dogs, nothing. When she reached the jet, she scanned the perimeter and then released the holding cables under its tail and wings. Crouching low, she stooped beneath the fuselage and emerged at the cabin door, inserting one of the five keys she held. *Fucking key! Work, work*!

Yes! Grinning to herself, she entered the cabin and closed the door behind her. She flipped on the main switch and saw that the fuel tanks were full and the batteries completely charged. She clicked her handheld walkie-talkie to signal Martinez, who was flying overhead, then hit the starter. The Rolls Royce engines whirred to life, but instead of moving in a forward fashion, the Gulfstream rocked back and forth. *Moron! Forgot to remove the chocks from the wheels*. With engines running, Mary raced outside, removed the blocks that held the wheels in place, and rushed back to the pilot's seat soaking in sweat. She screamed, *Full goddamn throttle—go, you little sweetheart—go, go!* The plane roared down the dark runway with lights out, racing blindly toward the directional radio beacon she had placed at the end of the runway, reaching one hundred-twenty knots before rising into the moonlight sky.

The walkie-talkie crackled. "Sister Mary, this is Jesus. You have sinned—again. Say ten Hail Mary's and I'll see you in El Paso."

THE Mexican caper was just another day at the office for their growing company, Charter Aircraft Leasing Ltd., or CALL, as it was known in the trade. CALL was the outfit you contacted if your firm leased an airplane to a client who decided not to make any more payments and disappeared into the fog of phony registrations and repainted tail numbers. Someone had to find and repossess those aircraft, often from criminals, deadbeats and modern-day pirates willing to go to extreme lengths to hide and disguise their booty. Mary, who liked to refer to herself as a CALL girl, and her partner, Jesus Martinez, often took on the repo jobs no one else could handle. The risks had paid off handsomely: in just three years CALL was bringing in more than $10 million in annual revenue. But, it hadn't been easy in the beginning.

Chapter One

BAD Sherif, the South Gate in the stone wall that surrounds Jeddah's Old City, was the coolest place that Air Force Captain Jesus Martinez could find in the muggy February humidity. He sat at a corner table by a thick wooden façade, called a roshan, which permitted ventilation and deflected the sun. Praying for a breeze, Jesus ordered a hookah pipe and a glass of thick, sweet tea. He would have preferred a snifter of good brandy, but in Saudi Arabia, that was out of the question. The tea was good, stimulating and strong, but the burnt smell of the smoke he sucked in from the pipe unsettled his stomach. He gazed lazily out through the roshan at the parade of goats, street vendors, Mercedes Benz sedans, and heavily veiled women. *Who would have thought that at forty-two I would be sitting in the middle of Arabia wondering if my career is finished, or if a Saudi executioner will lop off my head some Friday afternoon before prayers?* As he sat gloomily pondering his fate, his cell phone rang. He figured the call had to be from his commanding officer, his lawyer, or the Saudi police.

"Hello," he whispered.

"Jesus Martinez…? The guy from San Francisco?"

A few seconds passed as he listened to the voice and then his own voice rose.

"Mary? Major Mary Jane? This is quite a surprise and it's made my day—which, by the way, isn't saying a whole lot. I haven't seen or heard from you since Istanbul."

"I know. You still do transport?"

"Tough times, Mary," he whispered, as though fearful of being overheard. "This place is a rat's nest of intrigue and my ass is on the line." He told her about a possible upcoming court martial. "You can't serve two masters, the CIA and the Air Force."

"What happened?"

"I really can't talk. But I'm in deep trouble."

"I guess you didn't hear about me," Mary said.

"No."

"I got drummed out of the Air Force for refusing to wear the burqua off-duty. It's been in all the papers."

A decade earlier she had flown A-10 Warthogs over Kuwait, busting Iraqi tanks and had enjoyed it, but the fun began to wear thin when the post commander ordered that she wear the Arab burqua headdress that the local women wore. She had complained to her father, General Charles Jane, about discrimination against women in the armed forces. A TV news reporter in Boston got wind of the controversy, interviewed Mary on-air and the story ran on national television. The Air Force brass—including Mary's father—didn't like it and was swift to move. After twelve years in the cockpit, Mary was discharged, with honors.

"I quit reading the papers. I don't hear about much of anything anymore."

"Smart man. Anyway, I'm on my own and better off."

"I'm sure you are." His tone was flat, depressive.

"Listen, Jesus, if you're in so much hot water, why don't you resign?"

"I've thought about it, but they might reduce my rank as punishment for my sins—and I'm innocent. I just flew the wrong cargo to the wrong place at the wrong time. Life is all about timing, isn't it?"

"Pretty much so."

"The Air Force has been my life. I wouldn't know what to do on the outside. I'm like a cop. I've got a lousy civilian mentality."

"Cut a deal with them, take a reduced rank and ask to resign at your current pay grade. That's what I did."

"There's a little problem with the Saudis—I was set up."

"Can't you tell me?"

Jesus looked around. The couple that had been sitting near him had left.

"Recently, I flew General Electric engine parts from a Saudi air base to Abu Dhabi. When I returned, I was arrested by the military police for theft of the parts. It's all bullshit. I was also accused of stealing the parts from the Saudi government. My commanding officer believed me, but that didn't alter the fact that three million dollars in engine parts were missing. The Abu Dhabi businessman who received the parts told the Saudis that a briefcase full of money was given to me as payment.

Which was untrue, but the lie provided the basis for my arrest. In this place, that kind of charge could cost you your head."

"That's some downer."

"Tell me about it. And a non-Muslim's testimony is credited by law with only half the weight of the accuser." He paused and sucked on his pipe. "So this call, Mary, it's unexpected. Do you have something going?"

"I can't talk on a cell phone. Go over to the Sheraton Hotel, use a pay phone and call me back collect."

Two hours later, Mary took his call and explained in detail what she had in mind. Jesus listened with a growing mixture of amazement and unease.

"You're asking me to help you steal a 747 airliner belonging to a prince? Right now all they can do to me is chop off my head. But if I get caught doing this, they'll hang me on the chain."

"What chain?"

"I've heard that some prisoners are hung by the neck to a long chain that's stretched across a room about five feet off the ground. The prisoners are spaced six feet apart and left to stand there until they collapse and strangle. The good news is that the last person standing goes free. Self-torture and certain death—apparently, that's the will of Allah. No, Mary. I can't risk it. I'm in enough trouble already."

The line went silent until Mary said, "This is a simple case of repossession—*not* stealing, by the way. The prince reneged on his payments."

"Who are you repossessing it for?"

"Too many questions, Jesus."

"I'm a pretty inquisitive person."

"What does your attorney say your chances are with the Saudi court?"

"Slim and none. The Saudis are looking for the U.S. government to pay compensation, and then they'll drop the charge."

"That's not likely to happen, is it?"

"No." Discussing the case frustrated and depressed Martinez. "I'm hoping our base commander will set up a court martial as a show trial. Maybe that will ease the tension."

Mary paused, and he could almost hear her thinking through the wire. "So Jesus, can you still fly in and out of the country?"

"Technically—legally—probably. I guess it's possible. Why?"

"This job pays a million five for delivery of the 747 to the U.S. I'm offering you five hundred thousand for your role in this."

"Five hundred thousand," he repeated, trying to get his mind around the figure.

"And there are more jobs like this," she said. "Maybe we could even set up a business repossessing airplanes." When he didn't reply, she continued. "You must know by now the Air Force doesn't give a shit if you resign. In fact, that could be the perfect solution for your problem and theirs. They can convince the Saudis they're taking care of the situation."

"I don't know."

"Your expertise is valuable to me Jesus. Nobody will ever offer you a better deal."

"But why me? There must be a dozen jet jockeys who would jump at a chance like this."

"I don't want to spend a lot of time buttering you up on

the phone. But you were a top pilot during the Bosnian War. We all knew about you. And when you and I spent some time together in Istanbul, I knew you could be trusted. You can just tell those things, Jesus." There had been a brief flirtation, which she thought it better not to bring into the equation.

"I'm blushing."

"You're the guy I want. I admire you as a professional."

"I just don't know, Mary. It sounds risky and risks don't seem to work well for me these days."

"Look, meet me in Paris in two days. We'll talk more then. Figure on spending a week with me. What do you say?"

"Give me some time to think about it."

"No, Jesus, I'm sorry. I need your answer now."

"Then it will have to be no."

After a moment's silence she spoke. "Take down this number. You have a pen?"

"I remember things," he said. "No need to write them down."

She read off a series of digits. "Shall I repeat them?"

He read them back to her and she smiled.

"Mind like a steel trap."

"Maybe a rusty steel trap."

"I'll wait twenty-four hours to hear from you. If I don't, the issue's closed. No hard feelings. OK?"

"OK."

She hung up.

As he sat staring out at the silvery, heated winter air, he thought, *that's the problem with the military. You feel that you're safe, you grow too cautious to buck the system, and you often end up watching your old civilian friends make something of themselves, while you wait for a pension and little pieces of metal to hang on your uniform or on some wall.* Making decisions in the field was one thing, but making a decision that would completely change his life? As Martinez thought about it he could feel his ass pucker. He held his breath and closed his eyes.

Two hours later he called Mary back.

"Okay, let's talk."

"I'm assuming 'talk' means yes."

"I'm in," he said.

"You're not going to regret it Jesus," she said softly.

"Sure," he said. "Then again, it's entirely possible I have a death wish."

"Can you be here tomorrow?"

"No way. If I get clearance to leave base, and that's a big if, I'll need at least two days to arrange things. Tentatively though, pick me up at Orly. I'll phone in the time when I'm in the air."

When Martinez hung up the phone, he was surprised at how heavily he was sweating in the air-conditioned lobby. His mind began to race, examining all the ramifications of his sudden and radical decision to team up with Mary Jane. Part of him thought, *you are going in way over your head, man.* Another part of him thought, *Why the hell didn't you do this a long time ago? You're a forty-two year old man in a rut.*

Chapter Two

THE commanding officer called Captain Jesus Martinez to his office the instant Jesus returned from the Souk. As he approached command headquarters, he wondered if the Army had decided to simply let the Saudi government try him in a civilian court. Asking for time off base was going to require a miracle, considering the legal quagmire he was in.

"Sir, Captain Martinez reporting," he said with a salute.

Lieutenant Colonel Stark stood up, and instead of a salute, he offered Martinez his hand.

"Sit down, Captain. This won't take long." Stark motioned him to a coffee table set. Although he was stunned by this crazy break in military protocol, Martinez showed nothing.

A handshake?

He took one of the two identical tan leather chairs and waited in silence for the colonel to begin.

"Apparently you, or someone connected to you, knows General Charles Jane. I received a call from him an hour ago and he offered a solution to your current situation. Do you know anything about this?"

A flicker of suspicion crossed the colonel's face. He felt compelled to proceed carefully as he had no idea what kind of influence this captain might have with General Jane, who was not a man to be trifled with. Jane had been an ace fighter pilot in Vietnam and had risen through the ranks. He was reputed to be both difficult and a genius. He also owned his own museum of antique airplanes and was independently wealthy.

"No, sir," Jesus answered. "I don't have a clue."

But, of course, he knew full well what had happened. Mary was the general's only child. He had taught her to fly when she was in her early teens, and Martinez assumed that he would worship and spoil his talented, beautiful daughter. Clearly, Mary had pulled strings.

"General Jane wants to avoid a civilian trial in a Saudi court. He thinks it would set a bad precedent, and he believes, as I do, that the charges against you are bogus. He suggested that you have enough time in the service to retire with a pension, and that is the course you should follow. We can arrange your retirement—at Captain's rank, of course."

As a young Mexican, new to the Air Force, Jesus had learned early to mask his emotions. Standing now in front of Colonel Stark, he showed nothing. Nor did he have to think twice. He could normally retire at full pay with time in, but not with legal matters still an issue. This could be considered a gift—a miracle.

"Under the circumstances, I agree that retirement is best. I would like to finish my training duties, though. Can that be arranged?"

Stark regarded him with cold, gray eyes, his thin lips lifted in what might have been amusement.

"General Jane's idea is for you to be discharged and off the base immediately. However, you will be seconded to Air Force intelligence during the next ninety days until your papers come through. Basically, you will be free to come and go as you please. We will advise the Saudis that you have been dismissed from the service and that should be the end of it. If they get difficult, we will press for the arrest of the syndicate that stole the aircraft parts to begin with."

Martinez looked up sharply.

"Sir, what syndicate?"

Ignoring him, the colonel arranged papers on his desk.

"Do we have an agreement on this, Captain? General Jane is eager to move this right along through channels."

"Thank you, Colonel, and thanks also to General Jane."

Jesus saluted and left the office with a bounce in his step and one thought on his mind. *Mary Jane—what have you gotten me into*?

Chapter Three

IT was chilly and overcast in Paris, and even in the heated lobby of the Ritz, Mary felt cold and feverish. She paced impatiently, waiting for the Orly shuttle to pull up to the portico. Finally, an hour late, Martinez jumped out of a taxi and walked quickly to the lobby.

"Reporting as ordered, ma'am," he said, giving her a jaunty salute.

She cocked her head as she stared at him. "You're late."

"Head winds will do that."

"You look older, Martinez."

"Could that possibly be because I am older?"

"Some men grow handsomer with age. Spencer Tracy, Cary Grant, Paul Newman—you..."

"You're going to make me blush."

"You're too dark to blush." She continued to regard him.

"How long has it been since we ran into each other in Istanbul?"

She knew exactly how long.

"Three years—give or take a month or two." He smiled. "And we didn't exactly run into each other."

They had a fling that lasted a week before they both had to report back to duty. She pressed his hand. "It's good to see you again, Jesus."

"It's good to see you, too. At least, I hope it is."

Over drinks in the cocktail lounge, they discussed their careers, both recently terminated, and skirted carefully around that week in Istanbul. After a polite interval of small talk, Mary briefed Jesus on the repossession project.

"A week ago," she said. "I met two British guys—Ian Roberts and Charles Kinsley. My father had once considered buying a plane from them, then something happened, I'm not sure what, and the deal fell through. But the General thought they were decent types and might want to hire me to fly expensive vintage aircrafts at air shows in Europe. I'd done that for the General a number of times—he owns some great old beauties, Stukas, Spitfires, a mint P-38—but I wanted to be on my own. So I contacted Roberts and Kinsley and, after a few weeks, they came back to me with an offer. Not to fly in air shows—much, much more interesting than that. They have a Boeing 747-400 worth a hundred million sitting on an airport tarmac in Jeddah. The prince who bought it—Dani Al-Jabeer, everyone seems to call him AJ—he's made exactly one payment on the plane and the British guys are going ballistic. They're terrified of what their board will do if they don't get that plane back, and they can't get into Saudi without a sponsor's stamp in their passports."

"Are you sure you can trust these guys—Roberts and what's-his-name?" Martinez drew on his cigar.

"Kinsley. Yes. They've given me a down payment."

"How much?"

"Fifty thousand."

Jesus nodded.

"Okay. So go on."

"It's a little hard to figure out why Al-Jabeer stiffed the leasing company. I've done some preliminary research on the guy and believe me, he's loaded."

"Anything else?"

"The cars are not included in the Global lease."

"What's the story about the cars?"

"According to the newspaper, Le Monde, one car is a BMW 740i and it is covered with $8,000,000 in diamonds. It's painted a high gloss black mixed with gold powder and the bumpers, headlights and other metal parts are all done in solid gold. It'll do over 175 miles per hour and has been a contender in some international car races. It's a big attraction and I guess with all those diamonds it's a good idea to have some security. They might have someone just looking after the car. We'll be mindful of that." She continued. "Al-Jabeer bought it in Paris from Prince Al Rashid, another playboy in his own right."

"What about the other car?"

"Another BMW, it's bullet and bomb proof and it has a retractable gun turret in the roof."

"They're not part of the Global lease?"

"No, Jesus. They're automotive jewelry designed for the super rich. They probably make doing business easier and the social advantages are obvious. Look at this picture." She paused, pushing a Le Monde tabloid photo across the table. "That's the Italian actress, Zeta Luna, half-nude sitting in the driver's seat."

"What about the plane? You said it's a 747."

"One of the best Boeing 747-400s built in 2004 as a commercial jetliner. It carries over 400 passengers. According to Roberts, the prince had ridden in a friend's 747 private jet conversion and loved it, so Al-Jabeer bought one and had Inter Jet Interiors of New York outfit it." Mary shook her head, her red hair gathering in glints of bright gold from the light, and smiled.

"Listen to this. The plane has solid silver faucets, a hot tub, four bedrooms with adjustable vibrating queen-sized beds, an entertainment center, exotic wood and gold inlays, showers, and a video conferencing room. They keep the BMW's in the cargo area behind the crew compartment."

"Maybe that's why the guy can't make payments."

"No, Al-Jabeer is rich. Not Arab oil rich, but filthy rich anyway. There's a rumor that frequent parties are held on the plane with high-class call girls from Europe. They're paid a fortune to look after the Prince and his wealthy friends."

"What do the girls consider a fortune?"

"I've been told forty, fifty thousand for a week, plus tips, and tips can run into thousands of additional dollars, according to my sources."

Martinez whistled.

"Maybe that's a new career for you."

"Don't get smart with me, Captain," Mary grinned and punched his shoulder.

"So, where is the plane now?"

"I think it's on the ground in Jeddah. The only thing I know about his schedule, for sure, is the annual Bohemian Grove encampment in Monte Rio, California in July. He attends it every year. It attracts some of the most powerful men in the world, and according to Kinsley and Roberts, he makes that trip in the

747 with a bunch of serious high rollers. It's a safe assumption he'll attend again this year."

"There are no safe assumptions. Didn't you learn that in the Air Force, Major?"

She nodded. "I'm following his movements. Within a week I should know more."

"That's encouraging."

"I don't remember this sarcastic side to you, Martinez."

"It's the onset of old age."

"The thing is, he's not in Saudi Arabia during Hajj, but he'll probably return to Jeddah shortly afterward. In theory, we could make the attempt in mid or late March, say three weeks from now, but I would be more comfortable knowing exactly what his schedule is."

Martinez nodded.

"What are the plane's performance stats?"

"Empty of cargo, which it would be, it has an extended range of a fraction over 8,000 miles and a top speed of 630 nautical miles per hour."

"Not bad."

"This is a very special 747."

"I'd say so. Would you like another drink?"

"If you do."

"I do." After ordering, Martinez said, "tell me more about the prince. What makes him so special?"

"I've heard that he was a minor prince with little money, but with strong connections to the Royal family. He went to San Francisco State to study business administration, but after a couple of years, he dropped out."

"State is not exactly Ivy League." Jesus had grown up in

San Francisco, in a three-room shanty, one of five children, and he had no fond memories of college boys, whom he considered a lower form of life.

"My information is he's a genius when it comes to dealing with people. At college, he made many Saudi and Iranian friends among the students, he threw parties for them and provided them with women. Students from other colleges transferred to State just to be part of Al-Jabeer's circle. This was when Saudi Arabia was on a worldwide buying binge for military and commercial products. They needed people they could depend on in America. Al-Jabeer's credentials were his trustworthiness and his ties to students who were connected to the Royal family."

"The guy sounds really crafty, which may not be so good for us. How did he make his money?"

"The Saudis needed a modern telephone system, and using his contacts, Al-Jabeer brokered the sale to Erickson Electronics in Sweden." Mary smiled. "Yes, he has Swedish friends, too. He had the connections and Erickson had the right system. After he accomplished that mission, he put together the purchase of an anti-aircraft missile system and a battle tank from American companies. Pretty soon, he became the go-to guy for doing business in Saudi Arabia."

Martinez finished his whiskey and raised a finger for another.

"He must be a billionaire by now. Why would a guy like that cheat on payments? You say he has no financial problems."

"To the best of my knowledge—no. But last year, he did sell his $145 million yacht for $90 million. It was just a year old. I searched the internet for news articles on him and found that his estate in London is up for sale."

"Maybe he's just scaling down? Putting his money elsewhere?"

"Maybe. But something is going on. Our job is to get that plane back."

Jesus regarded Mary seriously.

"You realize that being a woman, you're going to be shot, stoned or whipped to death if you get caught. You do realize that, don't you?"

"Yes."

"That's what they do to women."

"I *know*," Mary said with a touch of impatience. "I've factored in the risks."

Martinez felt uneasy. He had flown for people involved in arms trafficking and knew it required a special type of person, someone very dangerous indeed.

"Mary, your research is largely based upon press coverage. This Al-Jabeer guy has the power to control much of how he's perceived in the media. I think you need to factor in the risk that he may be a good businessman and a dangerous criminal."

"I've thought of that. Maybe my reading of this material was partly wishful thinking. I'll be honest with you, I'm more afraid than I want to admit. I've never done anything like this before."

Martinez smiled. "If it's any comfort to you, the prospect of being in Saudi Arabia on a dangerous mission *is* pretty damn scary. It's a dictatorship, you know."

"I'm well aware of it. When I agreed to take on the repossession, I made a lot of assumptions. With my Air Force credentials, it's fairly easy for me to get in and out of Saudi Arabia. But once I got to thinking about actually seizing the 747, I wondered if I was in over my head."

"What we need is excellent intelligence on Al-Jabeer's movements, his security and his itinerary. No mistakes."

"We need more than that. Pictures of his wife and mistresses would be helpful. So would photos of the uniformed personnel around him—pilots, security, domestics, names of hangers-on."

"We need the guy under a microscope," Martinez said.

Mary smiled and raised her glass.

"Time for you to start earning your money, Martinez. Tell *me* what you think should be done."

He nodded. "OK. Let's divide the tasks and see what we can put together in the next week. I've been seconded to Air Force intelligence in Saudi Arabia and I know people there. I'll see what I can dig up. They must have a line on who comes and goes through the main airports. If they'll talk, I might find an itinerary."

"Good. I'll chase down the personnel and mistresses. I hear AJ has several. Also, why don't you see what you can find in the way of a pilot's uniform? Got to look the part." She cocked her head and squinted at him. "You could pass for a Saudi."

"I could pass for a lot of things in any country among the permanently tanned." He rose and dropped twenty Euros into the dish with their bill. "This one's on me, partner."

"The next is on me."

He leaned across the table and kissed her cheek.

"Is that the best you can do?" she said.

"This isn't Istanbul," he reminded her. "This is business."

"You don't believe in mixing business with pleasure?"

"Let's let it play out. That's the best way."

"Okay, Mister Philosopher. I'll heed your advice."

He bowed deeply, mockingly, and left.

Chapter Four

MARY headed straight to Bibliothèque Nationale de France to sift through news articles relating to Al-Jabeer, his wife, children and mistresses, and searched for information on his financial problems. In her zeal to put together a complete dossier on the prince, she worked through the dinner hour. She found that the more she learned, the more intensely she disliked the man. It took some reading between the lines for her to conclude that he was a womanizer and a very high-end dealer of everything from electronics to munitions, with connections worldwide. His press persona was carefully managed. He was seen to be reliable, trustworthy, a high flyer, and someone everyone needed to know.

Loaded down with a stack of photocopied articles, she took the Métro back to the hotel. She ordered a light room service supper, took a long hot shower and lay in bed until sleep came. She began thinking of Jesus, remembering their time together in Istanbul and wondering whether the good things in life could ever repeat themselves.

THE next morning over croissants and coffee in her suite, Mary spread the articles out on the table and told Martinez about her research.

"*The London Herald* essentially describes Al-Jabeer's mistress, Sandy Blair, as a blonde bimbo, but that's tabloid talk. Actually, she's a vice president with the Charter Bank of London, in their international department. Reading between the lines, I'd say she comes off as really smart. *The London Times* hints that our prince is in trouble in America for having paid a kickback on a big munitions purchase. *The Associated Press* is more helpful. They mention two other mistresses. One in New York—a young blonde with no known occupation. The other is a fashion designer right here in Paris, in her early thirties and divorced." Mary looked up and winked solemnly.

"He also has a wife named Safi and one child. Not exactly my candidate for man of the year."

"I'm not sure we're in a position to be judgmental when we're about to steal his airplane."

"Not stealing, Jesus, repossessing. Repossession is perfectly respectable."

Martinez shrugged. "His wife Safi—I've read about her."

"You told me you're not a newspaper reader."

"I used to be. Wasn't she born and educated in the United States?" he asked.

"From a very distinguished, upper middle-class Pakistani family, somehow related to the ex-king." Mary nodded and leafed through her file of clips as she spoke. "Oh, by the way, AJ is not a prince, although some articles make that claim. He's a Sheikh, but the tabloid press likes the notion of his being royalty and that's how it got perpetuated. It makes a better story, and nothing stands in a tabloid's way when it comes to a better story.

"You know, I'm a little surprised that Roberts and Kinsley, our current employers, keep referring to him as a prince. Shouldn't they know better?" Mary looked thoughtful.

"Maybe they read the tabloids. Or then again, maybe they don't know as much about Al-Jabeer as they should."

Mary shot Jesus a quick glance. "What do you mean?"

"I'm not sure. But I promise to let you know when I do." He waved at the rest of the articles scattered across the breakfast table. "Anything else of interest?"

"Not really. Various versions of envy, sour grapes and rank sensationalism. Al-Jabeer is involved in a secret gun running scam with the U.S.; Al-Jabeer is the world's richest man; Al-Jabeer is the playboy of the Middle Eastern world. And so on."

"That's a good start," Martinez said. "You did your homework."

"And did you?"

He bit into a croissant, frowned and pushed the plate aside.

"I thought the French were good at this. I've had better croissants in the Texas panhandle."

"You just can't take the boy out of the panhandle."

He leaned on the back two legs of his chair.

"I went to a couple of high-fashion houses downtown and asked if they could recommend a first-class purveyor of custom made uniforms for my pilots and staff. I got three names, and one was only two blocks away, so I wrote down the address. You have no idea the money rich people spend on the appearance of their staff. Butlers, maids, chauffeurs, pilots and crew, maintenance and security people—you name it."

"How long will it take to get an appointment?"

"I already have one for tomorrow afternoon, late in the day."

"Good work," she patted his shoulder. "You get a gold star."

"My first one. As a kid I spent half my time in the detention room."

"For fighting?"

"Fighting, smoking, cutting class, sassing the Catholic teachers. I was known as an incorrigible."

Mary studied Jesus.

"Did you go to college?" He shook his head.

"Got my high school diploma, though, and I'm damn proud of it. I also spent a lot of time in flight schools."

"You're so smart, Jesus. You should have gone to college. Harvard, Yale, one of the good ones."

"I went into the Air Force instead. That was my prize at the end of the rainbow."

"In Istanbul, you never told me much about yourself."

"We were too busy. Anyway, there isn't all that much to tell."

"Are you married? Have you ever been?"

"Negative to both," he said. He felt uncomfortable talking about his past, but knew that one day, if they did a lot of business together, or did more than business, he would have to unravel aspects of his life for her. He was more than ready to change the subject.

"There's something I don't understand. Why did you decide on meeting me in France? We could have met anywhere."

"I thought you knew. I grew up on the Left Bank. The General was stationed here."

"That still doesn't answer my question."

"I met a lot of people here I liked. Some were close friends of my father. This is the first time I've tried anything like this and I thought it might help to reacquaint myself with people in my old neighborhood. I might find someone who could be useful to us."

"You've been seeing too many Bond movies. I hope you're not creating a fantasy around the intrigue."

"Well, France is closer to Saudi than London is, so for now, just indulge me, okay?"

"Okay. You're the boss."

AT noon, Jesus and Mary took a taxi to Le Bistro du Beaujolais on the Left Bank, where the owner recognized Mary instantly.

"Mary—Mary Jane," she said, kissing her on both cheeks in the French style. "How wonderful to see you. It's been so many years. My God, I can still remember you as a little girl. You took piano lessons across the street, upstairs from Girard's butcher shop. My, my, haven't you grown into a beauty."

"Thank you so much, Bridget. You look the same to me as you did when we left—gorgeous as always."

Bridget Claudette was a product of what Mary considered the old Paris. She did not tolerate drug dealers or users in her establishment. However, she did cater to what she referred to as her regulars—old-fashioned criminals, the ones who held the respect of the police and their elders and who still had the manners to say "stick 'em up" before robbing anyone. Not like the new scum, who were ready to kill regardless of how petty the crime. Le Bistro du Beaujolais had always been holy ground for those who needed the recognition, admiration and camaraderie of fellow criminals, and it was one of the reasons Mary wanted to be there.

"Are you in Paris long?"

"A couple of weeks probably," Mary replied. "I was hoping to catch up with some of our old neighborhood friends."

"You've come to the right place. Everybody who's anybody eventually shows up here. You just missed Peter—you remember Peter Jarbon? He'll be back later."

"Bridget, you haven't changed at all. I'll bet you're the best-known woman on the Left Bank."

She struck a sultry pose and pushed her breasts forward with both hands, still coquettish in middle age.

"Ah! The young ones, they don't know anything about love."

Sitting in the bistro with Martinez over half a bottle of complimentary Montrachet and a sampling of special cheeses, Mary felt that she was truly back home. She gazed at the other customers, looking for familiar faces. A former fencing teammate arrived with two children in a stroller and they kissed and embraced. On the way to the restroom, Mary passed a table secluded in an alcove and recognized three classmates. Thirty minutes went by before she returned to Martinez.

"You're pretty popular around here. And I'm really impressed by your perfect French."

"I loved living in Paris. I never wanted to move to the States."

Bridget personally served them a platter of sweetbreads en brochette with mushrooms and bacon, and cabbage leaves in puff pastry.

"I suggest the Château Cheval Blanc," she said. "It's on ice in the bar."

"Thank you, Bridget."

"And after that bottle, there is another bottle on ice."

Mary laughed and turned to Martinez.

"When we lived here, my parents walked me through the menus of every restaurant on the block. I came to really appreciate the food, the people and the atmosphere of each place. It's so wonderful to be back." She grinned. "If I'd never moved away I'd weigh two hundred pounds by now. The food is just too fabulous."

Two older men entered the bistro and came by to pay their respects. Marcel Brione was a retired house painter that lived in the neighborhood and occasionally gave Left Bank walking tours to visitors. Mary remembered him from years ago, but the other man, Peter Jarbon, she knew more intimately. He had struck up a friendship with the Jane family when Mary was a small child. Jarbon was a street artist who had spent thirteen years in prison for counterfeiting francs and who now created chalk drawings on sidewalks for tips. Both sat at Mary and Jesus' table without waiting to be invited. That was the way in the old neighborhood—no one stood on ceremony. Martinez ordered three flagons of house Burgundy and sat back watching Mary glow with the recounting of neighborhood stories and of old friends remembered.

THE sun was still high in the sky when Mary and Jesus took a cab to the Marquee Costume and Accessories Shop on the Left Bank. Mary, in her flawless French, asked the proprietor what was available in Arab dress and was guided to two racks.

"Madam, so many Arabs come to Paris to enjoy life. We find the men particularly attracted to these." She whisked five hangers of belly dancing garments off the rack as she spoke. "This one is particularly provocative."

Mary shot a glance at Jesus, her lips puckered in a smile. Then, she spoke to the proprietor.

"I'm attending a series of important embassy functions. These won't do, I'm afraid. Let's see if we can assemble a wardrobe an Arab princess might wear."

"That would be the basic burqua, all black, probably silk. Generally, royalty wears a burqua in white with gold embroidery."

Mary turned to Jesus. "What do you think, dear?"

"The choice is yours, dear," he said with a shrug and a straight face.

"I would like one each in white, black and cream," she told the proprietor. "Leave the black one plain, but the others should be embroidered in gold. I'll want them with a series of pockets, which I'll draw for you. Use only the finest fabrics and include an assortment of veils."

"Yes, Madam. May I help you with anything else?"

"Jewelry," Mary said. "Something a prince would give to his wife. Any ideas?"

"You are fortunate to be attending a party in Paris. If it were in Saudi Arabia you would not be allowed to wear jewelry in public."

"I'm not planning to wear it. I'm going to carry it in an elegant jewel box, probably a Gucci attaché case with special slots for the valuables. Every Arab at the party will know what's inside."

Martinez reached for her arm and held it firmly, telling her by the gesture that she was talking too much. She shrugged him off.

"We have some items that should work beautifully," the proprietor said. "But if this is an important event, I would suggest cubic zirconium. To an untrained eye they look like diamonds." The storeowner walked to her desk and quickly scribbled a name on a business card. "This is an excellent wholesaler, Claude Gabin. Tell him you work for me."

"You are very helpful," Mary said. "When can I expect delivery?"

"If you are in a rush, I can have them ready in, say, seven days."

"That's fine," Mary said, favoring the older woman with a brilliant smile.

When they left the store, Mary quickly turned on Jesus. "Don't you dare treat me like a school girl."

"You were chattering too much."

"You just don't understand the relationship between two women, when shopping is involved."

"Probably not. I hate shopping."

"That's such a male attitude."

"There's nothing I can do about that, is there?"

She took his arm.

"I forgive you for being a man. You can't help it." She smiled up at him and squeezed his arm. "I really get the feeling that everything is beginning to fall into place. Don’t you?”

“I sure hope so,” he said.

Chapter Five

EARLY the following morning while Jesus rode a cab back to the Left Bank, something scratched in the back of his mind, but he knew that Mary wouldn't be up until eleven o'clock. While sitting at an outdoor café, he noticed Peter Jarbon sketch a chalk drawing on the sidewalk. Jarbon had struck Martinez as overly friendly at the restaurant the day before. He spoke eloquently and appeared to be well educated. Martinez wondered why he was doing street drawings. What caught his attention was Jarbon's almost constant use of a cell phone. It was unlikely that the man was taking orders for future street drawings. The more Martinez watched, the more fascinated he became. Slowly, a dim recollection began to take shape in his mind. He hurried back to the hotel to meet Mary.

Mary rushed into the lobby.

"Let's go. We're supposed to see the uniform people."

"I was at the Left Bank this morning," Jesus said. "The old man doing the drawings, Peter Jarbon, the guy we met yesterday…?"

Mary nodded. "What about him?"

"I saw him doing his street art, pretty good I'd say. Why is he doing street drawings, though? Do you suppose he's fallen on hard times?"

"It's probably more like a hobby. Maybe he fancies himself some kind of sidewalk Picasso. Let's go, Jesus." She tapped his shoulder impatiently.

Martinez shook his head. "We're going to have lunch with him. On me. My treat."

"For heaven's sake, why?"

"Be patient. Something tells me Jarbon could be valuable to us. It's just a hunch, but I believe in my hunches."

"You're being very mysterious," Mary said with a trace of impatience.

"Just trust me on this." He checked his watch. "It's 11:15. We'll have a bite of lunch with him. All we have to lose is an hour of time."

"But *why*?"

"Come on; let's take a taxi back to the Left Bank. I think I remember something about him."

Jesus paid the fare and took Mary's arm as they strolled over to Jarbon's section of the sidewalk. Martinez pretended surprise at seeing him. He examined the sidewalk rendering of the Eiffel Tower.

"Peter—fancy meeting you again. That's a real work of art."

"Thank you so much for your kind words." He inclined

his head toward Mary and smiled. “I hope you will remember me to your father. We had some good times together while he was stationed here.”

“I certainly will,” Mary said.

“You’re quite a colorist,” Martinez said. He continued to examine the drawing. “How much do you want for it?”

Puzzled, Jarbon rose from his knees.

“I don’t understand. How can I sell it to you? You can’t take the sidewalk away. But I do take donations.”

“We’re going to have lunch across the street at Armond’s. You’re invited, and because people will walk on your masterpiece once you leave, you’re going to lose money. So I’m offering you seventy-five Euros to not finish the work and join us.”

“I would be stupid to turn down such a splendid offer. With my meager pension, how can I refuse?” Jarbon rose slowly to his feet with a grunt and a creaking of his knees. His English was good, with just a shade of a French accent.

Jesus shot Mary a glance, which she quickly interpreted: the man was lying.

Inside the restaurant, Jarbon excused himself and went to wash up. Jesus ordered a good bottle of Bordeaux along with a bowl of fresh fruit and enough appetizers to make a full meal.

“Jesus Martinez, what’s going on?” Mary said.

He smiled and leaned close to her. She could smell bay rum and a slight burning odor, which was not at all unpleasant.

“I suddenly figured out who Jarbon is. This morning it kept nagging at me, there was something familiar about him. Then it came to me as I watched him on his cell phone. He’s a counterfeiter. He was arrested in Munich a year or so ago. Probably more like two years ago, although he was never convicted. I was still reading newspapers then. His picture was in *Le Monde* and when I saw him using his cell phone constantly, it all clicked into place."

Mary frowned.

"He was in prison years ago, but I'm sure he's been clean since then."

Martinez shook his head.

"This was recent."

"Are you sure he isn't just what he seems to be, a foolish old sidewalk artist who cons drinks from tourists?"

Jesus shook his head.

"I've definitely ID'd him, Mary."

"Is he a big time counterfeiter?"

"Seriously big time. And I think he's into other things."

"But it makes no sense. Why is he doing sidewalk art?"

Martinez shrugged.

"His idea of a cosmic joke, I guess. Or a Gallic joke. Maybe he thinks it's romantic to be taken for a poor artisan of objects the rain washes away." Martinez took a sip of wine and nodded in appreciation. "I think his street art is a cover, and I have a proposition for him."

"Like what?"

"If we can obtain Saudi passports or pilot identification papers, I'm guessing he can craft duplicates with our names on them."

"That's kind of risky, isn't it? I mean with his record."

"So what? The reward will be well worth the risk."

It took no more than a glass of wine for Jarbon to feel comfortable. At first he protested his innocence on counterfeiting charges and claimed that he had been on the straight and narrow for years, but after sensing that Mary needed his help, he admitted to "knowing people" who might be useful if she needed anything in particular. After another hour, he admitted that he "knew people" who had a thriving business forging immigration documents of all kinds, along with passports, birth certificates, police clearances, work histories and just about any conceivable kind of official paper that anyone might ever need. The street art, he explained, served two purposes. It created a perfect cover for him—an eccentric old man puttering away coloring sidewalks—and it was also an avocation he loved.

"Tell me," he said. "What gave me away?"

"I used to read the papers," Martinez said.

"Pardon?"

"You were famous a couple of years ago."

"That is true," Jarbon said with a touch of embarrassment. "Infamous, actually."

"Also your cell phone was a giveaway. You kept using it and that made no sense. Then, somehow, I connected the dots. Peter Jarbon, the noted French counterfeiter."

Jarbon finished his glass of wine and Martinez immediately replenished it.

"You didn't bring me here to pass the time of day. What is it I can do for you?"

"We need copies of certain documents. A pilot's identification, a Saudi passport, that kind of thing. Can you help?"

The Frenchman regarded Jesus as he weighed the offer. "You also met my colleague Marcel Brione yesterday. *Avec folie des grandeurs*, but brilliant at his trade. It's too bad he isn't sharing this delightful meal with us. He could tell you everything you could possibly want to know about original documents."

"But isn't he a house painter?"

"Nothing in our world is quite as it seems," Jarbon said with a smile. "Marcel is—how do you say—quirky. You have to know his history. He fought with the French resistance. Nothing new about that. Almost everybody in France makes that claim. But Marcel's story is unusual to say the least. He grew up in Berlin and fought with the Germans at Stalingrad. He was lucky enough to get wounded and that was his ticket out. He was among thousands of French who were brought up to believe in the new united Europe, but later in the War, he became disenchanted with the Germans, deserted and joined the resistance. That's his story anyway. He was only sixteen."

"He must be in his seventies by now. Is he still active?" Mary asked.

"Marcel is into everything. If you need documents, he will have originals stolen for you and I can reproduce what you need. If I vouch for you, he will agree to cooperate. He is simply the best at what he does."

Mary looked into his eyes. "And will you vouch for us?"

The Frenchman nodded.

"You are the General's daughter, my dear. You are a good friend from the past. I trust you. I trust you both. I have been in the business long enough to follow my instincts."

WHEN Jarbon returned to his street art, Jesus and Mary took the Métro from the Left Bank to Montmartre and exited at the Blanche Station. They walked across the street toward the Musée de l'Erotisme on Boulevard de Clichy. Behind it, on Rue Coustou, inside an 18th Century building of red brick, was the uniform maker Albert de Marie. The windows on the left side of the shop featured an assortment of police uniforms on mannequins, complete with gun belts, holsters, badges, name plates, chevrons, batons, caps and raincoats. Inside the shop were commercial uniforms for household maids, cooks, chauffeurs and man servants. There were uniforms for bank tellers, bus drivers, maintenance crews, pilots, air stewards and yachtsmen lining one of the walls. A separate room displayed military uniforms from all the French services and a few German uniforms.

Jesus and Mary approached the center of the shop and stood at a polished mahogany counter, alone except for a young Frenchwoman with her black hair done up in a bun. Seeing them, she approached the counter and rang a small brass bell. Her reserved manner, bordering on the severe, suggested that they should have had the sense to ring the bell on their own. A small man dressed in a dark suit that Mary told Jesus later was something she might expect to see in the Moulin Rouge cabaret, approached.

"What can we do for you please?" He frowned, his thin lips pinched even thinner.

Jesus regarded him with a flat gaze, refusing to react to his subtle arrogance.

"We need new uniforms for our pilots, stewards, drivers and security people," he said. "Only the best will do. If you don't have time, perhaps we can stop in on our next trip."

The man answered with aplomb, sensing the sale.

"Please follow me. I will show you catalogs of uniforms that we have provided to the most discriminating clientele."

He introduced himself as Claude Juillet as he escorted them into his office. Jesus was not interested in looking at stacks of catalogs as if he were shopping for wallpaper and tried to speed the process along. He declined the offer of fizzy water with a wave of his hand. Mary, however, accepted with a smile and a sharp look at Martinez.

"Mr. Juillet, we charter luxury private jets to Middle Eastern clients. We are looking for something that would appeal to a Saudi prince. Perhaps you can show us what you have," Martinez said.

Mary's time at the library had been well spent. She handed Juillet a color copy of a photograph of an Al-Jabeer pilot and the Sheikh in front of a new aircraft. Juillet studied it with a frown. Catalogs rolled off the shelves one after another, and within thirty minutes Mary pointed to one page in particular.

"This looks like it would work," she said to Martinez. "What do you think, dear?"

"I think I'll leave it to you, dear," he shrugged.

"I particularly like the light green," she told Juillet. "I presume the flight jackets are gabardine."

"They are, Madam."

"Very Islamic, especially with the dark green epaulettes and pocket piping." She began the process of putting together a sample order, which she claimed would be sent to Saudi Arabia for approval, but in fact the material and colors were exactly the same as the AJ uniforms.

ON their way back to the Métro, Jesus and Mary passed the Musée de l'Erotisme and Mary suggested they stop in for a look. They both were amused by the collections that featured the erotic passions and practices of generations of Parisians. They were so absorbed that a museum employee had to track them down on the second floor to announce the closing.

As they strolled from their Métro stop to the hotel, Jesus admitted that he had never seen such a variety of sex paraphernalia.

"The sadomasochism, lesbianism, domination—those wine bottles with the erotic themes. I mean the Picard and Wolinski bottles. They couldn't have been more explicit. Maybe I should order a dozen bottles and send them to my Air Force buddies."

"Would they be turned on?"

"I imagine so."

"Were you?"

Jesus gave a slight dismissive shrug.

"Not really."

"I wonder why."

"Don't laugh at my answer, okay?"

"I promise never to laugh at you."

"All I have on my mind right now is a certain 747, a phony prince and a five hundred thousand dollar paycheck. Everything else is sort of beside the point."

"Isn't that a little too focused?"

"I guess it is."

Mary stopped and turned to him.

"You've changed since Istanbul. Three years ago you were so fun loving."

"It was different then."

But that wasn't the reason. The reason was overwhelmingly emotional and complicated. It had everything to do with his late wife Isabel, and there was no way he could tell Mary about her without the real possibility that he would lose his temper. Isabel had been pregnant in her seventh month when she lost the child. In the third year of their marriage, she lost her life in a ski gondola accident in Italy. The moral principle on which he had based his existence died with his subsequent discovery of her infidelities. He often thought about Mary after that, but circumstances kept him from trying to get in touch with her.

"What do you plan to do with your half a million?"

"I have a few thoughts, but nothing is settled."

"Can you give me just one thought?" Mary said, breaking the ensuing silence.

"I might buy a boat in the Caribbean and hire out as a fishing guide."

"Do you know anything about fishing?"

"As a kid, I fished with my father and grandfather on San Francisco Bay. They did it for a living."

"Any other thoughts?"

He smiled at her.

"I'm trying not to fantasize, Mary. Fantasizing is a dangerous habit."

THAT evening, they decided to try a neighborhood bistro. Over a dinner of Sole meunière and a bottle of expensive Pouilly-Foisse, they discussed their progress so far.

"I put a call in yesterday to a friend at Air Force intelligence in Saudi—Skip McFarlane," Martinez said. "I guess the closest military friend I have. He was certain he could find Al-Jabeer's travel itinerary and promised to call me back last night. I still haven't heard from him."

"Don't wait, Jesus. Call him and offer five thousand dollars for solid information. If he asks questions, say we're doing business with one of Al-Jabeer's subsidiaries but are anxious to track him down directly. There's no need to be too specific."

Martinez nodded.

"I'll ask him to email me color photos of Al-Jabeer's flight crew's uniforms. I'm uncomfortable relying on your photo from the library and material samples we saw in a catalog. It could be out of date. I'll tell him we're brokering the deal for the sale of a plane to Al-Jabeer and the plan is to outfit the plane with a uniformed crew done exactly to his specifications. I'll say it's a sales gimmick. He can do all this stuff pretty quickly if he'll just get off his ass."

"The five thousand should help."

"It always does." They sipped in silence.

"This is good, right? Rich and yet subtle," Martinez said.

"It depends. Who's paying?"

"You are. It's your turn."

Mary swirled the liquid in her glass, tasted, bit her cheek and looked thoughtfully at the ceiling.

"Actually it's a little corky."

Jesus stared at her with a frown. "Corky? Are you kidding?"

"Yes, Jesus, I am kidding. Just trying to lighten you up a little."

"Just for that I'm ordering another bottle. On your tab."

"Live it up, Martinez. Tomorrow night you pay and I'm reserving us a table at the Ritz."

Over dessert and coffee, Martinez began again.

"You need to get on the horn to Roberts or the other guy and demand a copy of the lease agreement for that 747 in Jeddah. We don't want to be stopped for some reason and not have legitimate backup. I warned you about Saudi justice."

"OK. I'll insist they fax a copy to the hotel before we go any further," she said.

"They should have given you the agreement when you made the deal with them. That worries me."

"I should have asked."

"That's okay," Jesus said quickly, sensing that she was upset with herself. "We'll sort it out. Let's make a list of things we might need when we get to Jeddah. It would be great to have keys to the aircraft, but we don't. We're going to need a good set of lock picks and a little practice using them. They're not easy to come by."

They worked on plans late into the night. Mary was confident that she could play the role of Al-Jabeer's Saudi wife, Safi, and Martinez would be the Saudi pilot who would fly her from Saudi Arabia to Paris for a weekend of shopping. The burqua would hide her face, and the costume shop would provide a black wig and jewelry of the best quality, lending verisimilitude to her regal charade. In the unlikely event someone at the airport attempted to inspect her, she would be naked beneath the burqua. They would not dare search her, because it is forbidden for a man, other than the woman's husband, to see the body of any woman—especially the body of a princess. It was unclear whether she would need a Saudi passport to leave the country. Given her high rank, customs might not bother to check on the assumption that she would show it upon her arrival in Paris. Of course, their assumption would be wrong because no Saudi woman can leave without her husband's written permission. She planned to use her American passport to enter France, dressed as an American. The Saudi passport was insurance to get out of Arabia. Martinez did not need a Saudi pilot's license or other identification, as foreign pilots were commonly employed in charter service or as private pilots. It was possible to use your own name and claim to be a new hire. Nonetheless, erring on the side of caution, he would carry a Saudi pilot's license and a Saudi driver's license, both stolen by Marcel and reproduced by Jarbon.

"Al-Jabeer's security will know I'm not a new hire. And if you're questioned, it will be obvious you can't speak the language. One of life's little stumbling blocks," Jesus said.

"Not really, Jesus." She smiled mysteriously. "Eucalyptus."

Martinez regarded her with a mixture of amusement and impatience.

"Don't go cryptic on me. I'm not in the mood."

"Eucalyptus is the smell they put in cough remedies. I will have it in my mouth and around my veil. If I'm asked a question, I will use sign motions to indicate that I can't speak. Bad throat infection. *Cough, cough.* How does that sound?"

"Well, it's a plan."

"As for you being a new hire, I'll write out an employment note for you in case anybody asks. After all, I'm Princess Safi. What Safi wants, Safi gets." She did a little lounge-act twist of the hips.

"Add eucalyptus and a prescription from a Saudi doctor to the list. It might even be a good idea for you to carry a letter of introduction from the Saudi doctor to one in Paris. You can't be too careful," he said.

"I have a feeling you are always careful."

Martinez disregarded the comment.

"I'm guessing a lot of Saudi women come to Europe for plastic surgery and don't want to admit it. A referral from one doctor to another might be more common than we think."

Mary nodded. "You have a low opinion of women,

don't you?

"Not of beautiful women. Actually, I approve of plastic surgery."

"For me, I suppose."

"Don't fish."

"Okay, Captain," she said absently as she studied her list. "Let's see—we have lock picks to obtain, a wig, eucalyptus essence, a Saudi passport for me with a French entry visa, ID for you, a wardrobe of burquas, a copy of the aircraft leasing agreement and a box of jewelry. Anything else?"

"You can see by the library photos that Al-Jabeer uses a monogram extensively. If you look carefully, there is one on his pilot's shoulder, although I can't make it out. There also seems to be one on his attaché case. We need copies of it for Princess Safi's luggage, the pilot's arm patch and maybe a ring for me. Speaking of rings, what are you planning to do with all that cubic zirconium jewelry we're buying?"

"We'll have several monogrammed boxes with velvet interiors made up. Each one will contain a three-karat zirconium pendant. They're intended to be a gift from a princess to the right people. Head of security, a customs official, an airport manager—whoever we run into where a little greasing of the palms is needed. Gifts to them in gratitude for all the service they are providing me. Nobody is going to refuse such a spectacular present and the officials are bound to be a little less official, maybe even careless. It's just insurance."

"Throwing them off stride."

"You're so quick, Martinez." She smiled sweetly.

"Add monogrammed jewelry boxes to the list. Out of your end of the cut, of course," he said.

"No way."

"All right, I'm a reasonable guy. We'll go halves. We also need to think about something for your personal protection. Maybe a pepper-spray canister you could carry in one of your pockets. Although frankly, I'd be more comfortable with a pistol."

"Jesus, did I tell you that Princess Safi is a real member of the Pakistani royal family? And she walks with a limp? A bomb blast in Karachi ripped out the front of the limousine she was in, killing the driver and blowing off two of her toes. Pro-Bhutto activists were blamed, but never caught. I got that information from the library. She has been seen with what looks like a tapered ebony walking stick about four feet long. I can have one made with a sharpened point. With my fencing skills, I'll be more than a match for any trouble that comes along. I fenced all through college. I do like the pepper spray idea, though."

"OK, one ebony walking stick and a canister of pepper spray to add to your list."

"Wait a minute, just hold on. Why does the woman always keep the list? *You* keep the stupid list."

"Sure," he said as she pushed the pad his way. "I'm easy."

"You are also outranked."

"You mean, I was."

"In my mind you still are and always will be...Captain."

"Whatever you say...Major."

She touched his arm.

"Hey, Mister Serious. You're fun in a really weird way." She turned the list around and studied it with a frown. "All this stuff should be sent to a post office box in Jeddah. It wouldn't be a good idea to have it with us entering Saudi

Arabia. Too much to explain."

"Some things we can buy in Jeddah at the Al-Basateen shopping center," Martinez said. "A Hajj belt for your U.S. passport and money, plus the fancy luggage Princess Safi will take to Paris. You'll also need a separate purse that you can carry in your hand for your Saudi passport and local Riyals. We'll need to get that and the luggage monogrammed there."

"Let's not stay in an Air Force facility," Mary said. "I know it's cheaper, but if something goes wrong, I don't want to involve them."

"Your father, the general, would not approve."

"He definitely would not. The downtown Jeddah Sheraton Hotel on North Corniche is only nine miles from King Abdul Aziz Airport. It's fancy enough to have a limousine take us to the airport without drawing attention—although maybe the limousine should pick us up at the shopping center. We need to do this in style."

"I've been thinking about a security man's uniform," Martinez said. "You know how the Arabs are. If Princess Safi or any woman is seen with a man in public who's not her husband, watch out. It could mean handcuffs and a very small, very dark cell. A guard's uniform might avoid a potential issue, and I can change into my pilot's uniform at the airport."

"Add one security uniform and badges," Mary said.

"We're meeting with Jarbon in two days to give him our need list. He hasn't mentioned a fee for his services—and Brione's. I'm sure they won't come cheap."

"I agree. My guess is twenty-five thousand."

Martinez nodded. "We can live with that. One thing neither of us has thought about is the cockpit layout. When we get back to the hotel, I'll download Microsoft's Flight Simulator. The 747 will be on it and we can practice."

"I can hardly wait."

"Are you being sarcastic?"

"You're the boy in this partnership. *You* play with the flight simulator."

Chapter Six

TWO days later, before their morning meeting with Peter Jarbon, they stopped by the costume shop to pick up Mary's Arab clothes and a black wig. With profuse apologies, the proprietor explained that the current transport strike had left her two employees short and their order wouldn't be ready until the following week. Mary started to complain, but Martinez intervened.

"Rule number one," he said, as they left the store. "Don't sweat the small stuff. Things are going to go wrong. Just hope that the big things don't go wrong. Like the plane won't be where it's supposed to be. Like your two English friends decide to screw us. Like Al-Jabeer finds out about us and has us killed. Save your energy for real contingencies."

"Don't lecture me, Martinez."

"Okay, let's make a deal. I don't lecture you; you don't act like a spoiled matron with the help. It's best to slide in and out of things without making ourselves conspicuous."

Jarbon met them at Le Vieux Bistro, but Marcel Brione was not with him.

"Marcel sends his regards," Jarbon said with a bow to Mary. "He says that your problem will be taken care of."

"If we strike a deal," Martinez added.

"That is correct."

They moved to a table in the rear of the restaurant and ordered coffee and an assortment of French pastries. A small boy came by the table selling chocolates. Jarbon brushed him off the way you might brush off an annoying fly.

"If you don't mind, please don't show me the list at the table. Just give me the general idea. When we're leaving you can place the list in my newspaper," he said.

"That's very cloak and dagger," Mary said with a smile. "My father would approve."

"He loves intrigue, doesn't he?"

"Yes, very much."

"Just an obvious precaution," Jarbon told her. "The police are beginning to lose interest in me. I don't give them any reason to be suspicious. Marcel also knows how to handle the police, and that's why he's not sitting with us. He plans to accidentally run into us while he walks his dog—" Jarbon checked his watch, "in about twenty minutes. I am rarely seen in public with Marcel."

"We need to lay out some ground rules," Martinez said.

"Yes, of course."

"We hire your expertise to secure certain things for us, no questions asked."

Jarbon nodded. "No questions asked."

"Another thing. We should set the price before we go on."

"I cannot do that without Marcel present. We can wait."

Martinez glanced at Mary and an unspoken message passed between them. Martinez nodded as though she had spoken. He leaned forward, close to Jarbon, and began to run through the list of items from memory. Al-Jabeer's name surfaced for the first time and Jarbon showed a slight flicker of surprise.

"Al-Jabeer is a big fish, a very big fish indeed."

"That's what we understand."

"I know he has offices in Paris, London and New York," Jarbon said. "You should visit the Paris office. You can probably pick up company brochures and an assortment of flyers advertising products the company represents."

At that moment, the same little boy who had attempted to sell them chocolates returned to the table and spoke to Mary.

"Madam, please accept these chocolates as a gift from Marcel Brione." The boy spoke a kind of gutter French, which Jarbon translated for Martinez's benefit.

Surprised, Mary took the box and thanked the boy in French. When she opened it, she was stunned to see her wallet and passport inside. Instinctively, she reached for her purse; it was still hanging on the back of the chair.

"We decided to have a little fun with you and to show you that we know our business." Jarbon chuckled at her discomfort. "You see, it is not so difficult to acquire what you want when you know how. Marcel will join us in a minute."

"I thought he didn't like to be seen in public," Mary said, fighting to regain her composure. She glanced at Martinez who shrugged as though to say, let's play this out.

"He makes exceptions. Marcel is not too old to appreciate beauty."

At that moment Marcel Brione appeared, carrying a white toy Poodle in his arms. He scratched the dog under its chin.

"Allow me to introduce Gigi, my current flame."

Mary gave Brione a somewhat cautious smile as he sat beside her.

"Thank you for returning my wallet, Marcel."

"I hope you forgive my little parlor trick. Peter says that I'm very juvenile for an old man."

"Well, I don't think I'll hook my purse on the back of a chair anymore."

"Then you have learned a valuable lesson, Mary."

"I need five minutes alone with Marcel. Is that acceptable to you both?" Jarbon said.

Martinez waved a hand dismissively. "Fine with me."

Mary and Jesus watched the two men talking quickly and earnestly in the street, clouds of vapor flowing from their mouths, and when they returned, Brione quickly got to the point. He explained that he could provide Mary with a Saudi passport as Princess Safi, and Martinez with AJ International Security identification papers. He could also help with any other documents they might need.

"We haven't discussed money. Maybe this is the time to see if we can afford to do business with you," Martinez said.

Brione's eyes narrowed as he regarded Martinez for a moment before answering.

"You Americans have an admirable way of getting right to the point, don't you?" He sipped coffee and studied Martinez over the rim of the cup. "We find ourselves in a rather difficult situation and you could be of great service to us."

"How is that?"

"Would you rather discuss money first?"

"It's your dime, Mr. Brione."

"Pardon?"

"He means you have the floor," Mary said.

The Frenchman nodded and flashed a brief grin.

"Peter and I have been discussing this matter and it has occurred to us that we are in a position to turn this entirely around."

"You're being mysterious," Martinez said. "Turn what around?"

"Normally, for all that you need, and even for support that you may not realize you need, our price would be one hundred thousand Euros."

The table fell silent. Martinez looked at Mary and an unspoken question formed between them: Are we in over our heads? Is this league too big for us? He turned to Brione, but before he could ask what the Frenchman meant by "normally," he continued.

"Perhaps you recall a television documentary about a French construction contractor who was prevented from leaving Saudi Arabia. It was aired a few months ago."

"It's not familiar to me," Mary said.

Martinez shrugged. "I don't watch television or read newspapers. I used to read newspapers, but it seemed to become increasingly pointless."

Mary shot him a sharp look, as Brione continued.

"In any case, as you know, all business people going

into Arabia must have a Saudi sponsor. The sponsor's name and authorization is stamped into the person's passport. If the sponsor is a crook, he can claim the business visitor cheated him or there's a contract dispute and have the visitor's passport seized. Without the sponsor's release, the person can spend years in jail, or if he's lucky, rotting in a hotel room waiting for the outcome of the dispute. Not great options. Most Saudi businessmen are honorable and ethical—more so than in France, in my opinion—but there are some that use the sponsor's power to extort more out of agreements than was originally intended."

Martinez lit a cigar and regarded the Frenchman.

"Where are you going with this?" he asked.

"Bear with me a moment longer. Our interest is in a Marseille construction firm called Sepi Limited. It recently won a contract to build a hospital and a floating dry dock in Saudi Arabia. The contract price was $112 million dollars. Sepi had completed more than half the work when suddenly, the local sponsors demanded a $15 million kickback on top of the $10 million they had already received. Such a demand was impossible, and the construction company officials, including Peter and myself, refused to pay. Our friend and partner, Pierre Picard, is essentially being held there. He has freedom of movement, but is not allowed to leave the country.

"We have entry passports made out for him—to countries such as the U.S. and Sweden that he might escape to—but obviously, we can't mail anything to him. If the documents were intercepted, he would be accused of conspiring to circumvent Saudi laws and would disappear into a dungeon, or worse. We can't use the French Embassy because the television coverage made the matter too high profile. If the Embassy was to help him in any way, and Pierre escaped, the event might trigger the cancellation of French development contracts in that country." Brione sighed and sipped his coffee. "If this happened anywhere in Europe, we would have had the Saudi sponsors…we would take measures to fix the situation. But our people have no power or connections in Arabia."

"Your people," Martinez said.

"Colleagues," Jarbon put in. "Associates."

"Let me see if I'm clear on what you're asking. You want us to carry a passport into Saudi Arabia and arrange for this guy Picard to escape with us when we leave in the Boeing 747. Is that about right?"

"That is the proposition. Of course we cannot have him back in France until the matter cools down, and since you are going to America we thought he could go along for the ride."

Martinez nodded but said nothing.

"I have a feeling there's a lot you're not telling us," Mary said.

"Absolutely," Brione said with a smile as he conducted a slow survey of Mary's body.

"We don't mind not knowing everything," Mary said. "But we're not looking for trouble."

"You will receive no trouble from us, Mary," Jarbon said. "On my honor as a friend."

"So he will need an American passport, right?"

"As I said, that has been taken care of," Jarbon said. "You have to understand that we have been working on this problem for quite some time. When we learned of your plans just now, we saw an opportunity. It's not often that two parties can seek and find mutual satisfaction. Call it serendipity."

"You say that Picard is part of your operation," Martinez said.

"That is correct. And also a close friend."

"Is it okay to ask about your connection with Sepi?"

"Marcel and I, and a consortium of which we are a part, own a controlling interest. You see, much of the money made by us in France must find its way into legitimate enterprises, and with this in mind, our group purchased Sepi Construction. Thanks to Pierre Picard, we became involved with Ibriham Development, a Saudi construction firm. A minor prince, with lots of contacts but no expertise, owns it and it looked like a great deal for us at the time. We were embarrassed to learn that we had entered into a contract with crooks."

"Now that is an irony," Mary said with a smile.

"There are crooks and then there are *crooks*, my dear," Jarbon said, unruffled by her comment.

"Pierre, by the way, can be very useful to you. He speaks fluent Arabic and English, and he is one of us. We will always be grateful to you for what you are about to do," Brione said.

"We haven't agreed to anything yet," Mary said. "My partner and I have to talk this over."

Martinez turned to Jarbon. "Why are you being so open with us about your activities? That puzzles me."

"There is the obvious reason. As you are aware, I am an old friend of the Jane family. And then there is an additional reason. I believe in leaps of faith. French Catholicism is still in my blood, and character counts for a lot in my value system. Trust does not come easily to me; I've lived too long for that. Mary, of course, I have no qualms about. And you, Jesus, impress me as both honest and forthright." He smiled. "I hope you don't prove me wrong."

Brione interrupted. "Perhaps it's time to discuss your compensation."

"We are willing to listen to whatever you're proposing," Martinez said.

Brione sipped his coffee and studied Martinez over the rim of the glass.

"Americans usually get right to the point when it comes to discussions of money. I admire your patience. Here is what we are prepared to do. We are willing to offer you two hundred thousand dollars to take on this assignment. Half when you leave for Saudi Arabia, and the remaining one hundred thousand when you arrive in America. And, of course, you will receive all documents we create for you as part of the bargain. Call it barter, an ancient economic system I heartily approve of."

"You're offering a lot for the safe passage of one man," Mary said, after a pause.

"The man is very important to us," Jarbon said.

Martinez glanced at Mary and again an unspoken message passed between them.

"I believe we'll accept," he said, still looking at her. "That is, if you agree, Mary."

She turned to Brione.

"Do we sign anything?"

"Our signature is the shaking of hands," the old Frenchman said. He raised a finger to the waiter. "We will toast our mutual success with the very best cognac this establishment has to offer."

Chapter Seven

BY the time they arrived back at the hotel, the Global Aircraft Leasing Company contract was in the fax machine and Mary tossed it on the table. Still thinking about their afternoon meeting, she posed a question to Jesus.

"I wonder if Sepi Construction is continuing the work they were contracted for in Saudi."

"I don't know. What difference does it make?"

"My guess is, the work is continuing. Once Picard is out of Saudi, though, I wouldn't be surprised to hear that some of Ibriham Development's people are captured in Italy or some other country and held for ransom."

"Or show up missing. Did you catch Brione's comment? In Europe he would have taken measures to fix the situation. Did you notice his hesitation? I think he wanted to say he would have them killed. That gave me pause. We're playing with some serious people here," he said.

"You read about this kind of thing in novels," Mary said. "I never imagined I'd be part of the drama."

"Let's hope you're not. Better to stay in the wings than to be on stage." Martinez picked up the leasing agreement and quickly read through it.

"Everything seems in order," he said. "According to this, Al-Jabeer has missed his last six monthly payments." He frowned as he studied the fax.

"Something still bothers me. I can't understand why Al-Jabeer is leasing the plane. Rich guys get off on owning things—especially big toys."

"I don't know. Maybe there's some kind of tax benefit to leasing."

Martinez gave the agreement to Mary who filed it in her briefcase. He lit a cigar and sprawled back in a chair.

"Anyway, it's none of our business, right? Global gave us a down payment and it's up to us to deliver the plane. It's as simple as that. So now let's go out."

"What do you have in mind, Captain?" Mary asked.

"The Latin Quarter, Major. I hear there's a large Arab community nearby. It might be a good time to try on your wig and Arab bag-lady costume for practice in public."

THAT evening, they took a taxi to the L'Etoile du Berger just off the Rue des Carmes. Mary sat in the rear seat of the taxi and Jesus in front. When it stopped, Mary exited first to open his door. She walked with a limp and slightly behind him as they entered the restaurant, carrying his briefcase in one hand and her recently purchased cane in the other. As she played the role, Mary could feel her frustration rising. Martinez whispered to her.

"It must be hard to see through that thing. It looks like some kind of grill. Can you breathe OK?"

"Get lost, Jesus," she whispered.

"My. Is that any way for a good Arab woman to talk to her superior half?"

"How can anybody wear this shit on a regular basis? It's humiliating and uncomfortable. There's no peripheral vision and I have to turn my body to look sideways."

"I believe it. I saw you bump into that table at the entrance."

As it happened, the restaurant, on that evening anyway, was populated with locals and tourists. There was not another Arabic couple in view. The fashionably dressed women at the bar stared at Mary, who was covered in a baggy dark black burqua. Some whispered to friends as she sat drinking wine out of a coffee cup, lifting her veil to sip and being careful not to reveal any part of her face. She overheard a man saying something about Islam bringing back the 12th century to people stupid enough to believe in it. She could see something between pity and loathing in the eyes of other patrons as they studied Martinez, whose dark hair and swarthy complexion lent him an Arabic look.

"I don't think our act is going over well," she said.

"Maybe too well. I may get punched out before the evening's over."

"I would like to rip this crap off me. I hate it."

"Drink your wine instead—I mean coffee."

"I need to go to the bathroom. I piss a lot when I'm angry."

"I guess that's what is meant by being pissed."

She rose to leave but forgot her cane. Martinez stopped her.

"Madam, your walking stick."

In the restroom, she overheard two women with Midwestern American accents whispering.

"I think it's a man under that hood," one said to the other with no attempt to moderate her voice. Mary was furious, but, given the neighborhood, a slumming haven for the rich out on the town for a few thrills, she thought their speculation was justified.

She returned to the table and noticed that several people were staring at Martinez. He seemed serenely unaware.

"Master, have you ordered something humble for me?" Mary whispered. "A bowl of rice would be sufficient, if you deem me worthy."

"Well, we have a good idea how Western society reacts to the way you look." He smiled. "And by the way, your sudden humility is a real turn-on. It's sexy. I could get used to it."

"Bastard."

"There, there. Arab women do not sass their men. They know what's coming to them."

"Just wait 'til I get you alone," she hissed with humor.

The meal was good and they were both hungry. Mary suggested that Jesus wear a 12th century European outfit when they went shopping in Jeddah.

"I wonder how the Arabs would treat someone who looked like he was going to a costume party. Probably have him arrested. Serve you right," she teased.

"Arab woman jealous of Arab man."

"Stop it now, Jesus. That's enough."

"Come on, let's get out of here. These tourists have had an eyeful for one night. We can take a stroll in the square—with you behind me, of course."

When they left the restaurant, Mary walked in front of Martinez out of defiance. To him, she looked like a shapeless black bag moving along the sidewalk, swaying from side to side. Her very being is deliberately hidden, he thought, less worthy of public respect than an ordinary goat. He searched the non-descript moving blob for hints of a familiar curve. Two blocks later, he observed Mary posing or exaggerating her movements, perhaps trying to express her femininity inside the bag. He noticed that she had begun to walk with a glide to her step, and when a breeze came up she stood immobile to allow the fabric to embrace and outline her body. If an Arab man became aroused by such a pose, he thought, he was within his rights to beat the woman for causing it. Mary had resigned from the Air Force for a number of reasons, but partly to avoid having to dress in these servile costumes. Yet, here she was, stuck in the black bag anyway. It was part of the job; that was the irony. He quickly approached her and tapped her on the shoulder.

"If you promise to wear a burqua on a regular basis," he said. "I'll marry you."

She whirled on him, her hands on her hips.

"You are unbelievable."

"So I've been told."

"All men are vain."

"I've been told that, too."

"I think I could grow to hate you, Martinez."

"No, you couldn't," he said, laughing. He threw back the heavy hood and studied Mary's face. "You look good with black hair."

"It will be red again soon, thank you."

"I'll say this for you, Major. You're a trooper. Most good-looking, self-respecting Western women wouldn't be seen dead in this mess."

"It's the money. The things we do for money."

Martinez pulled her toward a waiting taxi. A mist of rain and ice had begun to fall on the city. Evening had brought to Paris a checkerboard of light and dark—lighted street lamps and windows, and dark buildings below a slightly darker sky.

"I hope we're not in over our heads," Martinez said.

The taxi was poorly heated and Mary shrugged tight inside of her burqua.

"Well, if we are, we're in over our heads together."

Chapter Eight

DURING the next two weeks, the "747 project," as they referred to it, moved slowly forward. Martinez's pilot uniform, done in pale green with dark green epaulets and pocket patches and with the AJ international logo in gold on the lapel, had been delivered. But then it had to be returned for further alterations—the waist was four sizes too large. Two monogrammed security uniforms, including pistol holsters, were already packed away in plastic. One was for Martinez and the other for Picard, tailored to Jarbon's best estimate of Picard's measurements. Also delivered on time were six burquas, a white maintenance crew jumpsuit marked Saudi Arabia Airlines, and three maintenance coveralls, two green and one orange, marked King Abdul Aziz Airport. French and American passports for Picard were in an envelope which also contained business cards indicating that Jesus Martinez represented Guardian Flights of Paris. The telephone number on the cards was an answering service. The jewelry had been deposited in the hotel safe, and the hotel desk had sent packing boxes up to their suites for the items being shipped to Jeddah. Most of the items on their list were ready. They were only a week behind their original schedule.

Mary came to Martinez's hotel suite, holding in her hand Air France tickets to Saudi Arabia.

"Three days to go, Jesus, and we're out of here. We leave at twenty-one hundred hours. Since it's a night flight, we'll be able to see the oil fields flaring their gas. It's an awesome sight. The fields light up like hundreds of giant candles."

"I've seen it more times than I care to remember."

"Me too. But the view still gets to me."

"To each his own. I equate Mid-Eastern oil fields with war and starvation."

Mary took that in and then spoke. "We'll be traveling first-class, but not sitting together. I think we should both wear our Air Force uniforms."

"So we really are doing this," Martinez said. "It's not a dream, right?"

"Definitely not a dream. We need to call Peter and meet with him and Marcel one more time before we leave. I just want to make sure everything's covered."

"By everything, I assume you mean Picard."

"Picard—yes…"

"Does he worry you? If Jarbon and Brione are willing to pay all that money, there may be some serious hitches. Maybe things we don't know and should know."

"Have faith, Martinez."

"I'm not much good in the faith department."

THE following evening, they met the two Frenchmen at Le Vieux Bistro for a late dinner.

"You look worried, Captain," Brione observed as they studied their menus. Martinez nodded.

"I haven't been sleeping well. The actual taking of the 747—so much could go wrong. I'm depending on a friend to provide me with Al-Jabeer's itinerary, maintenance record and perimeter security layout. He hasn't come through yet. That could mean all kinds of problems."

"What kind of problems?" Jarbon said.

"Well, for starters, getting off the ground."

"Can you be more specific?"

"There may be cable locks securing the plane to the tarmac. My friend is supposed to provide me with special cutters. It's possible the plane is equipped with a thruster lock—it's like a metal box that fits over the throttle, or a square one fitting over the thruster levers. Worst-case scenario, we need a set of lock picks that are no thicker than toothpicks. With practice, we can use them to spring a lock quickly, but the hitch is Mary and I don't have much time to practice, so let's hope we don't need them. The airport will be swarming with Saudi guards. And any successful outcome assumes my Air Force friend delivers the tools on time."

Martinez lit a cigar and blew smoke toward the ceiling.

"I'll be glad when the French invoke some smoking rules," Mary muttered.

Jarbon smiled sympathetically.

"There's this new tool," Martinez said, ignoring them both. "A thin flat syringe-looking device—the latest in lock-picking technology. It's a CO2, or compressed air cartridge. You insert the flat shaft into the lock and push a button. The explosive release of compressed air will force the lock tumblers to rise and open most anything that's not supposed to open. I'm not going to say it works every time, but if it doesn't, I'll still need a set of special picks to work with. My friend is supposed to deliver CO2 cartridges. I'm still waiting."

"Well, at least we can give you some good news," Brione said. He pushed a package across the table to Martinez. "Inside, you'll find two Chase Manhattan credit cards. There is a prepaid credit of one hundred thousand to your accounts, and another hundred thousand will be transferred when Pierre leaves Saudi Arabia and arrives in America. Your billing address is in the Cook Islands. No one will ever know you have been paid these sums. Here is a business card with the name of our contact there. If you need offshore business matters handled, we recommend him." He placed the card in Mary's palm. She studied it.

"You really want Picard out of Saudi Arabia in the worst way, don't you?"

"The very worst way," Brione answered. "But we also want what is mutually beneficial for all of us. After all, we may do business again in the future."

"I also have something for you," Jarbon said, "which I'll deliver to your hotel. It's a cell phone that is designed to make one call only—a call to us. Press the redial button and we will receive the call. It will signal that you are in trouble and cannot otherwise contact us. We will mobilize lawyers and other assets to help you immediately. Seven minutes after you push the redial button, the telephone will explode unless you press the number nine. It's a gadget we obtained from the Israelis. They are a smart bunch, aren't they?"

"Don't tell the Saudis that," Martinez said.

THE Air France flight to Jeddah was uneventful. When they arrived in the ancient city, humid and clammy even in late winter, it was still dark. Martinez was the first to go through customs, Mary followed and there were no problems. Both noticed the usual post—9/11 focus on incoming luggage, but they were carrying little. As they were being processed, they witnessed an argument between a customs official and an American businessman who was trying to bring in a sample desalinization device. The official insisted it was a distillation machine used for making whiskey. Although the official could read English, he apparently had no idea what desalinization was. The American demanded that the official produce someone who could speak and understand English. He refused and instead called over the Mutawa, or morals police. They began to beat the businessman with truncheons. Martinez came close to intervening, but Mary held his arm in a tight grip and they hurried out of the airport. In the taxi to the hotel, Mary leaned over and whispered.

"These people are crazy. That guy was completely innocent."

"It doesn't always matter here. Innocent, guilty—it can all be the same. They're probably thinking of those two guys they clapped in jail for making whiskey in a small still. Remember that case?"

"Vaguely. What will happen to them when the case gets heard?"

"They could get the death penalty. Beheading in the square on a Friday. They're British and that isn't good."

"This is an awful place."

"Not really. There's a lot of history here. It's the madness on the part of some that ruins everything. Last year a woman was given a hundred lashes when she was raped by a gang of Saudi youths. I don't remember if the whipping killed her, but I do remember that was about the time I stopped reading newspapers."

The downtown Sheraton Hotel's eleven-story twin glass structure loomed ahead.

"This is where the rich and famous stay when they're in town. I plan to enjoy it. A few weeks ago, I didn't know if I would be a guest in one of the Saudi prisons or have my head lopped off in the square," Martinez said.

"Lighten up, Jesus. We still have to figure out if I can walk around in Western dress inside the hotel or if I have to wear the black bag."

"A burning issue."

"You're damn right it is."

"Let's just stay with tradition. If we leave the room, you can wear the bag."

The hotel provided them with adjoining rooms on the ninth floor looking toward the Red Sea and the Old City. Major Mary Jane registered in suite 914 and Captain Jesus Martinez in suite 916. Their packages would not arrive from Paris for three more days, and they did not expect to hear from Pierre Picard until some time the following day. Once they were settled, they met in Mary's room.

"I think I'll telephone Charles and Ian in London and tell them I've arrived in Jeddah. I imagine they would like a progress report for their money. They gave me a cell phone to use before I left," she said.

"Don't even think about it," Martinez responded abruptly. "I'd rather not let anyone know where we are or what our plans are. We're still not sure they can be trusted. There's just something fishy about them."

"You're overly suspicious, Jesus."

"With what we're doing, you can't be overly suspicious. And that telephone they gave it to you thinking you might need to make a free call? No way does that make sense. Get rid of it. I hope you haven't used it already. Our only obligation is to notify them when the plane arrives in America, and where."

Mary hadn't given much thought to the cell phone. She was upset with herself that she hadn't been more suspicious. It was clear that Jesus was more street-smart than she was, and it threw her off balance. A certain naiveté clung to her—my white, all-American innocence, she thought disgustedly—and made it increasingly difficult for her to feel that, having contracted with Martinez, she was still in charge.

"The only time I used it was when I called you in Jeddah from London. So if there's anything sinister, all they have is your number."

Martinez nodded, his mouth tight.

"I'll have my mobile number changed. Another thing, while we're on the subject. I don't like the telephone that Jarbon gave us either. The fact that it explodes after pushing the redial button is taking our enterprise too far. I don't know what those guys are into, but we're pilots, not commandos. If repossessing an airplane results in someone being killed or injured, I don't want any part of it."

"Me neither," Mary said. "We can give the phone to Picard. If he doesn't want it, we can get rid of it."

"Get rid of it, Mary. That's the safest thing to do. It's just another complication we don't need." He yawned. "It's been a long day, night, whatever, and I don't know about you, but I'm beat. I'm going to get a few winks. Lock your door from the inside. Some bad vibes are reaching me from somewhere."

Chapter Nine

PIERRE Picard had watched Mary and Jesus arrive at the Jeddah airport. He wanted to make certain they had no problems with Customs and that they were not being followed by Saudi security. He trailed behind them in his rented Mercedes sedan and, when they arrived at the Sheraton, he listened as they registered in separate, but adjoining rooms. Satisfied, he telephoned Paris to report that everything had gone smoothly. He then checked into the hotel and was issued a key for room 812.

Picard was a handsome man in his early 40s, often involved in love affairs, but never married. He enjoyed the travel and challenges of foreign assignments and had become fluent in Italian, Arabic, Spanish and English. He was, by nature, a wanderer. His father, Colonel Charles Picard, had been a founding member of the Organisation de l'Armèe Secrete, or OAS, dedicated to keeping the French colony of Algeria from becoming independent. Pierre was born in 1959, the same year that

President Charles De Gaulle permitted Algerians to vote for independence. Algerian nationalists murdered Pierre's mother in 1962 during a riot. Filled with rage and despair, Colonel Picard returned to France with his son and participated in a failed assassination attempt on De Gaulle outside of Paris. With the OAS coup in disarray, he fled to Marseilles and, with secret help from sympathizers, he disappeared into the underworld of the criminal elite.

Young Picard spent his youth in boarding schools. Although he had little contact with his father, he did inherit a hatred for De Gaulle and the French government, a strong sense of military honor, and the ability to shred the center of a target from a distance of 1,500 yards. He graduated from Montpellier University in France as a naval architect, and shortly afterward, joined the French Army as a lieutenant. He then spent three years in northern Africa. In his final year, Pierre was transferred to military intelligence and promoted to Captain, in hopes that he would re-enlist. There was no chance of that. He believed that he had fulfilled his father's military expectations and that it was time to do something useful with his degree. Within a few months, he landed a job with a company called RAMAT that specialized in developing offshore drilling rigs. A joint venture of Chevron and Esso Oil, RAMAT assigned him to work on gas extraction projects in Angola, Nigeria and Newfoundland. He started as a supply administrator and gradually worked his way up to Project Manager for offshore drilling and mooring systems.

Picard was temporarily assigned to Sepi Industries in Italy as an offshore specialist, where he learned of that company's involvement with desalination projects in Libya and Saudi Arabia. Marcel Brione, and the organization of which he was a part, controlled the majority of shares in Sepi. Pierre's father held a minority interest, under an assumed name. Pierre's knowledge of the Saudi Arabian business climate prompted Sepi to contract with the firm of Ibriham Development and to invest in projects there.

When the owner of Ibriham Development, Zayed Al-Heid, attempted to extort millions from the Sepi Industries joint ventures in Saudi Arabia, he had Picard arrested and alleged that Sepi was corrupt. The government seized Picard's passport and he was thrown in jail for nearly three months before Brione was able to arrange for his release. Picard was furious and plotted revenge on Al-Heid, but Brione cautioned him not to jeopardize their investment.

"Be patient," Brione had told him. "We are working on a plan to get you out of the country. After that, we will take care of Mr. Zayed Al-Heid."

"CAPTAIN Jesus Martinez?" A deep voice with a pronounced French accent came through the telephone. "My name is Pierre Picard. I trust you had a pleasant flight. Perhaps we could meet for coffee."

At 6:30 in the morning Martinez was never at his best. When Picard's name clicked in, he responded.

"Would you like to meet downstairs around 9:00? And I'm no longer a captain, by the way."

"I would like to make it earlier, if possible, Mr. Martinez. Perhaps 7:30?"

Martinez agreed reluctantly.

"7:30 then," he said, making no attempt to conceal a yawn. "In the lobby."

"Very good, but since the lobby is so public I would prefer that you come alone. Please leave Major Jane in her room. After our initial discussion, we can meet later at a more appropriate place."

Martinez did not like excluding Mary, but again he agreed reluctantly. He called her room.

"Picard's downstairs. He wants to meet with me alone."

"Why? Did he give you a reason?"

"No. Something about security, I guess. He sounds a little paranoid."

"Well, he's got his reasons, doesn't he?"

"I guess."

"Meet with him, and then report back to me."

"Okay. And maybe you should call the number of my contact with the Air Force, Skip McFarlane. You've got the number. Say you're my secretary and ask for an appointment with a location place downtown, preferably the Old City. Make it this afternoon. We need to get this show on the road."

On the way down to the lobby, it occurred to Martinez that he had no idea what Picard looked like or how he was supposed to identify him. As the elevator doors opened and he started toward the lobby, a voice behind him startled him.

"Good morning, Captain Martinez." The man extended his hand. "Pierre Picard."

For some reason, Martinez had been expecting a Hollywood style gangster in a trench coat, but Picard, tall with distinguished features and dressed in tailored military style khaki, could have passed for a college professor.

"Let's have coffee in the lobby where we can talk. It's pretty empty at this hour," Martinez said.

Picard studied the lobby area with intense dark eyes.

"Being in the military you may not be aware of some of the business customs in this country. It is common to discuss deals in a hotel lobby. Once there is a meeting of the minds, they go to an office to continue their business. As a result, Saudi security personnel commonly congregate in lobbies to pick up stray bits of intelligence."

"Okay, you've convinced me. The restaurant is right around the corner."

"But observing the social manners in the lobby can be very instructive," Picard continued, as though Martinez had not spoken. "There is a reason the lobby is larger than one you would see in America."

"I'm afraid you've lost me," Martinez said, working to control an incipient headache and rising impatience.

Picard pointed to the portico outside of the hotel. "A chauffeur-driven Rolls Royce has just pulled up to the hotel. Now watch. You will see an important figure with an entourage of people sweep through the front door into the lobby. They will walk slowly and nod acknowledgement to various persons sitting in the lobby, some of which will rise to greet the great man. You will notice a slight bowing take place. The entourage will move on and finally be seated at a spot in the lobby already reserved for them. You are going to witness an exhibition of power, wealth and elaborate networking on a high level."

Martinez regarded the Frenchman. "There is no one in the lobby. There is no entourage."

Picard smiled. "That is true. It was purely a hypothetical."

"I think you're telling me that your little lecture has a moral," Martinez said.

"Perhaps."

"The reason is we will be part of an entourage as we leave Jeddah. Royalty taking off in the Boeing 747, am I right?"

Picard continued to smile. "Let's have that coffee. We've got a lot to talk about."

"I'll be honest with you," Martinez said. "I don't take well to hypotheticals, especially at seven-thirty in the morning."

"I don't blame you."

"Actually the lobby wasn't empty. There were two women sitting near the front desk," Martinez noted.

"I saw them."

They entered the restaurant and ordered coffee and honey cakes with sesame seeds.

"Are things proceeding according to plan?" Picard asked. "Marcel suggested that I help in any way I can. I know the territory."

"We have a few glitches," Martinez said. "But nothing we can't work out. I'm waiting for a call from a friend in U.S. Air Force intelligence. He's trying to get Al-Jabeer's aircraft itinerary, information on his security and the departure procedures. He's also working on getting me some hardware I need."

Picard listened intently. "May I speak frankly?"

"Sure. Frankness saves time."

"Unless you know this man extremely well, and can trust him implicitly, I would forget about him." Picard quickly added, "I sense I'm offending you."

"I'm listening."

"I want you to understand my feelings, Jesus. May I call you Jesus?"

"I prefer it to Captain."

"I know this is your show—yours and Major Jane's."

"She's no longer a Major."

"I'm simply saying that I don't want to intrude on your plans."

"Intrude all you want. We can always use another head. You obviously know your way around here. But we do need information quickly—information I'm trying to get from my friends. We don't have any time to waste."

"I understand that. I have a few thoughts for you that may be of help."

"Fire away."

Picard paused to sip his coffee.

"All commercial aircraft coming into Jeddah, including private jets, have their culinary needs filled by the same company. This company has the trays, trolleys and food specifications for different aircraft, down to the last detail. It's a huge operation and the choices of menus they produce vary from Chinese to Russian, and everything in between. Jeddah is a hub—like San Francisco, Singapore and New York. You or Ms. Jane can telephone them and ask to review the menu choices for all Al-Jabeer aircraft."

Martinez nodded. "You mean pretend to be attached to his organization and maybe recommend some changes. Is that it?"

"Exactly."

"You feel I can pick up information that way."

"It's possible."

"How many planes does Al-Jabeer have besides the 747? Our research came up with three."

"He has two Lear Jets and one helicopter that I know of.

I've also heard of a Gulfstream. For all I know, that's just the tip of the iceberg."

Martinez nodded. "We know that one jet is here and the other is in Riyadh. My guess is there are several more planes."

"I should think so. He is immensely wealthy," Picard said.

"How wealthy is wealthy?"

Picard shrugged. "Add up enough zeros and you may have an idea."

"Tell me something. Do you think a man like that would lease a plane?"

Picard's brow wrinkled in puzzlement.

"Pardon?"

"Don't you think Al-Jabeer would buy anything he wants outright? No interest, no monthly payments, no matter how big the tab?"

"I would certainly think so."

Martinez lapsed into thoughtful silence.

Picard continued talking. "I've been out to the King Abdul Aziz airport a number of times since Marcel put me on alert. I've seen the 747 you'll be flying. It's one of a kind."

Martinez nodded. The two men chatted for a few more minutes. A getting-acquainted conversation about Picard's recent experiences with Ibriham Development and Martinez's recent decision to leave the Air Force, which he glossed over without saying much of anything. They finished their coffee and shook hands stiffly.

"Thank you for letting me come along with you. My life isn't worth much here," Picard said.

"We're being well compensated."

"But the risk is great."

"Just one more risk piled on the ones we already have." Martinez dropped the man's hand after a few hard pumps. "What do people call you-—Pierre?"

"Yes."

"Well, let's hope you're lucky, Pierre."

LATER that day, Martinez met with his Air Force friend, Skip McFarlane. The two men had flown many missions together, and McFarlane was the kind of friend only a war can make. They drank together, they shared confidences, and they often fought over ideas, but with the deepest respect. He passed his friend an envelope packed neatly with $5,000 in American tens and twenties, and sipped the thick sweet coffee he griped about in Jeddah, but had missed in Paris.

"Nasty," he said. "But the stuff is addictive."

"You have strange tastes, Jesus. That shit burns a crater in your stomach."

"Not in mine. I'm impervious to small assaults on my person." He lit a cigar and blew smoke toward the ceiling. "So how do you think the Air Force will hold up without me?"

"It will barely survive. In two weeks, the morale will sink to a new level. With that fuck up Martinez gone, who will the finger point at now? That's the general thinking."

"Have another coffee, Skip. You're funnier when your battery is charged."

"I see," McFarlane said with a grin, revealing a treasure trove of gold. He fingered the envelope, picked it up and slipped it in the pocket of his flak jacket. "Have you got everything organized?"

"Yeah."

"Well, I've got some stuff."

Martinez regarded him but said nothing.

"I telephoned departure control and got next week's schedule," McFarlane said.

"With security so tight that must have been tough."

"Piece of cake," he said. "You can see the tail numbers from the private passenger lounge. I used Al-Jabeer's corporate name and gave the tail number to the dispatcher."

"I just met with the Frenchman I told you we're carrying. He said the 747 is on the ground now."

"Yep. It arrived two days ago and was towed over to a maintenance hangar for servicing, cleaning and refueling. Big trip planned."

"Sounds like it."

"But not the one they plan, right?"

Martinez blew a smoke ring and said nothing.

"I imagine Al-Jabeer's security will sweep through the plane for electronic bugs and bombs before it goes online," McFarlane said.

"So what about the take-off schedule?"

"I couldn't get a precise, but it looks like Wednesday or Saturday before twelve hundred hours. But you know the Saudis. It could be next week."

"They're not the British," Martinez said.

"Anyway, you need to get in there for a visual and, without keys, that could be a problem. I don't have any idea how you do that. Even with keys, there's often some failsafe mechanism or code that prevents unlocking, which could mean springing the lock."

Martinez nodded. "I'm working on that side of things."

"You may need cutting-edge lock picks. I'm checking out prices. It may cost you some bucks."

"Just get them."

"The techies have created some serious security safeguards for the military. It would take a Houdini to bust through some of their puzzles," McFarlane said.

"Who is Houdini?"

"A master magician. He's dead now."

"Don't sweat the money, Skip. Get me whatever will help us get out of here."

McFarlane nodded. "You told me you have airport maintenance and AJ security uniforms coming. Here's the way I see it." He glanced at Martinez, hesitated, and held up a hand, palm outward. "Stop me if I repeat stuff you and the Major have already nailed down. I know you brought me in for hardware concerns. But I do have some thoughts."

"Thoughts are welcome. Your brain is going to hurt."

"What do you mean?"

"I plan to pick it seriously."

"Can you blow that cigar smoke the other way?"

"Sure, Skip. I don't want to interrupt your train of thought, such as it is."

"OK, here's the way I'd do it. When you get your gear together and all systems are go, you, Major Jane and the French dude should take separate taxis to the airport. You change into uniforms there and scope out the aircraft and the private terminal. Keep your eyes peeled for wandering eyes. But I'm getting ahead of myself. My next job is to get a precise on the planned departure date."

"How will you do that?"

"I've got my sources. Now, the French guy—is he just extra baggage or can you use him?"

"He seems sharp. Mary's very impressed with him and she's good at judging people. And let me remind you one more time, she's no longer a Major. If you meet her, I'd advise you not to call her that."

"And in a few weeks, you'll no longer be officially a Captain."

"You've got that right." Martinez studied his friend. "Picard thinks he can use food service delivery as a source of information."

"That sounds promising. He must be a bright guy." McFarlane started to sip his coffee, and then pushed the cup away. "You asked me to check out this Princess Safi's whereabouts. She's here in Jeddah working on fundraising activities. The noblesse oblige thing, you know. It's the same the world over. She's always in the papers."

"I don't read the papers."

"I know that."

"You have any idea how her security is handled?"

"Not specifically, but I have an idea. Islamic rules forbid direct contact between the sexes, so a new type of bodyguard has sprung up for wealthy women who want to keep tradition intact, not to speak of themselves. It's called European Security Services, and the company is based in Dubai. ESS provides mostly women bodyguards—not all, but mostly—and they're former police or military police officers for the most part. They take care of the wives and children of wealthy businessmen and Sheikhs. It makes sense. Male guards can't follow their female charges into a toilet—not in these parts."

"Are these guards dressed in uniform or in the traditional dress?" Martinez said.

"I've seen them both ways. I don't really know what the regs are, but mostly I see them in khaki and a headscarf."

Martinez took a deep drag on his cigar as McFarlane watched him intently.

"You inhale that thing?"

"Sometimes. Depends on my mood."

"You're going to die a miserable death, pal. Look at the color of that cigar wrapping. That's the color of your lungs."

Martinez shrugged. "I'm trying to imagine Mary dressed as Princess Safi and her female guard dressed in the burqua. I don't see how a bodyguard could work dressed that way. How could they carry a pistol or two-way radio? How the hell could they even see out of that veil? I think we'll go for uniform style khaki and a head scarf."

McFarlane nodded. "I have a question," he said. "Can you trust the Frenchman?"

"You already asked me that. The answer is yes."

"I'm thinking you can get him to pose as her security guard. As I said, male guards can be used. The airport uniforms will accept him as her guard and won't make a fuss. I imagine he speaks Arabic."

"Fluently."

"He does the talking," McFarlane said. "Mary Jane stays silent with the sore throat ruse you mentioned on the phone. Her face will be veiled, so that will help."

"So we just sail through the airport, our tiny entourage of three, get into the airplane and take off?"

McFarlane smiled. "The same old cynical, skeptical Jesus I've known and loved for far too long. Don't worry. Departures are routine."

"It just can't be that easy, Skip. We've got to have every base covered. One misstep and we're in trouble."

"Understood. But let's take a good clear look at this. The private terminal departure officials have no idea if you're going to Brazil or Riyadh. You know what to do. File a flight plan with the tower for a destination like Tabuk, which is less than a hundred miles from the Jordanian border. No one will question you or your passengers about an internal flight."

Martinez finished his coffee and reached for McFarlane's shoulder.

"Okay, so we don't land at Tabuk," he said. "I doubt if they'll send up F-16's to shoot us down."

"You know the procedures as well as I do. Private jets are always changing course because their rich owners decide to skip Nice and go to Paris instead. Ground security figures it's your problem getting into a foreign country and it's up to you to have the right visas and passports."

"The flight plan sounds doable," Martinez said. "We can refuel in the Canary Islands before heading for America. This 747 has extra long-range fuel capacity—just over eight thousand miles, so one refuel stop might be enough, depending on what we start with."

"That leaves you with entry into the plane."

"We need to go into that more."

"Hey, haven't I already earned my keep?" McFarlane joked.

"You may be working on a bonus."

"I sure hope so. I doubt there will be an alarm, but if there is, and it goes off when you spring the lock, you'll have to abort. I don't have a good answer on this. If the lock picks don't work, you move out fast." McFarlane hesitated. "But there is one thing you might consider. If you can get into the plane while it's being serviced, or on the pretense of doing some kind of repair, you might be able to create a way to enter the plane later without using the doors."

Martinez puffed on his cigar, which had gone out, as he stared at his friend.

"You just lost me. What do you have in mind?"

"The toilet compartment. There are snap-out knobs at the base of the toilets. You release them; you can pull out the toilet, which is a self-contained plumbing unit."

"I know the set up," Martinez said, nodding. "Go on."

"Beneath the unit is a hatch cover for the vacuum hose used to service the plane on the ground. If you can create a work order to fix that toilet the day you plan to leave, you can pretend to be putting it all back together in time for the flight. It's the perfect excuse for being on the inside of the fuselage, and from there, you can open the doors from the inside."

"Skip—you're smarter than I thought. That just might work."

"I look at it as your last resort, at least until a better last resort comes along."

"I'll work on it and see if I can fine tune it a little."

Martinez dropped his dead cigar stump in an ashtray and leaned back in his chair, regarding his friend with a thoughtful frown.

"I appreciate your help, Skip. Tell me something. Is it all

about the money?"

"I'm a mercenary," McFarlane said. "You know that."

"I don't think so. What you are is, you're burned out and want out."

"What makes you think that? Maybe you're just projecting your own situation onto me."

"The wars we fight around the world, and you and I have had our share—do they make any sense to you? Do they really add up?"

"My job is to fly, not to think."

"Come on, Skip, don't give me that. We don't lie to each other."

"That's true."

"We've both seen too much. It's all about international business, it's all about oil and propping up dictators we can control. It's never about good stuff. Maybe it was once, but it isn't anymore. And let me tell you something—if I die, the cause I die for, had better be worthwhile."

"Jesus, my man, you should have been a preacher."

"Am I right or not, Skip?"

"Okay, you're right, but who cares?"

"I care."

McFarlane shoved to his feet and extended a hand.

"I think I was followed this morning. Unfamiliar faces, Arabic faces that seemed to be staring extra hard. I don't like it. Let's break it off for now. I'll call you within four days and by then, I should have a set of world-class tools for you."

"You're amazing, Skip. You're an Air Force Intel guy. What gives you access to lock picks?"

"I'll answer that question with a question. Why did you

come to me for help?"

"Because I knew you'd come through for me."

McFarlane grinned and grabbed his shoulder.

"Well, there's your answer. You know I'm into things."

Martinez stared at his friend, a small smile playing across his unshaven face.

"Be careful, Skip. My long-range plan is to bring you out to California and teach you how to fish."

"You be careful too, old buddy. I'll beep you down the line when I'm ready. Ciao."

"Ciao," Martinez said.

HE called Mary's suite from the lobby and, after ten rings, she answered.

"Let's take a stroll," he said. "Breathe in some of this murky Jeddah air."

"You know we can't be seen in the street together unless you get some Arab gear for yourself. Why don't you go shopping? I'm doing my nails now anyway—come back in an hour or so."

"Is that an order, Major?"

"It sure is. I've been in this room alone too long and it's giving me the creeps."

Two hours later, Martinez entered Mary's suite wearing a Bish—a loose white robe—and beneath it a Throb, or white cotton shirtdress. On his head was a white Ghutra folded in a triangle and held on his head by an Agal, or black rope-like cord. A white Taiyay, or skullcap, covered the Ghutra. He wore a wedding ring on the third finger of his left hand.

"Good job, Jesus," she said, surveying him from head to

foot. “You look more Arab than Omar Sharif. I wonder what’s under that robe,” she added, with a slow wink.

“You’ll never know.”

“Never say never.”

They both broke out in laughter, Martinez, with an edge of nervousness tightening his lips.

After he reported on his meeting with McFarlane, they changed their plans for the rest of the afternoon. Martinez’s left knee was throbbing—he had suffered a high school football injury, which still acted up occasionally—and the thought of a stroll had lost its appeal. He left by taxi for the airport to do some reconnaissance and Mary decided to visit the “Women Only” swimming pool on the hotel roof. She was dressed in a caftan with a scarf around her head. Most of the other women, though, including the Arab women, took dips in the pool wearing modest Western bathing suits. When she joined them, Mary felt the lightness of the pool water, which, like all water in Jeddah, came from a desalinization plant and contained no salts or minerals. The day was clear and the pool temperature warm. Mary could see the Red Sea from the roof, shimmering silver blue in the distance. The minarets below broadcasting daily prayers lulled her into a state of relaxation. She knew how much was riding on the success of her plan—financial freedom. She thought of her father. She respected his intelligence, but they did better at a distance. Charles Jane had swallowed his disappointment when his only child was born a girl. Nonetheless, he had planned out her life as though she were a boy: an intense regimen of sports and a pilot’s license by the time she was sixteen. She knew that she had gained his respect through the years by excelling in her studies, and in sports, especially fencing. She had become a pilot of skills approaching his own, but she also knew that deep down, as much as he loved her, she was still a girl after all.

MARY swam a few hard lengths in the lap lane, and then sat under an umbrella eating honey cakes and sipping thick black tea with sugar. Arabic music provided a moody background. She read a few pages of a new Harry Potter novel, which she had bought in a stall in Paris, and then dozed as the sun moved westward toward the sea. When she awoke, a strange woman spoke to her.

AT ten that evening, Mary and Jesus ventured out for dinner at Al-Kassim. It would be Mary's first time out in Saudi Arabia with a burqua. The restaurant was within walking distance and Martinez's knee was feeling better. They strolled slowly through the muggy night air, which was redolent with the smells of barbecue, tobacco and incense.

"Good smells," Mary said.

"This is the best time of day in Arabia," Martinez said. "No sun, no flies, and most of the animals are asleep. You wouldn't need a blanket to sleep outside."

After being seated on cushions on the floor, Martinez continued. "I'm not all that hungry. Are you?"

"Peckish."

"What about Mezzeh—you know, an assortment of appetizers. It looks like they have thirty or forty different kinds."

"Sounds good."

The mystery that shrouded Martinez confused her, annoyed her and intrigued her all at once. She had once slept with this man. He had been different years ago in Istanbul—sexy, passionate and carefree. He was still sexy, she thought, but the light had gone out and he carried darkness around with him like an extra layer of skin.

A parade of small bowls began to appear: rice combinations with lamb, curries and raisins; chicken rolled in flat bread and sliced; barbecue beef strips; prawn kabobs; hummus; curried lentils, called Dahl; banana in peanut sauce; cucumber in yogurt; fresh and dried fruits; nuts and sweet cakes. Most patrons ate with their fingers, but Mary and Jesus requested forks and spoons. It was the second time she had been forced to eat by lifting her veil without exposing her face, holding the food at the level of the tablecloth and then lowering her chin to accept the fork.

"You know what? They feed their dogs in public without a veil. I think I'd rather be a dog."

Martinez grinned at her discomfort.

"Here's an exercise for you. Divide the number of hours of humiliation into the money you're about to make, then ask yourself this—is it worth it? If it is, then just go with the flow."

"Sometimes I think I hate you, Martinez."

"Well, what is it the song says? 'There's a thin line between love and hate,' or something like that," he teased. "I guess I should report on my day."

"It's up to you," she said with a hint of chill.

"Well, I went out to the airport to see which firms handle aircraft maintenance. I also wanted to see if I could get close to the 747, or if access was going to be a problem."

"And? Is it going to be a problem?"

"Yes and no."

"Yes and no? What is that supposed to mean?"

"If you have a uniform marked Rahmad Maintenance you

can pretty well walk anywhere. That's the good news. They have badges with photo identification, but we should be able to create that on the hotel computer. I'll just scan my photo into it and frame it with the appropriate wording. The bad news? The place is crawling with security. Without ID, I couldn't get close to the plane."

"You'll need to create some kind of special order to service it, won't you?"

"I'm not sure. With the maintenance uniform I might be able to bluff my way into the hangar and tell them I need to inspect the toilets because of a complaint about smells. That's my plan."

"*Our* plan."

"OK, I stand corrected. Our plan."

"But doesn't it all depend on having a maintenance uniform? You don't have one."

"That's true. I don't."

"So we have a problem."

"Not necessarily. Most of the maintenance crew guys are European, and I asked one of them in English where he picked up his uniform. He gave me a name. I'll go around there tomorrow. Air and maintenance crews around the world speak English."

On the walk back to the hotel, Mary spoke. "Even stuck in this hideous old bag, I can't help admiring the evening. Arabia can be very beautiful, can't it?"

"As beautiful as it can be cruel. Did you enjoy your swim in the pool?"

"Very relaxing. But something strange happened while I was there. I meant to mention it earlier but it skipped my mind."

"This country can have that effect on people."

"An Arab-looking woman stopped me as I was about to leave. She called me by my name, but refused to give me hers. She used to be an American citizen, she told me that much. I gather she gave up her citizenship, or it was revoked. She seemed anxious to talk to me, but I could tell she was really frightened."

"Frightened about what?"

"I'm not sure. But she knew my room number. And she knew who I was. She asked if she could call my room."

"What did you say?"

"I told her she could."

Martinez shook his head in irritation.

"Not smart. Definitely not smart. She might be spying for someone."

"I don't think so. She was too unraveled."

"But you don't *know*, Mary. Our first commandment has to be, trust no one."

"She seemed okay. I felt sorry for her."

"But how would she know your name? That's what bothers me. We just got here."

"I have no idea. Maybe she'll call, maybe she won't."

When they entered the hotel it was one o'clock in the morning. A red light was flashing on Mary's telephone. She picked up the recorded message dated twelve thirty-five. A woman's voice, low pitched and tremulous, spoke slowly, pausing for breath every few words.

"Ms. Jane—I hope you will remember me. We bumped into each other this afternoon. If I sound frightened, it is because I am. Please forgive me for this late call. I, I will telephone you at eleven tomorrow morning and I pray you will be there to take my call."

Mary hung up and turned to Jesus. "Could you hear her?"

"Yes."

"Well, what do you think?"

"I think I'm worried. Since she knows your name and that you're here in this hotel, then others might also know. I can see a lot of bad reasons for that, but none that seem promising."

Chapter Ten

AT exactly 11:00, Mary's telephone rang.

"Ms. Jane, I am in the lobby," the woman said. "Please meet with me for a few minutes. I'll be wearing the burqua and sitting on a chair near the front desk with a black leather brief-case in my lap."

"Can you tell me what this is all about?"

"When I'm with you, yes. Not on the telephone, please."

"Okay," Mary said after a brief hesitation. "I'll be right down."

She entered the lobby dressed in a black burqua and scanned the room for indications of trouble, or for people who might be watching her more closely than necessary. Cloak and dagger, she thought. Definitely not in the repossession playbook. She approached the veiled woman and sat next to her without a word or a glance.

"Thank you for coming," the woman said. "Let us pretend we've just met and we're making small talk."

Mary nodded as her eyes continued to sweep the lobby. When her gaze returned to the cloaked woman, she noticed a long black cane propped against her chair. She glanced sharply at the woman, alarm bells going off in her head.

The woman began slowly, "I'll introduce myself. My name is Princess Safi Al-Jabeer."

Mary was momentarily stunned, at a loss for words. She gave the lobby another quick scan, carefully examining every face. A man dressed in a dark suit was reading a newspaper but she sensed that he was not staring at them.

"I know who you are," she said in a low whisper. "And I don't believe in coincidences. You have obviously sought me out for some reason. Somehow, you know me. I'll give you two minutes to explain yourself, then I'm out of here."

"My bodyguard is sitting over on that striped lounge chair."

"The man in the dark suit? I see him."

"We will appear to him as strangers that have met by chance in a hotel lobby," she said. "Just let your body relax. Don't appear tense. We're two women who have met for a chat."

"I don't feel very relaxed." Mary glanced at her watch. "You have two minutes."

"I'm afraid it will take me a little longer to explain why I'm here, but I'll try to be as concise as possible." The woman extended a hand and touched Mary's sleeve, the lightest of touches, and yet it exerted a strange resisting force.

"All right," Mary said reluctantly. She sat back in her

chair, trying to obtain a sense of ease she did not feel—all for the benefit of the man whose eyes she thought she could feel. The woman began her story.

"I graduated from Stanford University ten years ago with a degree in Engineering. I was on scholarship, my family had no money. Perhaps you've read that I'm a cousin of the Pakistani King Abdullah Kahn. We are the poor relatives." She laughed softly. "I mention this connection only because I soon learned that my background was what attracted my husband Dani Al-Jabeer to me. We met at a business seminar on the Middle East, held at Stanford. Once the seminar was over, he came on to me with this incredible charm. We had dinner that night, and then each night for the next two weeks. He dazzled me with stories of the luxurious cosmopolitan life he led abroad. He was in his early thirties then and already very wealthy, but he felt I had something to offer—a royal title and the prestige that it could bring. Six months later, we were married at a lavish wedding ceremony in San Francisco. We were very much in love.

"The next few years, I lived a dream come true. He showered me with clothes and jewelry; we traveled around the world in his private jet. He was completely attentive and kind. But when my son was born with Down's syndrome, everything changed. He felt disgraced. It was as though I'd shamed him somehow. He insisted on shipping my baby to an institution in Switzerland and forbade me to see him. That was when everything ended for me. He began to spend his nights away from me. It got to the point where the mere sight of me repulsed him. I had brought him defeat in the form of a damaged child.

"Still, he has uses for me. He insists I stand beside him

at official functions—embassy affairs and the like. Other than that, I am essentially a prisoner with no social contact except for a few government-sanctioned charities." She turned her veiled face to Mary.

"So many times I've wished I could be an ordinary Arab woman. Then I could have the comfort of an extended family, a network of women friends. I am utterly alone." She paused.

"Go on," Mary said.

"So—things grew worse. During our few private moments together, he became brutal. Mostly in his language, not physically. I began to dream of returning to California and finding work as an Engineer. Without my husband's permission, though, I'm not allowed to leave the country. I don't know how familiar you are with customs in Saudi Arabia. A man wishing a divorce, has only to publicly repeat three times the words 'I divorce thee' to end his marriage. A woman has no grounds to end her marriage. She has no control over her fate at all, and certainly not over family assets. Not a penny of my husband's millions belong to me, or so he says. He has large financial holdings in the United States, and for that reason alone, he has no intention of permitting me to travel there. American law would entitle me to a huge divorce settlement because that's where we married. About a year ago, he hired guards to continually hover around me. Their job is not to protect me, but to make sure I don't flee. They monitor my every movement and report back to him."

She tapped Mary lightly on the arm, giving anyone that might be watching the impression they were engaged in idle gossip. The woman impressed Mary; she had grace and great presence, but who was she really? She said that she was Al-Jabeer's wife, but was she?

Why has she picked me, of all people, to tell this sad story to, the very person who is planning to repossess her husband's plane—the very person who is pretending to be her? Is it remotely possible this could be a coincidence? Mary thought. This woman could be an impostor, after all, with some secret agenda of her own. Jesus would urge caution and Mary had to admit that he was right. Listen, but give away nothing. Mary would listen to the story and then judge the truth of it.

"Then one day, I read a piece in *The London Times* about a Major Mary Jane who refused to wear the burqua during off duty hours in the City. It said that the stand she was taking could lead to her court martial. BBC News carried the story and so did the local television stations. I think they liked the idea of an American woman being told where her place is. The story stuck in my mind and I thought about this woman often. She was brave and her position had complete moral justification. I would like to meet such a woman, I thought. I even had fantasies of calling the Air Force and trying to get in touch with this remarkable woman, but of course, I did nothing.

"Then, yesterday, I saw you lying in the sun beside the pool. Your head was uncovered, your hair was blazing red and I remembered that Major Jane had been described as having bright red hair. I looked at you and thought of Major Jane. I wondered whether this could be the miracle I had dreamed about. I listened intently as you ordered tea in tourist Arabic. Definitely an American accent, I thought to myself. And you gave your room number to the waitress—914. You may remember I left a moment later and was gone for perhaps ten minutes? I rushed to the desk and asked for the person registered in 914 and they gave me your name—Mary Jane. Ordinarily, they would not give out such information, but one of the benefits of being Dani Al-Jabeer's wife is the power to demand and get what you want—at least the small things.

"So it was you, after all. The former Major, the woman I had thought about for so long and so admired." Princess Safi forced a laugh for the benefit of the guard in case he was watching them. She continued.

"I am desperate. I am followed everywhere. I live in a prison—a prison of immense wealth, but it's a place where there's no love, no companionship—only watchful servants. I've been robbed of my child. There is nothing for me any longer."

"What are you asking from me?"

"When I saw you at the roof pool, then learned who you were, it all began to fall into place. Maybe there *is* hope. Maybe I can get away from here—with your help. I can't stay here. My life is intolerable." Her voice thickened as she continued.

"If my husband even suspects—if he could read my mind…." She shook her head. "I can't bear to think of what he would do."

"Again—what are you asking me to do?" Mary insisted.

"I need your help to escape from here. Money is not a problem. If you can get me to America, I will pay you one million dollars."

"You're not serious."

"I am very serious."

"You just told me you have no money. You said your husband controls everything. And now you're offering me a million dollars? Can you see why I'd be skeptical of your story?"

"Everything I'm telling you is the truth. And the money—I have all that I need. But the money means nothing to me if it can't get me out of here."

Mary regarded her for a long moment.

"What makes you think I can get you out of Saudi Arabia? You must have a reason to think I can. I would like to know what it is."

"You are a pilot."

"A pilot without a plane. The Air Force is not going to lend me one to fly you to America. You must think I have some way to accomplish miracles."

"I have a feeling that you do."

Does this woman know more than she was saying? Could she possibly know about the 747? Mary thought.

"You can rent a private plane," Princess Safi continued. "I would pay for its use, of course, apart from the money I'm offering you."

Mary started to rise.

"This has been a very interesting talk, but I have to go. I'm late for a meeting."

"Please." Again, the woman touched her sleeve, a kind of begging gesture. "You are my only hope."

"Look, Princess Safi, if that's who you really are, even if I could help you, which I doubt, why should I? You're a complete stranger to me. And how do I know you are who you say you are? I have no proof."

The woman nodded her veiled head.

"In my briefcase are materials relating to our Islamic version of the Red Cross. I'm a sponsor and a member. My bonafides are inside in an unmarked envelope. I'm going to leave you in a minute and go to the restroom. Follow me a few minutes later and I will give you materials that relate to your potentially becoming a donor and volunteer. In that capacity, if we come to an agreement, we will have a perfect excuse to meet." The woman rose slowly and reached for her cane. "If you don't join me in ten minutes, at most, I'll know your answer and I promise that I will never bother you again."

"SHE'S very believable, Jesus. I want you to meet her."

"No. No way. I don't believe in coincidences. What we should do is check out of here right now."

"I believe her. She is who she says she is. The woman is desperate."

Martinez regarded Mary with a smile that held no warmth.

"I'm desperate too," he said. "I am about to fly a plane out of a country that will consider this out-and-out theft, not repossession. In Saudi Arabia, a lease is the same as ownership."

"But we know Al-Jabeer has defaulted on his payments. That's why Ian and Charles have hired us. They sent us contracts and a retainer."

"This could still be a con," Martinez interrupted. "Everything right now depends on a fax and a $50,000 check. And now this woman comes along? Al-Jabeer's wife? How convenient is *that*? For Christ's sake!"

"Don't raise your voice to me."

"Mary, if we can't pull this off, we face the possibility of rotting in prison for the rest of our lives, or if we're lucky, being shot or hung. And now suddenly, a strange Middle Eastern woman enters the picture?"

"She is Princess Safi. She had the proof in her briefcase."

Martinez crushed his cigar out violently in the ashtray and began pacing the room.

"I don't give a damn, frankly. She may be Al-Jabeer's wife. She may be a saint—a candidate for the Nobel Peace Prize. Mother Teresa's secret daughter." He turned quickly and stood inches from Mary. "I agreed to do a job, and I'll do that job, but only if we keep our priorities straight. Otherwise, I'm out of here."

"You're threatening me."

"No. I'm stating a fact. Look at what you're suggesting, Mary. You really have to think this through. The wife of the man whose plane we're repossessing is willing to pay us a million dollars—*she* says—to get her out of the country. Isn't that just wonderful? Is there something wrong with your nose? I mean this smells to high heaven. Okay, so we stow her away—in her husband's plane, no less—which, trust me on this, she will recognize immediately—and we take off for America. What are you, crazy?"

"She hates her husband. If you'd only talk to her, you would understand."

"It's the money, isn't it? All the money you're getting for this gig isn't enough. You're willing to jeopardize the operation for more. Assuming there is more, which I seriously doubt."

Mary shook her head, red hair flying. "I admire you, Jesus. You're smart and you make good decisions, but this time you're wrong. Princess Safi is on the up and up. I just *know* it."

"Come on, Mary. You spent all of a half-hour with this woman. How much can you possibly know?"

"I believe her and promised her that I would help."

"You believe in the money."

"It's not fair of you to impugn my motives. I'll tell her we won't take a penny if that makes you feel any better. But I want to help her."

Martinez threw her off balance by reaching for her hand. He held it in a tight grasp as his eyes searched hers.

"There's something you're not telling me. There has to be more to it than this. You're willing to risk everything for a woman you've just met and I'm having trouble buying it. You better talk to me, Mary."

She pulled away from him and slumped into a chair. She bridged her eyes with both hands and for a long moment she was silent. When she finally spoke, she did not look at him.

"I have reasons why I have to do this." She rolled her eyes and gave him a grin. "You must think I've totally lost it. But believe me, my mind has been blown."

"Well, I have to know those reasons. So far, this looks like a prescription for failure." He slumped into a chair with a sigh. "I'm willing to listen. I owe you that much."

Mary sat opposite Jesus and folded her hands on her lap like a dutiful schoolgirl.

"This isn't easy," she said.

"Take your time. I'm not going anywhere."

"Have I ever told you about my mother?"

He looked at her in surprise. "Your mother? Is she joining us on the journey too? The 747 has plenty of room, it usually seats about four hundred passengers."

Mary's intense blue eyes shined suddenly with amusement.

"Cut it out, Martinez. Just listen."

"Believe me; you've got my complete attention. And no,

you've never mentioned your mother."

Mary hesitated. "My mother—oh God, is the world screwed up or what?"

"Screwed up for real," he said. "But that's yesterday's news."

"Okay, let me tell you some things before I lose my nerve. My mother was born to a family of perfume makers in Grosse. When she was a little girl, her father told her that imperfection in any form would not be tolerated in the Breton household—Breton is my mother's maiden name. She never attended a regular school. Only French was spoken at home, even though she was studying English with a tutor who came to the house twice a week. Her formal education, if you can call it that, ended when she was fourteen. My grandfather apprenticed her, for no wages, to make waxes, pomades, creams, soaps and sachets. Under his tutelage she became an expert perfume maker. In 1971 she met my father.

"She was on a rare day trip to Paris with a friend, the Air Force had just transferred him to Paris and he swept her off her feet. She was eighteen, totally unworldly and a virgin. What did he see in her? Her physical beauty aside? I think he saw what her father saw—a mind that could be molded. She knew that her parents would never approve of her relationship with an American—probably sensed that her father would never approve of anyone—so her friend went home without her. She stayed with my father and, two weeks later, she agreed to elope with him. Nine months after that, I was born. We lived in Paris for the next twelve years and what I remember most clearly about my childhood were their nightly quarrels. They fought in low bitter voices, but I was in the next room and I could hear them. Most of all, I could hear my mother's suffering. I would lie in bed crying, a pillow stuffed against my ears to shut out the sound. The General, like her father, would not tolerate imperfection—and her imperfections were numerous. She was poorly educated, inhibited, socially inept, and worst of all in his eyes, she was obsessed by the perfume business. Rather than stay at home, at his beck and call twenty-four seven, she was begging him to let her open her own shop. Imagine how he felt! Humiliated by a woman!

"Of course, he put his foot down. By the time I was ten, I knew he was rarely at home. He always had an excuse to be somewhere else. The following year my mother started having visions. I remember her racing from room to room muttering under her breath, her eyes wild, wearing nothing but a nightdress. The General had her committed. A few months later, she killed herself. Shortly after that, my father was transferred to the States. After the funeral, we never mentioned my mother's name again. Her name was Lisa, by the way. Isn't Lisa a beautiful name? My mother was prettier than most movie stars and obviously he married her for her beauty. But the inside of her? He never bothered to take a look."

Mary hated herself for telling such outrageous lies about her mom and dad. But, she thought, she'd make up for it later, somehow. She glanced up at Martinez. She was dry-eyed and her expression was perfectly composed.

"I replaced her in the Jane household and for many, many years did my father's bidding until I moved out on my own." She shrugged. "You're wondering what this has to do with Princess Safi."

"Not anymore," Martinez said. "I get all the connections. And I think you have to do what you have to do. And believe me,

I feel sorry for what you went through. The thing is, I only have one life, and as insignificant as it is, I'd like to hold onto it a while longer. I'm sorry."

Mary rose and moved to him. She leaned forward and kissed his forehead.

"Please, Jesus," she whispered. "Do this for me. I'm begging you from the bottom of my heart. Have you ever known anyone who needed to be saved and no matter how hard you tried, that person slipped away from you? If you've had that happen to you—if you lost someone that way and then you're given a second chance to make things right—I mean, think about it. Don't you have to do it?"

Isabel... All those years waiting for her, praying, hoping, only to lose her. On the day she died, he had closed his heart like a door on the world of feelings, lightness, and silly hope, preferring to live in darkness and safety behind that door. Martinez felt the warm imprint of Mary's lips where they had lightly touched his forehead. When she moved away, he stared into her eyes.

"Arrange a meeting," he said. A slow grin creased his face. "I guess I'm just as crazy as you."

Mary was disgusted at herself for telling such atrocious lies about her family.

Chapter Eleven

TWO days later, Martinez stepped out of a taxi at the Jeddah airport just after dawn. He ducked into a restroom and slipped into his maintenance uniform, put the red and white Ghutra on his head, pinned his picture identification onto his breast pocket and walked purposefully, but without undue haste, to the maintenance area. He grabbed one of the golf carts parked haphazardly in the open square and drove it to the hangar, pulling up to the 747's wing door. A burly guard approached him as he alighted from the cart. He stared at Martinez' ID and then scowled at a clipboard he held no more than two inches from his eyes. He mouthed a few words to himself, his brow wrinkled in puzzled concentration.

"Martinez," he said in heavily accented, broken English. "Your name is not listed."

"I'm new. I just started this week."

The guard shook his head. "Your name should be listed."

He peered hard at Martinez. "You are not Arabic."

Martinez grinned, showing evidence of easy relaxation.

"Half," he lied. "My father is Mexican. My mother was born in Riyadh."

The guard nodded. He worked his tongue around his teeth, found a morsel and spit it out. Under Martinez's intent, open gaze the man's eyes started to slide away.

"Security has become a problem. Last year people came and went with very few checks, but now, it is tight."

"Makes your job harder," Martinez observed. He continued to smile, but the guard did not join in. His frown suggested a concentrated effort to think the situation through as well as the difficulty of doing so.

"Perhaps you should accompany me to the traffic shed." He shrugged apologetically. "Just a precaution, you know. I don't want to…"

Martinez sensed his uncertainty. If this were a high-stakes poker game, he thought, the moment to bluff would be now. The guy is slow and even this little complication is giving him a headache.

"Let's go to the shed and straighten this out," Martinez said glancing at his watch. "I am already twenty minutes behind schedule, but you've got a job to do. I respect that."

The guard continued to stare at him. "Did you grow up here?"

"No. My parents moved to America when I was a kid. I returned after I completed my education," Martinez continued.

The guard's small eyes opened slightly more widely.

"America." He spoke the word with reverence. "Where in America?"

"California," Martinez replied.

Now he had the guard's undivided attention.

"I have heard about California. The big trees and the desert like here. Movie stars live there. Jennifer Lopez and Tom Cruise."

"That is so."

"And you left to come back here…?" Martinez detected the note of skepticism, of disgust.

"Yes, I returned with my mother." The conversation was growing too complex for Martinez's comfort. The more he told the man, the more he would stand out, and the more lies he told, the more lies he would have to keep straight. He looked pointedly at his watch, and then studied the guard's badge.

"Muresh," he said, reading the man's ID from his jacket. "If we have to go to the shed, we'd better do it now. I don't want to get in trouble my first week."

The guard gestured at the 747. "Clean up duty?" He pointed to Martinez' tool bag.

"Yes."

Again, the guard frowned and thumb licked his way through the sheets of paper on his clipboard. He shook his head.

"Clean up is scheduled for tomorrow, not today."

"That's what I thought, too. The flight plans must have been changed."

"I know nothing about that. My job is to open the hatch, wait around, then lock it again. You're lucky."

"Why is that, Muresh?"

"If I hadn't come by right now, you'd have been waiting here with your thumb up your ass."

Martinez laughed. "That is true. I'm a lucky guy all right."

The guard unbuckled a huge set of keys from his belt and climbed, grunting and sighing, to the hatch. He fumbled through his keys until he found one that fit. When he lowered himself to the tarmac and returned the key chain to his belt, he peered closely at Martinez's uniform.

"Where's your cell?"

Martinez patted his pocket.

"I'll be waiting for you over there." He pointed to a bench beside an empty hangar. "But if something comes up—like if I get called away—you wait beside the plane and call 313."

"Okay."

"That's some plane, that 747. Like a flying casino," he added confidentially. "It belongs to Sheikh Al-Jabeer."

Martinez nodded.

"Be sure to call in when you complete servicing. That's standard procedure."

"I know."

The guard clapped him on the shoulder and smiled for the first time, a dark cave with many missing stalagmites and stalactites.

"You'd better get to it, friend. I was about to go off duty. I've been on since midnight, so don't hold me up too long." He gave a jaunty salute, turned on his heel, and walked with a loping, heavy pace to the bench, collapsed on it and closed his eyes.

What if he decides to check my story? I'm dead, he thought as he stared up at the massive aircraft. I guess this is what they call the moment of truth. The point of no return.

He climbed up to the door nearest the cockpit using the aluminum steps, and passed through the unlocked hatch. He examined the door for signs of an alarm, but there were no keypads or anything unusual. His eyes did a quick survey of the interior. He proceeded to the toilet nearest the entrance and examined it to see how hard it would be to take out and open the service door to the outside. He was confident that he could manage to dismantle the toilet and crawl out, but it would take some time.

He moved quickly to the cockpit. It was identical to the one in the computer flight simulator he had practiced on—no fuel or thrust lever locks or special radio equipment. He did a quick search in the side pockets of the captain's chair, hoping he might get lucky and find an extra set of keys, but there was nothing except a pack of tissues, two sticks of Juicy Fruit gum and a tube of Visine eye drops. He examined the ignition and fuel thrusters and found they were standard, without locks. He finished his inspection in fifteen minutes and stepped into the main cabin. Toward the middle, he saw an elegant bar and in front, on the floor, was a glass partition. He bent down to have a look and saw the diamond covered BMW in the cargo hold. He wanted desperately to have a closer look, but there was no time. He hurried out; the guard was fast asleep on the bench and Martinez had to shake his shoulder to wake him.

WHEN he returned to the Sheraton, he went directly to Mary's suite.

"How did it go?" She asked.

"Okay. I'm still alive and I made a friend. He is missing many teeth, as well as a number of brain cells, and I'm thankful for that. With a little luck, I think flying out of here is doable."

"While you were gone, I arranged a meeting with Princess Safi—just the two of you. She suggested lunch."

Martinez waved her words away.

"I've changed my mind. It strikes me as awkward—like I'm interviewing her for a job." He drummed his fingers nervously on the side table. "I'm going to go along with you on this one, Mary. It may be the stupidest decision I've ever made, and I've made some beauties. But I have a feeling this is a deal breaker for you."

"Not exactly. Don't take this the wrong way, but I could still manage to repossess that plane—even without you."

A slow smile spread across his features. "I'll bet you could."

"You sure you don't want to meet with her?"

"I'm sure." He removed a cigar from his jacket and studied it. "What about the money."

"What about the money?"

"I'm asking you."

"We take it and split it. Why not?"

His grin grew wider. "Why not indeed?" He rolled the cigar between his thumb and finger and then returned it to his pocket.

"Thank you, Jesus."

He looked at her, an eyebrow raised slightly. "For the Princess or the cigar?"

"For not lighting that thing."

"You're welcome." He sprawled out in a chair and pinched his temples. "I'm way too old for this, you know. I should be wearing Bermuda shorts on some Caribbean island

and doing a spot of fishing while sipping a rum drink."

"Don't complain," she said. "You're about to come into money."

"Okay, we now have another passenger and luckily, another paying passenger. We need to know the depth of her security problems—for instance, is there any time in the day she's alone? We need to know more about Al-Jabeer's movements and travel plans. If she's with us, she has to help us."

"She's practically a prisoner, Jesus. Don't expect too much."

"But these are things to ask her. He probably has personal security and we don't know if there's a special detail looking after the plane. Maybe she knows that—anyway, there's no harm in asking. We want a list of names for those security people. Let's make her earn her passage."

"She's already paying us a fortune."

"Not enough. And as far as I'm concerned, it doesn't even exist until I see it."

"I made a few notes this morning," Mary said. "Maybe there are regulars at the airport—you know, people she sees each time she takes a trip. We have all those jewel boxes. Maybe she can make good use of them. I also want to know where she can move around inside of Arabia without arousing suspicion.

"Also, we'll need a way to lose her security when we are set to move her to the airport. A conference at the hotel maybe? Once she's alone in a women-only meeting, we can take her out of the hotel using another exit. So, let's see—we need to add signs to our list. We need at least one for the conference room door. Something that says 'National Health Conference: Women Only.' Another thing—we can do up a phony agenda. If anybody asks, she can say it's about the AIDS epidemic in Africa."

"Sounds good."

"I'll run it by her. I've got a question, though."

"I've got about a thousand. What's yours?"

"If she's on board as herself and you're the pilot, then who am I supposed to be? I just lost my starring role," Mary said.

"You catch the next plane."

"Seriously, Jesus."

"I'm stumped at the moment."

"I'm thinking Picard can go as co-pilot and I'll be her female guard. Of course, maybe Picard can't fly a plane."

"It doesn't matter. All he has to do is sit in his seat and look professional. I'm doing the flying."

"The uniform shouldn't be a problem," Mary said. "We don't have a jacket for him with the AJ logo, but he can wear a shirt with epaulets and he can wear your cap; if we can't find another one. A plastic badge that says 'Captain Pierre Picard' should do the trick. I can't imagine anyone asking to see his pilot's license."

"Just consider it one more risk," Martinez said. "A guard almost blew my cover today. I wonder how many lives I have left."

"I'm going to ignore that comment. I can't stand negativity."

"Sorry."

"As Princess Safi's guard, I'll need the proper ID. Something that identifies me as a member of ESS—European Security Services. My American passport and other Air Force papers will stay the same."

Martinez nodded, and gave a huge yawn. "I'm beat."

Mary was pacing back and forth, running a hand through her hair.

"The hotel handles conventions," she said. "And they're likely to have some of those plastic name badge holders. I'll pick up a few. I guess I'll be on the computer for about four hours doing the sign, the agenda and the various ID badges. Maybe you should go up on the roof and get some sun. You'll look even more like an Arab."

"I'm going back to my room where I can smoke my cigar in peace."

"When is Picard contacting us again?"

"Tomorrow morning."

"He should meet with Safi. We can brief him, and after my meeting starts with her, he can slip in."

EARLY that evening, Mary produced her artwork.

"Here it is—signs, badges, the lot. What do you think, Jesus?"

"Picasso comes to mind."

"I'll take that as a compliment. I even scanned your pilot's license and put Picard's name and information into it. All we need is his photograph. Now you are both licensed. I got his plastic badge engraved at a Kinko's, which is right down the street from a Starbuck's. Things are sure changing around here, aren't they?"

"American influence at its best. Pretty soon the Arab nations will be feasting on pork and Twinkies. And talking about food, why don't we get something in the hotel tonight? I don't feel like sitting on the floor while I eat. It's hard on the knees,"

Martinez said.

"Fine with me. Incidentally, when Safi is here tomorrow, I want you to have Picard sitting in the lobby. Make sure he's in the lounge section near us. Ask him to wear a white shirt with the new engraved plastic ID. And put your captain's hat on him."

"Don't you think exposing him like that might be a risk?"

"This risk is worth taking. Safi's bodyguard will be hanging around. I want him or her to get a good look at Picard as an airline pilot. While he's in the lobby you can have him paged. Something like 'Captain Picard to the house telephone please.' The bodyguard will notice him and maybe later it will trigger recognition. He'll see Picard at the airport with us and think, oh yeah, the pilot, no big deal."

"I like that." Martinez nodded. "I know how much you hate it when I'm not positive. Now I'm being positive."

"Thank you, Jesus," she said, smiling. "You've just made my day."

Chapter Twelve

AT exactly two o'clock the next day, Princess Safi Al-Jabeer exited her Mercedes limousine and entered the Sheraton Hotel. An ESS bodyguard dismounted from her motorcycle, entered just ahead of her and sat less than thirty feet away. Mary, dressed in her burqua, walked slowly up to Safi. They shook hands, sat and chatted for a moment, then rose to take an elevator to the mezzanine. As they were about to enter the conference room designated as the National Health Conference, Safi gestured to the guard to take a chair in the hallway. She nodded, and Safi and Mary entered the room and closed the door. They were alone.

"Your bodyguard seems pretty docile," Mary said.

"Actually, she's very intelligent. But she obeys my husband's orders, the most important being to keep a close watch on me. The other is to treat me with the abject servility befitting a princess. As you can imagine, these orders sometimes are at odds."

Mary led the way to the mezzanine conference room and after sitting, she was the first to speak.

"Safi—I am going to tell you a story that will be difficult for you to believe. You came to me seeking help and I'm willing to help you, but I want you to know I'm taking a great risk. And in coming to me, you don't have any idea what you've gotten yourself into."

Princess Safi met Mary's eyes with a calm expression.

"Nothing can surprise me anymore. Go on."

"I should also explain that Jesus Martinez, my partner, was completely opposed to your proposal. It took whatever persuasive powers I have to bring him around." She knew that Martinez and Picard, waiting in the adjoining conference room for Mary to call them in and introduce them to Safi, could probably hear her words.

Princess Safi slightly inclined her head in a bow.

"I am grateful to you."

Over the next twenty minutes, Mary outlined plans for the repossession of the 747. When she was finished, Safi shook her head in wonder.

"My husband's plane," she said, a smile twitching at the corner of her lips. "What a delicious irony. I will escape in the plane my husband made into a flying whorehouse. Am I dreaming?"

"I hope not. Because if you are, then I am."

"Is there any information I can provide?"

"Only everything," Mary said, reaching out and touching her hand. "We need to know about your husband's security arrangements. We have some information, but the more the better. We need to know of any planned trips for the 747, the routine we should expect at the private plane air terminal, details about his routine, where he goes when he's overseas…"

"I don't know how much I can help, but I'll try." Safi sighed and slowly shook her head. She stared at her lap. "This is very painful for me, but for years I've been loyal to Dani. No matter what he did, even the most outrageous behavior, I looked the other way. But it's over—that's what I have to keep telling myself. He used up the last ounce of my sympathy and loyalty, and it's over now."

Mary said nothing. She put a hand over Safi's and gave a gentle squeeze.

"Sandy Blair is his mistress in London," Safi said after a pause, a new firmness in her tone. "She's a blonde in her early thirties and he's with her right now. Then there's Shari Armand, his Paris girlfriend, a playgirl from what I've been told, and very wealthy. And Carla Santonio is a recent acquisition. She's very young and does some modeling for top agencies in New York." Safi's smile was rueful.

"My husband believes in having a woman in every port. He takes his women to various resorts along the Mediterranean. I have reason to believe he will leave London with Sandy Blair this week and fly to a resort in Sardinia. He generally stays with one or another of his women for at least ten days at a time. I guess you could say he rotates them, but I also think it's part of the image he wants to project—dashing, panache, successful. You know the kind of man I'm talking about."

"So he doesn't use the 747 for all of his trips."

"Oh, no. That's for special occasions. His Gulfstream IV is his usual transportation. He has a fleet of planes, but the 747 is his special business tool, that's what he calls it—personally designed for him without a care for the cost. It's used as a flying brothel for his local cronies and for business contacts all around the world. It may be the world's fanciest, most expensive whorehouse. Girls from France, Morocco, England and America are recruited to fly to spas and resorts with wealthy businessmen. They're paid a flat fee of fifty thousand dollars for a week's work, and the guests usually provide huge gratuities above that—cash, jewelry, villas, that sort of thing. The airplane picks up its pornographic videos and liquor outside of Arabia—usually somewhere in Italy. Then it collects the guests wherever they are. The 'sin tours' are especially popular during the religious holidays—for instance the Five Pillars of Faith or the Holy Hajj, which just ended. That's probably why the plane is being serviced.

"I hope that clears up the mystery a little. The Boeing 747 often has a schedule that is different from my husband's. He goes on these trips when the guests are very important. The man that arranges the 'sin tours' is a Lebanese named David Sassoon. He calls himself a security advisor—at least that's his cover. Sassoon visits Arabia often, but he lives in Beirut, probably because of the Morals Police and the possibility of scandal in this country. I get the feeling he does a lot of dirty work for my husband. Sometimes, I hear his name mentioned when things are fixed to Dani's satisfaction. Every time I hear the name David Sassoon, my skin crawls."

"What's he look like?"

"I've never met him and I haven't seen a picture."

"My partner has an Air Force friend working on when the next flight is scheduled," Mary said.

"That's good, because I have no connection with David Sassoon. My husband has forbidden it."

"Your husband seems to live his life totally on his own terms. How did you put up with him for so long?"

"Oh, these things are never easy to explain. Commitment, inertia, the desire to make something work when you know in your heart it never can. And there's his charm. I can't begin to describe the man's incredible electricity. When he chooses to use it, he can be absolutely mesmerizing. But I learned that it's all about business. He truly believes that money is the sum total of life—women and power can be bought with money, and money is the only god he knows. He creates success for his associates. He provides a fantasy lifestyle probably unmatched anywhere. His friends trust him and his absolute discretion. He is a god to them. I've heard Dani brag about the deals he made on these trips and how many of his friends he's made rich." Safi paused and seemed to struggle for the right words to go on.

"Sometimes I think that under all his macho posturing, he fears me. In his mind I'm a liability. I'm not sufficiently subservient. That was fine when we first met—we were living in the States. But here, my behavior is unacceptable. He thinks that America ruined me and he would kill me before he'd ever let me return."

Mary regarded Princess Safi for a long moment. "I have to ask you a very tough question."

Safi smiled slowly, revealing perfect white teeth.

"I've learned there are no tough questions. Or easy ones either. Only questions—many, many of them."

"I'm not trying to pry into your personal life, but this is crucial. Do you still love your husband?"

"No. It's been burned out of me. There's nothing left."

"Are you totally committed to your decision? Once this is set in motion, there's no backing out."

"Totally. This is no sudden act of revenge. There is no way I can continue to live this life of emptiness." Safi paused and then added in a low, flat tone, "I've come to hate my husband. I would kill him to escape from here. Murder is not always immoral, you know."

Mary, unsure of how to respond to that sudden burst of passion from such a seemingly gentle woman, glanced at her watch.

"This room connects to another conference area. Jesus Martinez and Pierre Picard, a Frenchman who is seeking asylum in America, need to meet with you. Pierre is trapped here just as you are."

Before waiting for Safi to respond, Mary rose from the table and quietly knocked on the door connecting the two rooms. The two men entered. After introductions, Mary outlined everything she had covered with Safi.

"I'm afraid we're in the dark about the 747's flight plans."

Martinez smiled at Safi and then turned to Mary.

"I talked to my Air Force contact this morning. He claims the plane isn't going anywhere for ten days, maybe two weeks. Pierre here can verify that. He has a connection with an official in charge of the food commissary that services Al-Jabeer's plane." Martinez nodded at Picard. "Why don't you tell them what you know?"

"The order has gone out to stock the plane on March 29th, five days from now," Picard said, in a deep, heavily inflected accent. "Judging by the menu, it's headed for Indonesia and that means it's likely to be gone from Jeddah for a week or more."

"How did you get this information?" Mary asked.

"A former Sepi Industry employee," Picard said with a smile. "He was head chef for the company and we've stayed in touch. The commissary he now works for has a contract to supply food to commercial and private aircraft using the airport."

"Is he French?"

"Syrian. And let's say he owes his life to me. I won't go into details."

"That doesn't always count for much," Safi said. "Not in this country."

"In this case it does, Madam. He'll do anything to help. No questions asked."

"Call me Safi, please."

Picard nodded.

"It looks like we should be leaving in about four days," Martinez said.

Four days. Those two words etched themselves on Safi's mind. She realized for the first time that her dream was more than merely a dream. She tried to sound businesslike, but her voice wavered.

"I'll write down all I can remember of my travels through the private air terminal," she said, then turned to Mary. "This is real, isn't it? This is actually going to happen."

"I appreciate how you feel," Picard said. "I began to despair I would ever leave here. We all have our reasons to make certain we do this successfully."

"I suggest a rehearsal at the airport in two days," Mary said. "Safi, make sure your guards and anyone else you deal with know that you're meeting a friend at the airport. While you go through the private terminal, we'll all be watching. Two days later, we'll simply repeat the process."

"On the day we leave, I'll enter the aircraft first with the co-pilot," Martinez said. "Then you, Safi, with Mary as your bodyguard. If we run into problems with the exterior door locks, you ladies will have to cause a diversion. Maybe use the jewel boxes—give some away as gifts. We need just enough time to spring that lock if there's a problem."

"Okay, that leaves the task of getting the 747 to the terminal from the maintenance hangar," Mary said. "What do you have in mind?"

"It's already half fueled up and ready to go." Martinez grinned. "My new friend, the security guard, has been very helpful. He's under the impression I know Omar Sharif. He's angling for a signed photograph of him."

"What's that got to do with fuel?" Mary frowned.

"Well, thanks to him, I walked right inside the plane and checked the instruments, pretending to be a maintenance man. He's really anxious to get to the States. Should we add him to our Noah's Ark?"

"Not funny, Martinez." But Mary couldn't hide her smile. "What else?"

"Pierre's contact in culinary will order ten carts of food. I'll telephone the hangar shortly afterwards, on behalf of AJ Enterprises, to inform them the plane is to be at the terminal at ten-thirty in the morning. That's pretty much the routine out there. It will be towed to the terminal and there's a good chance the doors will not need to be unlocked."

"We should be so lucky," Mary said.

"Not really. I've sat in the terminal and watched other private jets being towed to the gate. Twice, I went down the ramp dressed in my maintenance outfit and saw that the ground crew opened the passenger doors and left them open. The Jeddah airport isn't exactly Fort Knox."

"When will you file the flight plan?"

"Seven, on the morning we're leaving, so the tower will know what the movements will be."

"Good. We've agreed that the flight's original destination, as far as the tower is concerned, is Tabuk near the Jordanian border. We can talk about the in-flight destination changes later, but for now, the authorities will see a local flight and that should look totally normal."

"I only have a photocopy of my American passport," Safi said. "But once I'm in the U.S., I'm hoping I'll be okay. They might hold me for a few hours."

"We talked about you taking some money out of the country," Mary said. "If you bring cash into America, it might be confiscated. Do you have an account here?"

"Yes. The last I looked there was four million or so in it. I was going to convert it into cash or a cashier's check. What do you think?"

"Does your husband have any control over that account? I mean, would the bank call him if you withdrew all your funds?"

"No, he has no authority on my account. I think he gave it to me so I could feel I had some kind of control over my life. Both of us were educated in the States and I went from being an independent woman to becoming a prisoner. When I complained—this was early in our marriage—he said I have everything a princess could ever want. But I kept after him 'til I got my own personal account." A brief shadow crossed Safi's features. "He wasn't all bad—especially in the beginning."

"Okay," Mary said quickly. "The day before we leave, stop by your bank and have them make up a cashier's check in your name for your money and one in my name for one million. What about other personal possessions?"

"There's some art work I'd like to bring, but how can I without causing attention? The only other thing of value is my jewelry, and I have lots of it."

Mary turned to Jesus. "Is that a problem? Can she bring in a fortune in jewelry?"

"Just declare it." Martinez shrugged. "Safi is a princess, after all. Jewelry and royalty go together, but if someone notices it is gone, it could be a problem. Forget the artwork."

Picard had sat quietly listening to the others, then looked at Mary. "Do you mind if I make a suggestion?"

"You're a member of the party, Pierre. A paying member, I should add. Speak up. We need good ideas."

He smiled and turned his gaze on Safi. "You will be arriving in your personal Mercedes limousine dressed in a black burqua. My guess is it will wait for you just away from the hotel portico. We'll need another Mercedes limo to take all of us to the airport."

"There's a sign in the lobby that advertises Hanco Limousine service," Martinez said. "We can reserve one. The only hitch is getting all of us out of the hotel without Safi's bodyguard or her chauffeur noticing."

"Not a problem," Mary said. "We'll have our limousine pull right up to the hotel portico and we'll just pile in. Safi's guard won't be looking for her wearing a gray burqua, or maybe one of my uniforms." She turned to Martinez. "What do you think about the uniform idea?"

He shook his head. "It won't work. There's no place to change at the airport without the risk of being noticed. If we're going to make a grand sweep into the private terminal by limousine, then Safi will have to wear a silk burqua. She'll have to leave the hotel dressed that way." He glanced at Safi and winked at her. She tried to return his wink but only managed to twist her features into a comic mask. "We can pick up a gray silk one in the lobby store and have it waiting."

Martinez felt a little uncomfortable raising the issue of Safi being nude beneath her burqua, but felt it was necessary.

"Safi," he said. "Will you be naked beneath your burqua when we go through the terminal? I mean, in case someone decides to challenge you?"

"Yes," Safi replied. "I doubt anyone would dare demand removal of my burqua, but if I'm naked, no Saudi man will dare look at me. It is a long shot, but I'd rather be careful than sorry. I will have a change of clothes in a small bag. Once we take off, I'll get dressed properly."

"Not to change the subject," Mary said. "But do either of you guys know what burqua actually means?"

"A bag to cover your face," Martinez answered.

"Yes, essentially," Picard agreed.

"It has many names." Smiling, Safi explained. "Some call it a hijab or borqua. It's a shawl or veil to cover a woman's 'Awra,' which means the shameful parts of the body."

"And rightly so," Martinez said with a grin.

After shooting a look at Martinez, Mary suggested they

set the departure for March 27th. Martinez thought that date was doable if everything went according to plan.

"Now let's get all the pieces together for the departure," Mary said. "Jesus, you'll be responsible for getting the plane to the terminal. I'll call that rental service and arrange for the limousine and buy Safi's burqua. We already have the uniforms, tools and other stuff. All we really have to worry about is the actual departure."

"Some worry," Martinez said.

"Don't be negative."

"Easy to say."

"Just try it, okay?"

"Whatever." Martinez nodded. "One thing we haven't considered. What if Al-Jabeer cuts short his visit with the London mistress? That could be nasty."

"You know where he stays in Sardinia, don't you, Safi?" Mary asked.

"Yes."

"We can telephone there and have him paged—just to make sure. It might be good insurance."

"And if he isn't there—what then?"

"Abort maybe. We could consider that."

"No abort," Martinez said. "At this point, we just trust to luck. We're in all the way now."

Mary smiled.

"I like that attitude, Jesus."

"There's the issue of guns. I understand you have one, Safi."

"I do. My husband insisted on it years ago, for protection."

"I suggest you put it in your briefcase, we'll take it on board for you."

"All right."

"I have one thought," Picard offered.

"Let's have it," Mary said.

"The early morning flight can be chancy. Safi would have to arrive here no later than nine in the morning. It's a weekday and the hotel is eleven miles from the airport. The Medina highway will be choked with traffic. Her security may also wonder what she's doing at the hotel that early in the morning. What about departure from the terminal at ten o'clock? Safi can then pretend she has a breakfast conference at the hotel."

"We had planned for a conference at seven," Mary said, "but it is early. I think you've got a point."

Martinez turned to Picard. "You're carrying both French and American passports so I don't see any problems there. Safi has a photocopy of her American passport and that could cause delays on arrival. Mary and I have valid passports. If there's a delay or some kind of glitch, I think we should stay together until everyone is through customs and established in a hotel."

"Why the concern?" Mary asked.

"The plane could be reported stolen. If we leave on March 27th and fly towards Jordan on the first leg, then to the Canary Islands for refueling, we should arrive in New York roughly sixteen hours from departure. If there's a plane theft alert, we might get arrested when we arrive. Sixteen hours is a long time to be in the air. Someone is going to know that plane is gone and that Safi has disappeared."

Mary chewed on her thumbnail as she stared at Martinez, a habit he had noticed before and that, on balance, he found more endearing than annoying.

"Al-Jabeer may not know the plane is missing even if he returns early and sees it's gone. David Sassoon manages the plane's schedule, and he's not in Jeddah. He lives in Beirut," Mary said.

"But with Safi missing that's sure to cause a major investigation, Mary. That's all I'm saying."

"We have the aircraft lease," she said. "Once we're in American airspace or on the ground, we shouldn't have to worry about being arrested, even if there is a Saudi complaint."

Martinez rose from his chair and stretched. "It looks like we've tied the pieces together. Let's hope it doesn't all unravel. Pierre, how about joining me for a cigar?"

Chapter Thirteen

DAVID Sassoon was puzzled and in a high state of alert as he gripped the telephone. The bank manager had just informed him that Safi had withdrawn $4,000,000 and that strangely, $1,000,000 of it was payable to a "Mary Jane."

"That is very unusual Mr. Sassoon. We tried to reach you earlier, but without success."

"Mary Jane could be a code name," Sassoon speculated. "Did she give you any reason for the withdrawal?"

"No, sir. The only thing she said is that she intended to open an account in the new shopping center near the palace."

Sassoon could smell the bullshit in that explanation. Something was going on, something very worrisome. But he remained calm with the bank manager, who must not suspect a problem in the Al-Jabeer empire.

"Okay, call me if you hear anything more," he said and immediately rang off.

Sassoon looked at his watch. It was 9:30 at night in Beirut. He had to be in Jeddah in two days for the 747's flight to Indonesia, and he really didn't want to rush to Jeddah ahead of time unless he had hard evidence that she was plotting in some way against her husband.

There's probably a simple explanation for the withdrawal, he thought as he reached into a file cabinet for his Saudi Arabian passport. I'll call Dani on the way. He telephoned London only to find that Al-Jabeer had left and was probably in Sardinia. Sassoon glanced at his watch again and then dialed his personal pilot.

"I'm on my way to the airport. Call ahead and have the Lear ready for an immediate departure. How long before you can be there?"

"I'll be there within an hour," the pilot replied. "I can't guarantee a co-pilot though."

"Just be there," Sassoon snapped.

The Lear jet's departure was delayed by a sand storm, and it did not arrive at the Jeddah terminal until 6:30 the next morning.

"Get this thing fueled up and ready to go if need be," Sassoon told the pilot. "Christ, we nearly ran out of fuel getting here. I'll call you in the next couple of hours at the transit lounge."

It occurred to him that he shouldn't leave his 9mm pistol inside the aircraft, but he was in a hurry and did not want to risk a problem with Customs.

PRINCESS Safi Al-Jabeer's Mercedes limousine pulled into the Sheraton Hotel portico at 7:30 the morning of March 27th for a conference on charity functions for Red Crescent,

Arabia's version of the Red Cross. On the way to the hotel she reminded her bodyguard, Marina, that the meeting might last four hours. When Safi suggested that it would be all right for her and the chauffeur to use the hotel pool and to have breakfast instead of just sitting around waiting, Marina discussed it quickly with the chauffeur and he accepted for both of them. Safi exited the limousine, explaining that she would be back in the lobby at 12:30. Marina escorted her to the mezzanine conference room, taking note of the sign on the door, and then rejoined the chauffeur.

"How did it go?" Mary asked as Safi entered. "Any problem with the guard?"

"It went just as you said it would," Safi replied.

"Jesus won't be checking us out of the hotel. We don't want our departure to coincide with your disappearance. We've made several trips from our rooms down to the lobby with our luggage. Everything's inside of the limousine. It's waiting for us now. I'll hold your cane under my burqua."

Safi nodded, breathing quickly with excitement.

"It might be better to take your ring off until you're inside of the limousine. Someone might recognize it."

Safi removed the ring.

"I left a pendant behind for the room attendant to discover," Mary told her. "I'm betting that it disappears and that the man will claim he never entered our rooms. That will make it more difficult for anyone to start asking questions."

Picard and Martinez were waiting in the lobby. They had observed Safi's entrance and watched the movements of the chauffeur and bodyguard. Mary and Safi, dressed in burquas, left the lobby together and entered the rented limousine. In

Arabic, Martinez directed the driver to the airport private terminal. Handing him a handful of bills, he then suggested that after dropping them off, the driver return to the Hilton Hotel to pick up three other people at two o'clock and take them to the British Embassy. The ruse would prevent the driver from being available for anyone attempting to track Safi's movements.

But, Princess Safi's guard was no fool. She had waited outside of the Sheraton Hotel just beyond the portico with the chauffeur keeping her company. She convinced the chauffeur that going up to the pool roof was not a good idea, that it was abandoning her responsibilities. She noticed the women in the gray burquas exit the hotel and enter a Mercedes with two other people. Something about the group caught her attention. Just seconds after the Mercedes pulled away from the portico, she turned to the chauffeur, her voice tight with anxiety.

"One of the women limped," she said. The chauffeur dropped his cigarette on the asphalt and ground it under his heel.

"So?"

"Goddamn it Malik, I just have a bad feeling. Quick—run upstairs to the conference room. See if the princess is still there."

The chauffeur took the stairs to the mezzanine level two at a time and threw open the conference room door. It was empty.

"What the hell," he muttered. He reached for his two-way radio and announced that the room was empty.

"I'll check the roof, all around the pool area. You check the restaurants," the guard said.

Five minutes passed before the guard radioed the chauffeur.

"Any sign of her?" The two-way radio crackled again.

"Negative."

Reluctantly, the guard called the news into headquarters. She offered the possibility that the princess was with the group she was supposed to be conferencing with. They might have gone off to have breakfast somewhere, or she might be in one of the hotel suites with the others, but headquarters was not reassured and went into a state of high alert.

Marina wondered how long she would keep her job. She knew that Dani Al-Jabeer could be ruthless and did not tolerate mistakes. She had an aunt and uncle living in Jordan; they would put her up and help her find work. It might be time to move on.

ONE of Safi's personal housemaids greeted Sassoon when he arrived at the palace.

"I'm sorry Mr. Sassoon, but Princess Safi has gone to a Red Crescent conference this morning. In fact, she left only a half hour ago. Shall I leave her a message?"

"No, that won't be necessary. Was she carrying anything...? Perhaps a suitcase?"

"Oh, no, Mr. Sassoon. She had only her briefcase, the one with all the volunteer materials she carries with her."

"Do me a favor and look into her jewelry case. I want to make sure nothing is missing. I'll wait."

Safi had left a good handful of Mary's cubic zirconium jewelry in her jewel box in the event that Dani conducted an investigation into her absence. The housemaid, alarmed by the note of urgency and anger in Sassoon's voice, rushed up a long flight of stairs. She returned from Safi's bedroom, stuttering breathlessly.

"Sir, I looked in her jewelry box and it seems to be all there. But, certainly, some could be in the safe. I don't have the combination. Is there anything else I can do for you?"

"Thank you, Medina. Take my cell phone number down and if you hear from the princess, please call me at once. If Mr. Al-Jabeer calls, tell him to phone me immediately."

"Is something wrong, Mr. Sassoon?"

"Just do as I say," he said as he turned on his heel and left.

So she's out of the palace and going to a conference without her jewelry. Not much help there, Sassoon thought, as he drove his rented Mercedes toward the Old Town. Who the hell is Mary Jane? He immediately dialed Dani's security service.

"Yes, we have the princess with one of our female security personnel," the dispatcher said. "The schedule shows that Princess Safi is attending a Red Crescent conference at the Sheraton. Nothing unusual about that, sir."

Sassoon had already turned his Mercedes around as he listened.

"Who is the chauffeur?" he demanded.

"His name is Malik. He is part of the Al-Jabeer household, Mr. Sassoon. Is there a problem?"

"It's possible there is a problem. Patch me through to the security person who's with the princess."

"I will need clearance from my supervisor to do that sir. Will you hold?"

Sassoon's chest puffed out.

"You stupid son of a bitch," he screamed. "Put me through this instant!"

The red rage that surged through his body was followed quickly by an attack of panic. What if the woman had gone off the deep end? True, there was no evidence of any wrongdoing, not yet anyway, but the $4,000,000 in cashier's checks nagged at him. He was on hold and then could hear a telephone ring as he was immediately patched through.

WHEN the limousine arrived at the airport, Mary jumped out of the Mercedes and scanned the surrounding area, playing the role of Safi's bodyguard. She was dressed in her khaki uniform, with a scarf on her head covering her black wig. Satisfied, she gestured to Martinez—making a circle of her thumb and second finger, the classic "okay" signal. The others exited the limousine and entered the terminal. Once inside, Safi recognized two airport security men whom she remembered from other departures and arrivals at the airport. She limped over to them and spoke in her husky, musical Arabic.

"You have been so gracious and considerate to my husband and me in the past that I want you to have a little something in appreciation. I am so pleased to see you today." She handed each of them a velvet jewel box. They showed their gratitude with smiles and repeated bows. Safi turned and rejoined Mary. They walked slowly toward the boarding ramp.

A large black Sudanese security guard approached them just short of the ramp. Safi recognized his face, but did not know him. When asked for her passport and her husband's written permission to travel, she froze for just an instant, and then assumed the hauteur of a true princess. She demanded to know what this was about and threatened to call his superior. He explained that he was just doing his job, but Mary understood immediately what was happening.

"He wants a gift," she whispered. "He's watching the two security men."

Maintaining a smile to hide her terror, Safi quickly reached into her burqua and produced another jewelry box and handed it to the security guard. He opened it, removed what he assumed was a diamond ring and beamed with pleasure. He nodded, gave a little bow and waved them forward. Using her ebony walking stick, she resumed her slow but regal walk to the ramp. In the back of her mind she shuddered to think how close she had come to having her burqua removed and exposing her nakedness to that grinning half-wit. She leaned close to Mary.

"How did you know what to do?"

"In this part of the world it's common to buy favors with cash or gifts. You're probably not aware of this because you're royalty; you travel with a large entourage. My guess is the big guy didn't know who you were and that's why he approached you. When he saw the two men bow and scrape in front of you it began to dawn on him—'Hey, she's important!' Giving him the ring overwhelmed any other thought he might have had."

"I'm so used to seeing Dani's security men around when I come to the terminal. It's strange that they're not here." She shot a quick glance at Mary. "But, then, they're not expecting me, are they?"

Mary returned her stare, the faintest hint of a smile in her eyes.

"You better hope and pray they're not," she said.

While Safi and Mary were in the terminal seating area, Picard, dressed in a co-pilot's shirt and with Martinez's cap, walked down the ramp to inspect the aircraft. Martinez, also uniformed as an Al-Jabeer pilot, filed a flight plan for Tabuk and then joined the Frenchman in the cockpit.

"Do you think they're held up?" Picard said.

"I just passed them in the lobby. I watched a little drama with the security people and was about to go to them demanding they hurry on board. But everything was suddenly fine."

Five minutes later, Safi and Mary boarded the plane, and right on their heels, an AJ uniformed female steward hurried up the ramp, apologizing in rapid fire Arabic for being late. Safi had forgotten that when she traveled an attendant was always on board. But how did the woman even know about this flight? That was the question running through everyone's mind.

Safi approached the stewardess and handed her a jewel box. "It's so nice to see you again," she said. "Look what I purchased for you on my last trip to Jordan."

The woman's mouth flew open in amazement and she fumbled for words. But before she could reply, Safi continued.

"This is a very short flight—to Tabuk—and we'll be back late tonight. Why don't you take the day off? My bodyguard will take care of the snacks."

"But this is my job," she blurted.

"Please go now, I insist," Safi said.

"Well," the stewardess said, hesitating, her eyes darting quickly at the others.

"When I return I have something else in mind for you. I promise to be in touch."

The stewardess left in a state of high excitement and Martinez watched her go.

"What the hell was she doing here?"

No one answered. Once the hatch was closed, Mary

spoke.

"We've chewed up fifteen valuable minutes. Let's get this plane in the air."

"Got to wait for taxi clearance," Jesus replied.

She moved into the co-pilot's seat, studied the controls with Martinez and listened to him as he explained that the layout was exactly like the Microsoft software except for a lever marked Auto Ramp.

"What's this for, Jesus?"

"I imagine it's for the gate that lowers the BMW."

"Christ, that's a lot of extra weight," Mary groaned.

"Yeah, but we don't have any luggage," Jesus quipped.

"Master switch on," he said.

"Avionics switches, fuel gauges okay, but we are only half full," Mary replied.

"Altimeter setting, lights, directional gyro—all normal," Martinez said.

"Check the flaps, Jesus. When we reach the hold position on the tarmac, set them at five degrees."

Martinez dialed the radio to frequency 121.6 and spoke in English, the standard language all pilots and air controllers use regardless of the country they're in. "Jeddah ground—Boeing 747-1441. Request taxi to holding point one-six-right."

BACK at the terminal, a telephone rang.

"Yes, Mr. Sassoon the princess is on board," the Sudanese guard replied. "The stewardess has just left the aircraft."

"I am ordering you to stop that aircraft from taking off. Do you understand?"

The security guard rubbed the beautiful jewelry piece

Safi had given him. He did not want to stop the aircraft, incur the wrath of the princess and possibly lose his gift.

"I cannot stop a domestic flight without police orders," he replied instead.

Sassoon, now feeling a full surge of panic, yelled. "She does not have her husband's permission." He could have predicted that woman would be trouble. She was too American, too independent. Sassoon did not know her personally, Dani kept her in seclusion from his business associates, but he had hinted at her failings more than once.

"But Sir, the princess has an ESS security guard with her."

"I don't give a shit who she has with her. Get down to the tarmac and throw chocks under the wheels of that aircraft. If it takes off, you are a dead man."

The big guard's eyes scanned the terminal. Everything seemed normal. He could hear the jet's engines turning in the distance. David Sassoon's words scared him. He did not know what to do. Finally he put the receiver down and began running towards the gate.

"Stop—stop that plane!" he shouted. He sprinted through the gate doors, picked up a wheel chock and began running toward the nose of the 747.

THE tower responded to Martinez's request. "Boeing 747-1441, you are clear to taxi to one-six-eight and hold short of runway. Tower frequency is 118.2."

The aircraft pushed back from the gate and began rolling, a behemoth rumbling awake from a deep slumber. Martinez was sweating profusely. He glanced at Mary.

"I must be getting old," he said. "My hands are clammy."

Mary saw him first.

"What the fuck is that nut doing?" she yelled into her headset at Jesus.

"Shit, he's under the aircraft. I saw a wheel chock in his hand."

"Move, move, *move* Jesus. He's going to jam one of our wheel pods. This guy is a security guard, not a cop. But he wants us stopped."

Jesus was breathing hard as his eyes studied the terminal gates. The 747's forward motion suddenly lurched left as the chock bit into a wheel pod. "We're stuck, god damn it, we're stuck."

"No," Mary screamed. "Roll over it. I don't care what you have to do, but get over it. Now—*now*!"

The engines screamed in protest as the fuselage swung wildly to the left, then suddenly the left wing swooped up and came down hard.

"You did it Jesus. Now taxi normally, we don't want to attract any attention."

"What if the tower saw the incident?"

"Tell them some asshole maintenance guy ran across your front and you swerved to avoid him." Mary shook her head.

"I've got a bad feeling about that Mercedes that just came onto the tarmac from the terminal. It looks like he's trying to force his way through the cyclone fence."

SASSOON dialed his Lear jet pilot as he approached the terminal.

"Get airborne," he yelled. "And fly to the private terminal. This is an emergency. I want you to land in front of the 747, it's taxiing down the runway as we speak and will be holding for takeoff clearance."

"What's going on?" the pilot asked as he ran for the Lear.

"Just do what I say. Land in front of it while it's on the ground and force it to stay put. Block it."

"If I do this, I'll lose my license and spend time in jail. This is crazy." But the pilot had already climbed in the jet and reached for the starter switches.

"I'll look after you. Don't worry."

The pilot ignored the control tower and all the rules of aviation as he roared down the runway. Shit, the private terminal is only four miles away, he thought. I'll barely be airborne before I have to land…heading in the wrong direction against outgoing traffic. He inched past stall speed and began looking for a way into the private terminal's runway without colliding with another aircraft. Christ, there it is. This is going to kill all of us! He swung the Lear in line with the runway. My God, all the arrows are pointing toward me. Shit, this is like some fucking nightmare! His landing gear was still down, and as he approached, emergency-warning lights flashed into his windshield. The rogue pilot had to land short or stall. He pushed the yoke forward and prayed for a safe glide down.

"IT'S okay, Jesus," she said with a wide grin. "That Mercedes won't get through that fence, and even if it does, there's not enough time for it to reach us."

"Yeah, right. I think my nerves are shot."

"Mine are shot too, but just hold on. Don't panic."

He frowned at the controls. “Who do you think is in that Mercedes?” he asked.

Mary sighed as she dialed in the tower frequency. “I’m trying not to guess.”

“I keep waiting for a call from the tower telling us to return to gate.”

“That’s why we’ve got to move it, Jesus.”

He nodded and then spoke into his throat microphone.

“Jeddah tower, Boeing 747-1441. Ready for takeoff on six-right departing south.”

“Good morning Boeing 747-1441. Jeddah Tower. You are clear for takeoff—one-six-right. After takeoff, call Jeddah control 119.1. Thank you, and have a good day.”

Mary pushed up all four thrusters, almost maximizing power. Martinez stared down the runway intently, leaning forward, unblinking.

“C’mon, Jesus, it’s all yours,” Mary shouted into the headset.

The four Pratt & Whitney PW4062 jet engines roared. Martinez blinked, seeming to emerge from a trance. The terminal between the two main runways rolled past on his left. Vehicles with blinking blue lights were on his right and Martinez followed them with his eyes.

“Maintenance vans, Jesus. Snap out of it,” Mary yelled.

“One of the guys down there—Muresh, my buddy. I’d love to see his expression if he could see me in the pilot’s seat.”

“No you wouldn’t,” Mary replied, trying to conceal her fear.

“Mary, that Mercedes is throwing up a lot of dust and it’s cutting across the runways toward our front. I think it’s trying to block or ram us."

"You can't stop now. Let the son of a bitch just try to ram us. We're bigger than he is."

"I'm at 125 knots, we need more. That Mercedes is going to outrun us before we're airborne." Then, almost panicky he shouted. "Release the ramp lever holding the BMW. We gotta lose weight fast."

Mary pulled hard on the lever. She looked down at the long runway and yelled at Martinez to keep going. Then she spotted it.

"Christ, there's a jet aircraft landing in front of us. It's going the wrong way."

"Set the flaps at ten degrees," he said. "I'm going up."

"You can't, it'll stall. The outside temperature is too high for this speed—we'll crash. Jesus, don't do it," she pled.

"No choice. Pray for that first BMW to drop. We're dead otherwise." Martinez pushed the thrusters upward for all the power the aircraft could muster and the fuselage shuddered. He heard the sound of an electric motor.

The 747 required a higher takeoff speed, but without cargo there was a chance it could lift, stay in the air and not stall. Martinez made that calculation. His eyes were riveted on the Mercedes converging on his left four hundred yards to his front. The rogue Lear was on the ground straddling the runway. The 747 bounced once, then again, but neither BMW fell, although Jesus could hear metal scraping the runway. The plane hung in the air for an eternity. It began to sink. The edge of the ramp, between the wheel pods, scraped the ground, sending out a shower of sparks. Suddenly the jeweled BMW shook loose, plummeted twenty feet and struck the ground; the rear section collapsed and the fenders fell away. Momentum hurtled it forward. With the extra weight gone, the 747 leaped into the air.

Mary and Jesus watched the Lear slide beneath them as the 747 clawed its way skyward. The roof of David Sassoon's Mercedes almost touched the 747's tail. At the last second, Sassoon veered away, but not before clipping the Lear and spinning it directly into the path of the careening BMW, with its nose poised up. Amazed air traffic controllers watched as the car bowled down the runway at ninety miles an hour trailing a fiery plume of sparks.

The giant plane rose and climbed to 10,000 feet before turning west. It was only then that they saw the wrecked Lear, its tail section gone and burning on the runway.

"I think our ten million dollar BMW just torpedoed that Lear. There must be thousands of diamonds scattered all over the runway," Mary said flatly, trying to mask her fear. "We're going to be in big trouble if the authorities order us back"

Mary levered the ramp closed.

"Maybe the confusion will give us time before they come for us," Jesus said, gritting his teeth and pushing the throttle levers back to maximum. "The Lear's on your side now. What do you see?"

"Right now, all I can see are flashing blue lights and a couple of fire trucks," she replied, craning her neck for a better look. "Let's hope those guys find the diamonds. Maybe we should follow the Red Sea. It'll take us out of Saudi airspace in six minutes. We can't risk being forced down."

"I know you're shook up Mary, but if there's trouble, we can land at an Israeli airport in about forty-five minutes."

The 747 pointed north for its 600 mile run up to Jordan.

Jesus' shirt was soaked in sweat and his hands held the yoke in a death grip. Mary's face was drained of its usual high color. Both understood that the crashed Lear would send major alarm bells ringing, but there was nothing they could do except fly as fast as possible.

The cockpit was silent until Martinez turned to Mary. A slow grin creased his face.

"I'm shaking like a leaf, but you know something? We made it. We got away. And this is the part the pilot in me loves—heading up into the sky. This is almost better than sex."

"You think so?" she said softly as she looked into his eyes.

"I do indeed."

"Well, speak for yourself."

"Why don't you go back and see how the others are doing? I'm fine up here. Shaky, but fine."

She nodded and unhooked her belts. As she rose, he reached for her hand. They stared at each other.

"We're doing it, Mary," he said.

"Yep. We're sure doing it. Want me to brew you some coffee?"

"That sounds great."

Before she could slip away, he leaned to the side and kissed her cheek.

"Is that for me?" she said, honestly surprised.

His answer was a brief kiss on the lips. "That's for both of us, partner. I guess I showed a chink in the armor back there."

"Not really. You've never done anything like this before."

"Neither have you," he replied.

"Well, I have in a way. I'm the General's daughter, remember? And my father has always been a real risk taker. He brought me up that way."

"Whereas I'm the son of a Mexican fisherman accustomed to the simple life?"

Mary laughed. "Not so simple. There's nothing simple about you, Jesus. But if you want to think so, that's okay. I'll go do the coffee now."

Chapter Fourteen

STRAPPED into her seatbelt and feeling the plane rise, Safi closed her eyes and fought to control her breathing. She had been so preoccupied with the boarding drama that she had forgotten she was still wearing her burqua. When the airplane reached cruising altitude at 35,000 feet she slipped into a bedroom, ripped it off, and let it fall to the floor. She was leaving her son behind, locked in his surreal world of the mentally ill—a prison from which he would never escape, but she tried not to think about that. She tried not to think about Dani and the rage that would erupt when he learned that she was gone. She tried to think about freedom. That was the one thing she had to hold on to. She must be strong. She must look ahead.

Entering the cabin, Mary tapped her lightly on the shoulder. "Feeling okay?"

Safi opened her eyes and smiled up at her. "I guess—I don't know. I guess I feel reborn. I still can't believe this is happening. I prayed so hard, and for so long. It's a miracle."

Picard was still thinking about Safi's nakedness beneath her burqua when he came into the cabin.

"I've made coffee," he said.

"You beat me to it," Mary replied. "I promised Jesus a cup. I'll take it to him."

Picard regarded Safi, a kind of questioning in his dark eyes. Now that he had a chance to see her without her burqua, dressed in jeans with a loose, pale blue, silk blouse, her beauty stunned him. But he knew that no Arab woman would expect a compliment from a man other than her husband, so he remained silent. He was aware that she was American born. Still, he had no way of knowing how liberated she might be.

Mary rejoined Martinez in the cockpit with two cups of coffee. They sat next to each other in silence for a moment.

"How strange all of this is," he said. "We started off with a simple airplane repossession—just the two of us—and now there are four of us."

"Our flying Noah's Ark," she said.

"Without forty days and nights of rain, I hope."

Mary studied his profile with its lean, slightly aquiline features.

"Why did you kiss me?" she asked after a long silence.

He took a moment to answer. "You've been very patient with me," he said finally. "I have a lot of baggage and I don't like to open it for you or anybody."

"That doesn't exactly answer my question."

He looked at her. "Mary Jane, I like you. You've got the guts of a cat burglar. But don't ask too many questions, okay? Is that a deal?"

She nodded. "I guess it's a deal."

"WHAT do you mean the 747 is not at the terminal?" an AJ security officer screamed at a terminal attendant, who held the telephone away from his ear. The security officer slammed down the phone and dialed Dani Al-Jabeer's private cell phone number. There was no answer. He drummed his fingers on the table, cursing under his breath. Five minutes later, he tried again. This time Al-Jabeer's mistress, Sandy Blair, picked up. She explained that AJ was on his yacht with a party of business people and was not expected back until three o'clock.

"Can you reach him by telephone?"

"No. He left his cell phone with me," Sandy responded.

"What about the yacht?"

"Sorry. He didn't leave me that number."

"Well, please get a message to him as soon as you can. It's urgent." The security officer hesitated, but in his desperation, decided to confide in this woman with the well-bred English accent. "Tell him we think Princess Safi may have left the country in the Boeing 747. We need to confirm that he did not order the aircraft out."

"I'll certainly relay the message."

She smiled as she hung up the phone. The plane was gone, Dani's wife had disappeared. This news, if it were true, would surely lead to a divorce. Sandy Blair understood Al-Jabeer's rigid code of honor. She smoked a cigarette, thinking things through one step at a time. She then dialed the dock to notify them that AJ was to call the villa when he returned.

But it will be far too late for him to stop her by the time he gets the message, she thought. Still, I will have tried. And I will be by his side to comfort him.

She poured a glass of Chardonnay and continued to smile.

"WE'RE approaching Tabuk," Martinez said. "It's time to radio in with a change of flight plan to Sardinia and ask permission to cross Jordanian airspace."

"Okay."

The Tabuk tower approved the new course and advised them of the Jordanian radio frequency for clearance. Everything went smoothly. It took only fifteen minutes to fly over Jordan and into the Mediterranean. Near the Italian island of Sardinia, Martinez again called ahead, this time to alter the course for Athens. Clearance came, but instead of heading east, Jesus dropped to 500 feet and flew west toward the Canary Islands. He wanted to be off the radar screen for at least 100 miles before returning to 35,000 feet. He then called the Tenerife air tower using a slightly altered registration number—1541.

Jeddah Tower frequency 119.1 suddenly came on. "Boeing 747-1441, this is Jeddah Tower requesting your return to base on 16 right. No clearance required. It is requested you land immediately. Please advise your current position."

Martinez had been waiting for that call. He knew it had to come but, instead of answering, he dialed in another frequency, aware that the tower would hear the clicking.

If they hear enough static they might think I'm on the blink. We can buy some extra time, he thought.

He dialed back to Tenerife's frequency.

"Tenerife, this is Boeing 747-1541 Delta 800 miles east of you. Flight level, one-eight-zero tracking for Tenerife. Request clearance to land and refuel."

The radio crackled. "Boeing 747-1541 Delta, this is Tenerife Tower. Maintain present course and flight level one-eight-zero. Advise when you are 100 miles from station for landing instructions. Permission to land, affirmative."

Moments later the control tower at Jeddah called demanding that the 747 return to Jeddah regarding its involvement in an air crash incident.

"Affirmative," Martinez answered.

"Do you think they'll buy that?" Mary asked. "I mean, it won't take them long to notice we haven't turned around."

"They don't know where we are. We'll be three hundred miles over the Mediterranean on the way to the Canary Islands by then. I don't give a damn whether they notice or not. They don't have any jurisdiction out here."

"We need all the distance we can put between us and Jeddah," she said. "There may be a theft alert out by now. It's been less than three hours, but still you have to think about the possibility."

Martinez checked his gauges. "Normal cruising speed for this plane is 567 knots per hour. I'm running it at 590. That puts New York within six hours after we refuel. We could fly into another airport—it doesn't have to be New York. What do you think?"

Mary nodded. "New York is too obvious. How about Cincinnati? Maybe the Customs is a little less intense there. Wait." She snapped her fingers. "Cancel that. I just remembered Cincinnati has no Customs facility."

"We could top up our tanks in Bermuda and then fly direct to San Francisco," Martinez said. "We don't need the fuel, we've got plenty of range, but it might help disguise our trail if someone is looking for a plane going non-stop from Arabia to America."

"A lot of my father's airplanes are at the Santa Rosa airport, about fifty miles north of San Francisco. It has an extended runway. Maybe San Francisco is the answer. Let's do it."

"I'm okay with that. But if we run out of fuel over water, I'm really going to hold you accountable."

Four hours later, they refueled at Tenerife and were flying over the Atlantic toward Bermuda. Picard looked after the food and drinks during the run to Tenerife and made a point of waiting on Safi, but she was eager to help and joined him in the gallery. She had heard so many lurid stories about what went on inside the aircraft and felt compelled to see it all. She paid particular attention to the bedrooms, which were whorehouse elegant. Later, she gave Mary a tour where they both speculated on the level of eroticism and debauchery that must have taken place on board.

"This puts my husband in an entirely different light," Safi said. "I knew about it, of course, but seeing it is different."

Mary was fascinated by the lavish and vulgar display of wealth and, fueled by curiosity, she began to look through the bedroom cabinets. In the second bedroom, a drawer pulled open only four inches. She pushed it back and tried again. This time, the drawer came out completely and she discovered that it was twice as deep as the others. She peered inside and could see a small brass handle at the rear. She twisted it, but it was locked. She went to the galley to retrieve the set of lock picks and managed to jimmy the handle open. A hidden motor moved the headboard away from the wall revealing a very large, long and narrow metal box flush with the fuselage. It resembled a rectangular electrical junction box, but when she sprung the lock and lifted the top, her startled glance swept over rows of gold bars each about eight inches long and three inches square. The depth of the box was approximately two feet, and the bars were stacked nine to a row—thirty-six bars total. She reached down to examine one of the bars. As she did, she could see bundles of cash lining the sides of the box, buried below the first row of gold bars. There were stacks of Euros, Greenbacks and English Pounds, too many to calculate a total. She removed one gold bar and a stack of cash and took them to the cockpit.

"Jesus, I think we have a problem."

Martinez hefted the gold bar in his hand. He shook his head and whistled. "Holy shit. I wonder what this guy was into?"

"It seems he was into collecting lots of gold and lots of cash. What do you think we should do with it?"

Martinez stared at the brilliant expanse of sky ahead.

"The plot thickens, doesn't it?"

"Day by day, it seems like." She rifled through the bank notes, counting under her breath.

"I would imagine the money doesn't exist," he said.

"That's my thought too. It's probably used for the sin tours—maybe for major contracts between the government and foreign businessmen. I remember the story of a General Electric vice-president who was accused of influencing a large jet engine deal with the Saudis. Al-Jabeer's company was supposed to have bribed him with something like fifteen million. Nobody could prove it, though."

"I smell drugs in it somewhere."

"Maybe, but I doubt it," Mary said. "He doesn't strike me as that stupid. He has other ways to make vast sums and then make the money vanish."

"Like I said, nonexistent money."

"Right."

"So what are you suggesting?"

A pensive thirty seconds went by. "I'm not suggesting anything."

"Oh, yes you are. You're saying it's ours to keep. Am I right?" Martinez asked.

"I'm not saying that. You are."

"But that's what you're thinking."

"So now you're a mind reader."

"What about Pierre and Safi?"

"What about them?"

"Do they need to be a part of this? I mean a part of whatever we decide to do?"

Mary regarded him for a moment, trying to read his expression.

"I don't know. Do they?" she responded.

"They weren't even supposed to be on this plane, remember? I see them as passengers, and the fact that Safi is Al-Jabeer's wife doesn't make it her money."

"Are you suggesting we split the money and gold between the two of us—I mean, if we decide to keep it?"

He hesitated before replying. "No," he said, shaking his head. "It has to be four ways. In the first place, there's no way we can hide this from them. They're going to know and we need their complete cooperation. Another thing, it doesn't really belong to anybody, does it? This means it belongs to them as much as it belongs to us."

Mary touched his hand and stared into his eyes. "It's one thing to repossess a plane, Jesus. This is something else."

"I know that."

"We're out of any gray area here, right into outright theft."

"I don't agree. We're still in the gray area. Al-Jabeer is the biggest wheeler-dealer in Arabia. He's a legend. Not to put too fine a point on it, but this is stolen stuff."

"You're rationalizing, Jesus. Trying to feel okay about taking it."

Martinez shrugged. "Look, if you don't want to touch it, put it back in the box. Lock it up. I can live without it."

Mary stared at the gold and money in her lap.

"I think we've agreed on one thing. If we decide to take it, we split with the others."

The "if" hung in the air like a cloud.

MARY returned to the rear cabin and explained what she had found and how she and Martinez thought things should be handled. After a lot of questions they agreed and sat down to count the money. Each stack of U.S. hundred dollar notes contained 200 bills, or $20,000 per stack. There were 300 stacks, for a total of $6 million. There was three million in Euros and English Pounds which, when converted to U.S. dollars, amounted to another $4.5 million. The cash, split four ways, gave each of them $3,375,000.

Picard went to the galley and found a small scale used for baking.

"Let's weigh one of the bars," he said.

Safi placed one on the scale and it registered eleven pounds. Picard pulled out a small calculator and tapped out a series of numbers.

"That's almost 400 ounces per bar and 36 bars equals 14,460 ounces. If an ounce is worth, say, $800, then that's $5,760,000 in gold. Give or take a million, we're talking about $20,000,000." He wiped his forehead with his hand, an exaggerated gesture of disbelief. "I feel like I'm in Aladdin's cave and this is really a pirate movie. Every kid has dreamed of running away and finding a secret treasure. I just never dreamed it would happen to me."

They gathered in the cockpit with Martinez.

"What's the verdict?" he asked. "Take the stash or forget about it. I'm fine with it either way."

"We've decided we can put it to better use than Dani Al-Jabeer," Mary replied.

Martinez glanced at Safi, who nodded her head in agreement.

"There are some real hazards here," he said. "We can't each carry a fortune of nearly identical sums through Customs without raising questions. They'll also have the plane's registration number and the point of origin we used to get here.

"So what do we do? Do we put the cash and gold into four separate luggage trolleys at the airport and just march past Customs? You know that won't work. The shit will hit the fan. Anyway, we don't even have luggage to put it in. What I'm thinking is, we continue the same roles we used to get out of Jeddah. Pierre and I are pilot and co-pilot. Mary, you continue as a bodyguard for Princess Safi Al-Jabeer, her jewels, cash and gold. It's not unusual for a member of royalty to have foreign security personnel and her own personal flight crew. When we're over San Francisco air space, we request an on-board inspection. At the same time, we ask them to arrange for secure transport of the cash and gold. They may have such a facility at the airport or they may give us the phone number of Brinks or another armored car service. The more open we are, the more routine this will appear to Customs."

"It sounds risky," Mary said.

"Everything we do from this point on involves risk."

Mary turned to Picard. "What do you think?"

"I would go with it," he said.

"Safi?"

"You have to decide. This is not my world."

Mary turned to Jesus. "Go on, Jesus. Tell us the rest."

"Well, the next thing is, the armored car needs a destination. I suggest they hold the valuables in storage. When we get to a San Francisco bank, we can open an account. We make arrangements for Brinks to deliver the gold and money there. Customs might try to give us some trouble, but we should be okay."

"So you really think it can work," Mary said.

"I'm not sure, to be honest. But it beats the alternatives. Trying to smuggle anything in is a lost cause."

"What happens if my husband puts out a theft alert for the 747 and we're stopped at the airport?" Safi asked. "Is there any chance we'll be arrested?"

"That's been on my mind," Martinez said. "Mary brought up the theft alert problem. But I think we'll be okay. The aircraft tail has the initials AJ painted on it and the fuselage has Al-Jabeer Industries lettered below the window line. You're an Al-Jabeer—

the copy of your U.S. passport says you're an Al-Jabeer, and there's nothing unusual about you flying around in a luxury jet. After all, you own it by virtue of your marriage. If there's a theft alert, you can state that you left Jeddah to divorce your husband after finding out he was cheating on you. We have the English woman's name and phone number if we need evidence. You were mad as hell. At first you decided to confront him in Sardinia, which is why we filed a flight plan for there. But you changed your mind and decided to return to the States and start divorce proceedings. Mary became your bodyguard because she had a U.S. passport and your regular guards did not. It's all been very emotional for you. I think you get the picture."

Safi slowly nodded. She seemed to swallow her breath as she gazed at Martinez.

"It makes sense. But what if Dani claims the aircraft belongs only to him or his company? What if he claims I stole the money and gold?"

"But he doesn't know we've found it, so he'll never bring it up. The last thing he wants is for anyone to know it exists. I think Customs or the police will see the airplane issue as a domestic dispute, and they'll take your side. This is America, not Saudi Arabia. In the absence of a court order from a U.S. judge, he would have no right of seizure. It would be different if you were only his mistress. Asking San Francisco for aircraft storage, having an armored car at the airport and not attempting to hide the valuables—that makes a really strong case." He turned to Mary. "So what do you think?"

"You're doing well today, Captain. I'm very proud of you."

The four of them put their fists together, one on top of the other.

"To success," Mary said.

"To success," they all said in unison.

Chapter Fifteen

MARY took a turn in the pilot's seat and Martinez lay back in his for a rest. He closed his eyes and sighed.

"I'm beat," he said.

"Get a cat nap, old timer."

"I guess we're about to be rich," he said. "Either that, or permanent guests of the federal government."

"Think positive."

"Impossible. My mantra is to think realistic."

"We have eight hours of flight time to destination," she said. "We should call Kinsley and Roberts and let them know we have the airplane."

"We probably should, but frankly, I'm in no hurry to do that. I'd rather wait until we're through Customs and get the banking sorted out."

"Why? What's bothering you?"

"Something just doesn't add up. That aircraft lease is for

$100 million. At nine percent, the lease payments come to just under nine million per year or $755,000 per month. When we first got into this, the sheer size of the transaction dazzled us. But now that I see all this cash lying around, and know that Al-Jabeer has other airplanes, I ask myself one question. Why would he default on the payments? I keep saying it makes no sense."

"Well, if no payments are made for a year he saves nine million. That's a huge sum, even for Al-Jabeer. The cash and gold may lever him into lucrative contracts, but somewhere along the line he might have had a cash flow problem. That happens to the Donald Trumps of the world." Mary thought for a moment. "Whatever his problem is, he'd never turn this plane back to the leasing company. It would eliminate his best business tool."

"So you're saying he does the next best thing and stops making payments."

"Right."

Martinez opened his eyes and regarded her for a moment.

"I still think we should clear Customs before you call those guys."

"Okay. But let's think about how we're going to make the actual delivery."

"DINNER is served," Safi announced. "Pierre and I have been slaving over a hot stove. The menu is lamb with fresh mint sauce, taboulleh, *very* spicy, baba ghannouj and a shirazi salad." Safi was enjoying doing ordinary tasks, particularly in the company of an attractive male. Picard made her realize how desolate her life had been. It felt good to work together in the galley, to sip wine and talk about her past without feeling she had to watch every word. She felt the bad years slipping away from her, evanescent as a slipstream.

The aircraft was on automatic pilot and for an hour they enjoyed talking and eating. Martinez was in the middle of recounting a funny story about his first week in the Air Force when he heard the cockpit telephone ring. He rushed forward and picked up the receiver on the sixth ring.

"Captain Martinez here." He waited through the crackling on the wire, aware that he was holding his breath.

"This is Captain Suleiman of the Jeddah Police Department. Sheikh Al-Jabeer has filed a complaint with us for aircraft theft. We are ordering you to return to Jeddah immediately."

"I'm afraid I don't understand," Martinez said.

"You had no authorization to take that aircraft, Captain Martinez. That is a serious felony."

"But I do have authorization. Sheikh Al-Jabeer's wife, Princess Safi Al-Jabeer, hired me and my co-pilot to take her to America."

"Captain, Princess Safi has no authority to leave Saudi Arabia without the written consent of her husband. You have committed an act of kidnapping. I must insist that you return to Jeddah immediately."

Before replying Martinez clicked the intercom on so that the conversation could be heard in the cabin.

"Princess Safi is on board with her American bodyguard and we are not over Saudi Arabia airspace. I do not believe you have the authority to countermand the princess' orders."

The voice at the other end was rising, losing patience.

"The princess has no authority to hire a pilot to take

her out of the country. If that were even remotely in dispute, Sheikh Al-Jabeer's word still carries more weight than the princess'." Suleiman was snapping off his words now, cold and sharp enough to slice the air between them.

"Captain Suleiman, the princess has every right to use an aircraft that is owned by both her and her husband, and that bears their family name. Every right in the world. Not that it has any legal bearing, but the princess became enraged when her husband stayed away from Arabia during Ramadan last November. He spent his time instead in Paris with his mistress, Sandy Blair, whom he then took to Sardinia. I know of this because Princess Safi originally hired me to take her to Sardinia to confront her husband with his infidelities and hypocritical religious piety." Martinez grinned at the phone. He was having fun.

There was a long, muted discussion between Suleiman and another voice. The Captain then came back on the line.

"Sheikh Al-Jabeer requests to talk to Princess Safi."

"One moment," Martinez replied. Mary and Safi were already in the cockpit. Safi took the phone.

"Yes. What can I do for you?"

"This is Dani. I don't know what you think you're doing, but you're mistaken if you imagine you can get away with it."

"Did you call to tell me that? Or did you call to offer me a reasonable divorce in light of your whoring around?"

"It's not adultery if I have an affair with a non-Muslim. You know that I have remained faithful to you and my religion in the eyes of Islamic law."

"That's interesting. Are you saying that I can have an affair with a non-Muslim man and not be stoned to death for adultery?"

"It's different for women, as you well know."

"What is different, Dani, is that I'm no longer in Arabia. I'm no longer subject to Islamic law. I'm still an American citizen. My married name is on this airplane and I have every right to take matters in my own hands. That's what I intend to do."

She heard his heavy breathing. She could imagine his soft brown hands clenching and unclenching with rage, desperate to reach through the wire and enclose her throat. But he hid behind his voice, which revealed nothing.

"You're making things more difficult than they need to be. Why don't you return here and we can discuss it in private?"

"You must be joking. Do you think I'm crazy? You would have me and this crew arrested."

"Don't make me do something I may regret," he spoke in a voice barely above a whisper, which strangely increased the menace.

"Let me tell you, Sheikh Al-Jabeer, what *you* are going to regret. *You* are going to read headlines in all of the world's newspapers about Princess Safi Al-Jabeer's escape from her cage. The press is going to get a tour of this flying whorehouse and they are going to get an earful from me on every television talk show in America. Everyone will know how you always leave Arabia during the religious holidays. And your mistresses—they will become household names. You think you're so high and mighty, above the law, with your money and mistresses and kickbacks. That may be a way of life in Arabia, but not in America. I can think of at least three American companies that received illegal kickbacks from you. I'm going to make sure those names are made public."

She leaned into the phone as she talked. Her pulse pounded in her temples, but she was giddy with a sense of release.

"I'll tell you something else I have for the press, Dani. I found a very pornographic tape in the pilot's compartment featuring some of your holy Muslim cronies having intercourse as a group with what looks like Arab women. You're not in that video, but your name is mentioned several times."

Al-Jabeer was surprised at Safi's forcefulness, and for a moment he was confused, even cowed. It was as though she had slipped into some other woman's brain—an American woman, liberated and disgustingly unfeminine.

"Safi," he said, managing to remain unruffled. "I am still your husband. I don't blame you for being angry. Think about our child and don't do anything foolish that might jeopardize our financial security. Call me when you land and we can sort this out. Let me know where to send a pilot to fly my plane back to Jeddah."

It was the last sentence of his appeal that made her realize how frightened he was. He wasn't worried about losing her. He wasn't worried about what she might try to do to hurt him. He was terrified at the thought of losing the money and the gold. The 747 was insured against theft if he could make that case. Losing it would not hurt him, and he had no more use for her.

"Our *child*?" she said. "You haven't seen him for years. And you never stopped blaming me for giving birth to a handicapped boy."

"That's not true. I never blamed you."

"Let's be clear on one thing, Dani. If you try to interfere with my landing in America, I will make your life miserable."

"Don't worry," he said. "I will not do anything to harm you. Just call me when you land."

The telephone connection went dead. Mary squeezed

Safi's hand.

"That was one hell of a show you just put on. Your eyes were blazing. Your words were like knife thrusts. Where did all that come from?"

"Years of repression," she replied.

"I'm beginning to think you're a natural red head like me, even though your hair is black."

The two women laughed and embraced.

THE final five hours of the flight to San Francisco were uneventful. No fighter plane flew up beside them to escort them to the ground, nor did the FAA broadcast a theft alert. The tension on board began to ease. The same question occurred to them all: Was it possible that they would actually deliver the plane and walk away rich?

Safi stared out the window during the landing approach. She could see the city of Palo Alto below and to her left, a reminder of her days at Stanford University. San Mateo crept by, just before the wheels touched the ground. Picard smiled and began to clap softly. Safi joined him. The 747 taxied to a terminal. A Customs inspector and an assistant came on board to examine the valuables. It took an extra hour to clear Safi, but her photocopied U.S. passport matched her Saudi passport, and her regal manner certainly did not hurt. Four Brinks guards were on hand with trolleys and canvas bags to take possession of the money and gold. As Safi exited the other side of the Customs gate, she tossed her headdress into a trashcan. They boarded a Hilton shuttle and left the airport for downtown San Francisco. The March wind had brought with it a soft rain and a silver clarity of air. So welcome after muggy Jeddah.

THEY met at seven the next morning in the hotel coffee shop. It was nearly empty at that hour, but even so, they took a booth in the rear. After ordering poached eggs on an English muffin and tea, Mary began.

"The Brinks receipt is in all of our names for thirteen point five million. I suggest using Wells Fargo Bank. They can receive the shipment from Brinks and a fourth of the total will be transferred into each of our personal accounts. We'll need four safe deposit boxes for the gold and we'll each receive eight bars. Safi, you'll hand the one million dollar cashier's check over to Jesus and me—the price we agreed on for this trip. You okay with that?"

"Of course," Safi said.

"I'll call Brinks and arrange for the delivery, hopefully early tomorrow," Martinez added. "Once the delivery's made, we can go to Wells Fargo and set up the accounts and the safe deposit boxes. The banking should be over with by noon tomorrow. Let's have lunch at the Tadich Grill. It's in the financial district on California Street, close to the bank."

Martinez regarded Safi, a line etched deep between his eyes. The worry line, Mary thought.

"Safi, whatever you do, don't telephone your husband. At least not yet. I don't want him showing up here with a regiment of lawyers. Right now, he'll have no idea where you landed until they track the airplane. That could take days, and by then, we'll have moved it for delivery," Martinez added.

"I'm not crazy," Safi said. "I have no plans to contact him. He needs to get used to the idea that I'm not going back."

"What about your son?" Mary asked.

"I'll make arrangements to have him brought to this country. The medical care is so much better here."

"Your husband may put up a battle."

"I'll barter with him for my child. Give him a free pass on some things he doesn't want made public. He is, first and last, a businessman."

Martinez turned to Mary. "In the morning I'll go back out to the airport, fuel up and then fly to Santa Rosa."

"Why Santa Rosa? We could let them take possession of the plane right here."

"I don't know really," Martinez answered. "I get the feeling that it's better to be in a place where we have more control. Maybe a smaller airport gives us that, especially if your father's people are nearby."

Chapter Sixteen

THEY called London from Mary's hotel suite.

"Global Leasing. How can I help you?" a female voice with an Irish accent asked.

"I would like to speak to either Ian Roberts or Charles Kinsley, please. Mary Jane calling."

"Mr. Roberts is on another call. Please hold."

A few moments passed. Mary could hear the sounds of muffled conversation and then Roberts came on.

"Mary, Ian Roberts here. How are you? Are you still in Arabia?"

"No. I'm in America with a very luxurious Boeing 747 ready to deliver to you."

"That's wonderful news. Charles will be very pleased. Where are you exactly?"

"In San Francisco, but the plane is on another airfield. I'll disclose the location when you fax me a copy of a certified check from Global Leasing in the amount of one point five million, less the $50,000 you already paid." She softened her tone, "just doing business the proper way."

"No problem, Mary. Let me have the fax number and I'll do it immediately."

She gave him the Hilton Hotel fax number. "When you take possession, will you have a pilot to move it? If not, I can arrange for one. You'll have to pay him for his trouble and for his return trip."

"Listen, if you have someone in place, by all means arrange for it. Charles and I plan to be on the West Coast in Reno two days from now for a conference—let's see…that will be April first. Convenient timing."

Very convenient, Mary thought.

"Okay, Ian, I'll call you when I see a faxed copy of the check." She hung up and turned to Martinez. "Everything seems legitimate. Now let's run through the delivery plan."

"I'm not expecting trouble," Martinez said. "But we are handing over a hundred million dollar asset and I don't want to be stiffed for the payment. We need to move the 747 from San Francisco to Santa Rosa when we see them arrive. If there are more people with them than seems right, we abort the delivery and I stay on the ground in San Francisco. If everything is okay, call me on your cell phone. I can fly there in less than an hour."

"That should work. I'll tell them you work for American Airlines and moonlight deliveries like this, and you're prepared to fly the 747 anywhere in America."

"Right. But in case things get edgy, it would be great to have some backup."

"You mean me?" Mary asked.

"Who else?"

"There's a Gulfstream IV at the Santa Rosa airport. I saw it when I visited my father recently. It belongs to a wine company. They might be willing to charter it to me. It's not as though we don't have the money. I'll follow you to wherever you take them. Roberts and Kinsley don't need to know about this."

"Let's get on the charter right away. I like the idea of you following me."

"You still don't trust them, do you?"

"In a deal like this I wouldn't trust my own mother."

"Let's go up to Santa Rosa in the morning," Mary said. "I'll call American Aviation, that's a flying school up there, and see who they know that's connected to the Gulfstream. I want to inspect it."

Martinez nodded. "By the way, I called Customs this morning and they agreed to release my 45-caliber pistol. We've still got Safi's pistol. You should take it—maybe use a leg holster."

Mary rolled her eyes. "We abandoned exploding telephones, ebony sticks used as a saber, lock picks, wigs and other James Bond stuff. And now you have me running around with a leg-holstered pistol."

"We didn't abandon those things. We just lucked out and didn't need to use them." Martinez sipped from a glass of ice water. She noticed that the deep line was back between his eyes.

"Something is stretching my paranoia," he continued. "We're talking about two guys you know next to nothing about. These guys are supposed to hand you a check for a million and a half. In exchange, you deliver an airplane to an unspecified location. It may sound logical, but the fax of a check is not the check."

"I know that."

"All I'm saying is that we have to take every precaution."

"Okay, I'll wear the gun. Does that make you feel better? Let's have lunch and check downstairs to see if the fax has arrived."

Later in the day, they sat in Mary's suite while Martinez examined a faxed copy of the Global Aircraft Leasing check made out to Mary Jane for $1,450,000. He frowned and tossed it aside.

"Still not a check," he said.

"Damn, you're stubborn."

Mary was upset by the implied criticism and frowned at Martinez while she picked up the telephone and called the Global Leasing number. Ian Roberts came on the line.

"Ian, Mary Jane here. When did you say you're arriving in Reno?"

"We are flying out tomorrow morning. We can take care of business before the conference."

"I'll be at the Santa Rosa airport day after tomorrow at eighteen hundred hours—that's a Thursday, April first. That should give you time to catch a Horizon Air flight and meet me there. One arrives at four in the afternoon. Can you make connections and be on it? Incidentally, the Santa Rosa airport is in California, maybe two hundred fifty miles from Reno. For you, that's a short hop."

"We'll be on the Horizon Air flight as you suggest," Roberts said with just a hint of coolness.

She hesitated. "It would be better if you and Charles are

the only ones meeting with me. I hope that's not a problem."

"Just the two of us. Will the 747 be there when we arrive?"

"I have it on standby. When I receive the check from you I'll make a telephone call. The plane will arrive in less than an hour. An American Airlines pilot, Jesus Martinez, will fly it. I've never met him. He's just a voice on the phone, but he checks out just fine. He has three days down time and he's agreed to do this little ferry job for you."

"Excellent."

"One more thing, Ian. I prefer not to board the aircraft with you for personal safety reasons."

"I understand. Prudence in all things." He tried to strike a note of levity, but she sensed flatness in his tone.

When Mary hung up, she nodded to Jesus.

"Did I sound okay?"

"A little on the cool side. I could feel my testicles shrivel." He drank the rest of his water and wiped his mouth with the back of his hand.

"In the morning I'll go to Santa Rosa and take the Gulfstream for a spin until I'm comfortable with it," Mary said. "I think I'll wear my Air Force uniform."

Martinez nodded. "I hope this rain clears up by tomorrow. It's supposed to, according to the weather report. I'd like Pierre to be on standby while we're delivering the airplane—maybe have him at the Santa Rosa airport just in case we need him. That's why I bought the extra cell phones, so each of us could have one."

"We've done quite a bit this morning," Mary said. "Let's get the banking done."

The quartet took a taxi from the Hilton to a bank on California Street. It was Picard's first time in San Francisco and the hills, the cable cars, and colorful street scenes absorbed him. He asked Safi if she would join him later on a cable car ride down to the wharf. The growing warmth between the Frenchman and the Pakistani princess was not lost on Jesus and Mary.

"Sure, Pierre, I'd love to do a tour," she said. "I'm so happy to see this city again. I feel I've come home."

As the cab pulled up to the curb, Martinez announced, "Wells Fargo Bank, friends. Time to do our business."

Setting up the accounts took less than an hour. The bank manager served coffee while they waited for the Brinks truck. When it arrived, the three guards escorting the trolley were immediately ushered into a secure room. The money was counted and the foreign currency adjusted to U.S. values and deposited into the four accounts. The gold was divided and placed into four safe deposit boxes.

That done, they walked to the Tadich Grill for a quick lunch. As Mary pointed out, she and Jesus had a little more work to do before they could truly celebrate. After lunch, the women went shopping. Picard and Martinez took the orange maintenance uniform to the hotel concierge and asked that the Saudi name be removed, leaving only "*Maintenance*" for anyone to see.

"We already have a belt and holster," Martinez said. "It was part of the stuff we thought we might need in Jeddah. There's a toy store up the street. Maybe we can find a realistic looking pistol to put into the holster. Pepper spray we have."

They entered a toy and model shop on Post Street and bought an air pistol that bore a close resemblance to a

45-caliber automatic.

"It's hard to tell the difference between the toy and the real thing," Martinez said as they left the store. "I'm not sure that's good for the kids of America."

Picard had been quiet and appeared lost in thought.

"I spoke with Marcel," he said, finally. "He wants me to do some business for him in New York. He's thrilled with the escape and congratulates you and Mary on your efforts. He said he might have a project for you if you're interested."

"I don't know. Right now I'm looking forward to some R and R."

"You deserve it."

"What's up with you?" Martinez said. "You seem a bit moody."

Picard flourished his hands, reaching for words.

"It's Safi," he said. "She's been on my mind ever since Jeddah. Watching the money go into our accounts this morning gave me the feeling that everything will be over soon and that she'll disappear from my life. Didn't you get that feeling at the bank?"

"Not really. I mean why would she disappear? Where would she go? She may have some old college acquaintances she can look up around Palo Alto, but let's face it—Safi's been out of America for ten years. What's left of her family lives in Pakistan under stressful circumstances, and the politics there aren't moving in her favor. I wouldn't look for her to be joining them any time soon."

"Yes, but her options of where to live are endless," Picard said. "She mentioned a large Pakistani community in London. And she told me she's thought about serving as a conduit for

Pakistani nationals in America, to fund human services in Pakistan. Plus, she's still a princess and, well, I'm a naval architect." He laughed, but not happily. "I must be out of my mind. You know, I couldn't take my eyes off of her while we were on our way over here."

"I noticed."

"This may be wishful thinking, but a couple of times I thought she showed some interest in me."

"Look, Pierre, Safi is scratching around for some kind of direction. Does that surprise you? She's a princess in title only. There's no kingdom, no servants, no soldiers to order into the field. Al-Jabeer glorified her title for his own purposes. I'd give her time and space."

Picard shook his head.

"I don't know how this happened to me so quickly," he said quietly. "But I've never felt like this, that someone is right, absolutely right, the only one. I'm afraid, I'll overwhelm her."

"Christ, man, haven't you been paying attention? The way she looks at you? It's obvious she has some pretty strong feelings. You're supposed to be the great French lover, right? Buy her some flowers—a lot of them. Let her know how you feel. Don't overwhelm her, but don't try to hide your feelings either. Timing is everything, pal, and you'd better grab your minute or it's over."

Picard's features collapsed in a boyish smile. "Thanks, Jesus."

"Okay, enough of this love talk," Martinez said. "I'm beginning to sound like a 'Dear Abby' column."

EARLY the next morning, Mary left the hotel with Picard, rented a car and headed north to the Santa Rosa airport dressed in her Air Force uniform. She approached the Gulfstream IV belonging to Korbel Winery and handed the hangar manager her pilot's license, log book showing she had been checked out on the G-IV, and credit card.

She spoke to the manager, and booked the plane for two days.

"I may only need it for one. Right now, I'd like to take it up and do a couple of circuits between Petaluma and Clear Lake," she said.

Rental agreements were signed and Mary did a pre-flight check and inspected every aspect of the aircraft. After flying the Gulfstream for half an hour, she touched down and taxied to an aircraft parking area just behind the tower's south side and shut the engines down. She called Martinez on her cell phone.

"How did she check out?" he asked.

"Beautiful airplane. Couldn't be smoother. We should buy one someday. I'm going into the terminal in a few minutes to see what Pierre learned, if anything. I told him to wear a jacket over the uniform to hide the printing. No point raising problems with the airport."

"Good. I'm inside the 747. It's been cleaned and it's parked in a holding area for an early departure." He paused. "Are you okay?"

"I'm fine."

"I hope you gauged these guys right."

"Stand by, Captain," she said, ignoring his comment. "I'm going inside the terminal. The next time you hear from me it should be approximately sixteen hundred-twenty hours."

She hung up and went to meet Pierre who was waiting in the empty airport restaurant. She ordered coffee, and they covered the main points of the transfer.

"I'm not sure why I have you here," she said. "But if something comes up, it's great to have backup."

"Well, I'm the only one that can call the police if something goes wrong. You'll be following Jesus in the 747 and anything can happen inside the plane when he flies those guys where they want to go. Bad things can happen."

"Yeah, I know, Pierre." She pushed her coffee aside and sighed. "But you know what bothers me most of all? April. The first is April Fool's Day."

THE following day, Mary and Pierre returned to the Santa Rosa airport. Pierre hovered in the terminal while Mary went out to the tarmac to greet the arriving aircraft. Under her right leg trouser, Safi's pistol was strapped and ready if the need arose.

"Good afternoon, gentlemen. I hope you had a pleasant trip." Mary beamed her 'cute' smile on the two Britons.

"Very pleasant indeed," Roberts said, his returning smile too forced, reflexive.

"Did you enjoy Reno?"

"Horrors!" Kinsley gave an exaggerated shiver. "Business does take one to some curious places."

We are talking around something, Mary thought. But what is it we're talking around? She fought against a flutter of anxiety that filled her diaphragm, conscious of each breath she took.

"Did you have any problems with the recovery process?"

Roberts asked.

"Not at all, Ian. It went according to plan."

As she checked her watch, she caught Roberts checking his.

"Perhaps we can conclude our business now," she said.

"I don't see the great hurry," Kinsley said, with a dismissive shrug. "The delivery of the 747 calls for a celebration. I've been looking forward to that. San Francisco is full of superb restaurants."

"Charles, I'm afraid I'll have to take a rain check. This is a very busy period for me, and I hardly have a minute to turn around."

"I understand," he said. But from the tightening of his mouth, it was clear that he was displeased.

"As we discussed," she said, turning to Roberts, who seemed the more businesslike of the two. "Once I receive the check, I can have the plane here in less than an hour. I hope that's satisfactory."

"Of course," Roberts said. He reached into the inside pocket of his Harris Tweed jacket and withdrew an envelope.

She broke the seal and examined the check. "OK," she said. "I'll make that call now." She pushed a button on her cell phone, waited a few seconds, and then placed the phone back on her belt.

"What kind of call was that?" Roberts said his blue eyes boring into her.

"I hit the redial button. When that number rings it's a signal for the pilot to leave for Santa Rosa immediately. My guess is, he'll be here within an hour."

"Anybody on board other than the pilot?" Roberts said.

"No, he's alone. His name is Martinez. Jesus Martinez. He's very seasoned and reliable."

"May I buy you a drink while we wait?" Kinsley said, his grin slightly lopsided and charming. "If I use all my blandishments?"

The conversation taking place on the tarmac offered an opportunity for Picard to get a good look at both men, so she agreed. They took a booth in the airport restaurant and discussed the possibility of Mary doing more repossessions for Global Leasing. They were clearly filling time as they watched the horizon for the 747 to appear. Mary saw it first. She pointed to the north. The two men glanced out the window, but did not react.

"It's coming in," she said. "His instructions are to taxi to that large hangar next to the American Aviation flying school. He will keep the engines running. You're to board and leave. That's it. A very simple plan." She smiled, but something was bothering her, something did not fit, and it left her with a chill of apprehension.

"Simple plans are best," Roberts said, not quite returning her smile.

They walked over to the hangar and arrived just as the 747 made its parking turn. A moment later the front-section door and steps swung down. Mary shook hands with both men, but the thin layer of bonhomie was gone. The engine noise was deafening and clouds of dust swirled as both Roberts and Kinsley mounted the steps and climbed into the cabin. The door closed and the 747 began to taxi. When the plane made its turn, Mary rushed back to the Gulfstream, started the engines and requested the tower for permission to taxi. She was advised to proceed, but to hold behind the Boeing 747, which she did.

Martinez delayed a moment at the holding apron and telephoned through to Mary.

"I see you are right behind me. Anything unusual to report?"

"Something's nagging at me but I don't know what it is."

"Did they pay us?"

"Yes."

"In full?"

"Come on, Jesus. They wouldn't be on board otherwise."

"We're getting richer by the day."

"If I were you, I'd turn on the microphone in the cabin so you can hear what they're saying. There's something creepy about those guys, especially Roberts. Any idea what the destination is?"

"Reno."

"Reno? They just came from there."

"Well, they're on their way back."

"Got the mic on?"

"Yep. Hey, I've noticed something really strange," Martinez said. "These guys are more nervous than we were when we left Jeddah. It doesn't add up, does it?"

"I'm beginning to think that nothing adds up in this business. Okay, Jesus, take off. I'll be right behind you. Take your pistol out of your flight bag and put it into your belt behind your back."

"My, my, now who's getting a little paranoid?"

"Just do it, okay? Just do it. I'm glad you didn't foist it off on me."

Once in the air, Martinez heard conversation from the

cabin coming through his headphones.

"Sadat Haif said it was in the bedroom. That stupid ass didn't mention there are four bedrooms. I thought you said he was on board partying it up with some bigwigs."

The hair on the back of Martinez's head stood up as he listened. He deliberately slowed his breathing, but could feel his pulse race.

"Chuck, you look in these two bedrooms. I'll take the other two."

"Right."

"But remember, Sadat said it was part of a panel—some kind of secret compartment. So take your time. Don't be in a hurry."

The cell phone rang in the cockpit, causing Martinez to jump.

"Me again," Mary said. "Guess what? I just telephoned the number on that Global Leasing check. It's a phony. I'm afraid we just got taken."

"Oh boy. Why am I not surprised?"

"And another thing. I know what was bothering me. When we were sitting in the restaurant and the plane was coming in for landing? They were oblivious. It was one of three that landed within ten minutes and they didn't recognize it."

"What are you getting at?"

"The plane isn't theirs."

"Well, I've got a hot bulletin for you. Those two guys are back in the cabin right now ransacking the bedrooms for the money and gold. They knew about it all along."

"Oh my God!" Mary exclaimed.

"Not good, huh?"

"Not good, but there's no need to panic."

"Why is that, Mary?"

"Because it does no damn good!" She took a deep breath and tried to fight back the fear. After all, Jesus was in the danger seat, she was safe, and she had to sound confident, reassuring. She had to control the tremor of fear in her voice. Still, the question had to be asked.

"So when they find out it isn't there, what then?"

"Well, if they think like me, they might conclude that you stole it before handing over the plane."

"Nobody thinks like you, Jesus."

"I hope not. But I wouldn't depend on it."

"What am I supposed to do? Go into hiding? I don't know what to do. Most likely they'll hold you as hostage to bring me back into the picture." Her voice caught. "I'm so sorry, Jesus. I'm sorry I brought you into this…"

"The search could take them a while," Martinez interrupted, not wanting to hear her in that mood. She was strong in some ways, and in other ways she wasn't very strong at all. He was beginning to be able to judge the line that divided her strength from her uncertainty. "By then, we'll be approaching Reno. I don't really want to be on the ground with them. No telling who they might be meeting, and whoever it is I'm not going to like much."

"As long as you're in the air, you're in control."

"Up to a point."

"Okay, let me think." The vision of Jesus being forced at gunpoint to another airport leaped into her mind. "I'll tell you what. When you get over the Sierra Mountains, call back into the cabin for one of them to come forward. When he does, tell him you've been in contact with the Reno tower, you gave them your call sign, and they informed you the Boeing 747 has a theft alert posted. Tell them you're being directed to San Francisco. Hopefully, that should give them something to think about."

"That's about the last place they'll want to land with a theft alert up."

"I know. They may want to return to Santa Rosa instead because it's so close," she hesitated. "And because I'm here. Tell them the alert system is now tracking the aircraft wherever it goes."

"Hold on, Mary. They're talking again."

It was Roberts yelling at Kinsley.

"I found it. The fucking box is empty. *It's empty*. How could that be?"

"Rubbish! Why would Sadat double-cross us?" His voice was close to a sob.

"It might be Major Jane," Roberts said. "Though that seems unlikely. How would she know about it? Or it could hae been taken by U.S. Customs."

"Impossible. Then Jane would definitely know. And why would she keep it to herself?"

"Sadat swore it was on board. He saw it, remember? He was a guest of the bloke who owns the plane—Al-Jabeer."

"Maybe Sadat stole the money and set us up. He's probably pointing the finger at us right now. That's it! He wants to put paid to us. If we get picked up in this airplane we'll have trouble denying we stole the plane, but didn't also steal the cash."

"Easy, Chuck. Let's take this logically, a step at a time. For the moment, let's rule out Major Jane. I mean you can't go on a search for something you don't even know exists. Sadat is a definite possibility, but I can't see him screwing up a deal. He's always been solid in the business."

"Honor among thieves and all that."

"Exactly. But there's also the owner of the plane to consider. Al-Jabeer could have removed the box contents without Sadat knowing. After all, the plane sat in Jeddah for more than a week."

"But why would he do that?"

"Maybe to point the finger at someone else."

There was a long silence in the cabin. Martinez held his breath, waiting for what came next.

"Maybe we should land and squeeze the pilot's balls a little to see what he knows," Roberts finally said.

"You think he might know anything?"

"It's worth a try."

"Okay—let's do it. We'll question him at the hangar. Corner him in the cockpit."

"We might have to threaten to neutralize him," Roberts said. "The questions we ask will reveal our complicity in this."

"We'll do what we have to do. Now let's get this bird on the ground."

Martinez quickly relayed everything he'd heard on to Mary. He threw a bullet into the chamber of his .45 and placed the gun under his shirt. He switched on the intercom and requested one of the men to come forward. Kinsley came into the cockpit. His face was pale and his features rippled with twitches. Normally the more affable of the two, he did not return Martinez's greeting but simply stood and waited.

"Reno tower has just advised me that there's a theft alert up for this aircraft," Martinez explained in a matter-of-fact voice.

"They're demanding its return to San Francisco."

Kinsley's mouth hung open in surprise and dismay. Without answering, he spun around and returned to the cabin. Again, Martinez listened in on the conversation.

"Ian—this is terrible. The Reno tower just advised our pilot that this airplane is stolen. A chase plane might already be on the way. What do we do now?" Again, Kinsley sounded close to tears.

"Well, Christ, man, it *has* been stolen. We just didn't expect to be on board when the news came out, now did we?" Roberts' voice dripped with sarcasm.

"The pilot is waiting for me to tell him what to do. If he's a stickler for the rules, we may have to force him to fly us to another airport. How much cash do you have with you?"

"Maybe five thousand. Why?"

"Reno tower can't possibly know we're on board. Their only concern is the aircraft. We can force the pilot to return us to the Santa Rosa airport, we can get out, and he can fly on to San Francisco. He would be complying with their order. I doubt they would notice the stop in Santa Rosa."

"So you want to bribe him?'

"You have a better idea?"

"We didn't steal the fucking plane, Chuck. Major Jane did."

"Okay. Maybe we should just land in Reno and plead innocence."

"What good will that do?" Roberts said, his tone nasty. "Reno security will check everyone that gets out of this aircraft. Besides, we can't risk bringing her back into the picture. We just handed her a phony check for one and a half million. I don't think she'd be a good witness for us."

"You've got a point."

"We could force the pilot to land in, say, Sacramento. We could make a run for it from there."

"But Ian, the instant we leave the aircraft the pilot will call the cops." He hesitated. "Well, of course, not if he's dead."

"You can't be that stupid," Roberts said. "At least I hope not. Jane knows we're on this plane. If the pilot shows up dead, we'll be wanted for murder. Right now nobody wants us for anything, especially if we can get off of this fucking airplane."

"I can't believe we're in this pickle. Everything was going so well. I hate to give up on it. Do you think we looked in the right place?"

"We're running out of time," Roberts said. "Go back to the cockpit and offer the pilot two thousand dollars to drop us back at Santa Rosa. We need to have a little talk with Major Jane."

Martinez had held his cell phone onto his headset and Mary had heard it all.

"Looking good, Jesus," she said. "Those guys are really rattled."

"Easy for you to say. They may decide to kill me yet."

"Take the money," she said.

"Well, hell yes. Do I have a choice?"

Martinez barely had time to set the cell phone off to one side before Kinsley reappeared in the cockpit.

"It seems there might be some sort of misunderstanding," he said, trying to sound official. "This aircraft has been repossessed for nonpayment of a finance contract. The owner probably thought it was stolen. We don't have time now to notify everyone and we'd rather not get caught up in the investigation. Red tape and all that." He attempted to chuckle. "The Americans are big on red tape."

"Sir, the Reno tower is calling me again," Martinez lied. "I guess you'd better tell me what you want me to do."

"Look here," Kinsley said, his face snaking with nervous ticks. "The best thing is to drop us back at the Santa Rosa airport. We can sort it out then."

Martinez regarded him with feigned puzzlement. "But the problem is this plane's been ordered to San Francisco. Reno tower has made that clear. How can I get around that? I don't need trouble. My license could be revoked."

"It would take an entire day if we become embroiled with authorities in San Francisco." Kinsley fought to control an urge to plead. "Look, as of right now, this trip is aborted. Why don't we just pay you two thousand dollars for your trouble?"

"Yeah," Martinez replied. "But, see, my fee for flying you anywhere you want to go is five hundred an hour. A short trip to Santa Rosa would hardly be worth my time."

"Okay, make it three thousand." When Martinez did not immediately respond, Kinsley added. "Never mind, we'll pay you four thousand."

Martinez hesitated a moment longer. "I accept, but I want the cash now, before we land. I won't let either Reno or San Francisco know you're on board. Is that a deal?"

Kinsley squinted and frowned as he examined Martinez. He wondered if the pilot knew more than he was letting on. The man revealed a slight insolence of manner and a knowingness that unnerved the Briton. But, without a choice, and with no time to investigate, he accepted.

"We have a deal, Captain. I'll be back in a minute."

Before Kinsley returned to the cockpit, Martinez put the 747 on automatic pilot and entered the cabin with his pistol showing in his belt.

"Gentlemen, I'm happy to accommodate you, but given the nature of these developments, I must insist on searching you for weapons. Both of you can oblige me by facing the wall and putting your hands up on the overhead luggage bin."

Kinsley gaped at him, at a loss for words. Roberts took one step forward, then stopped as Martinez's hand slid toward his belt.

"It looks like you came prepared, Captain," Roberts said. "What's this all about? You have absolutely no right to threaten us."

"This is not a threat," Martinez said. "I was hired for a rather mysterious job by someone I don't know. I wasn't given a destination, just a cell phone call to let me know when it was time to leave San Francisco for Santa Rosa. I have my safety to think about. For all I know, this job could have been to run illegal drugs. With the theft alert up, I don't want you to be tempted into hijacking the plane for another destination."

Roberts shot a quick glance at Kinsley.

"That makes sense," he said. Both men put their hands in the air. Martinez searched them. They had identical Smith & Wesson 9mm pistols. He shook his head.

"I don't know why respectable gentlemen like the two of you need to carry guns. I'm going to take these from you, just in case you aren't. When we get to Santa Rosa, we'll separate and that will be that. Meanwhile, don't come near the cockpit if you value your lives. Understood?"

Kinsley nodded, but Roberts gave him a cold, appraising stare. He was the one to worry about.

Martinez took four thousand dollars from Roberts, returned to the cockpit, and locked the door. Taking the controls, he banked steeply and set a southwesterly course for the Santa Rosa airport. He then picked up the cell phone and explained to Mary what had just happened.

"Should we still use Pierre?" Mary asked.

"Yeah, I think so. My idea is to tell them there's a security man at the airport waiting for us to arrive. I'll suggest to them that the best I can do is let them out on the tarmac just as I begin the taxi run back from the south end of the runway."

"You're a devil, Martinez. I never want to be on the wrong side of you."

"I'm happy to hear that."

"Those two crooks will be on the tarmac miles from nowhere. It's probably going to continue raining." She giggled. "You know, I kind of feel sorry for them."

"Don't bother. You overheard them talking about getting rid of me in Reno. Four thousand bucks and a long wet walk out on the tarmac is a just sentence."

"You're a devil *and* a hard man."

"Get in touch with Pierre. Have him stand in front of the terminal without his jacket. I'll do a low pass and point him out to Kinsley and Roberts. It might be hard to see the lettering on his uniform, but they'll get the idea when they see that he's armed."

Mary laughed. "With an air pistol no less. I can hear their voices. What are they saying now?"

"They're screaming at each other as you might expect.

That's what cornered rats do. Scream and show their incisors."

Martinez clicked on the intercom and told his passengers there was a security guard on the ground.

"Probably someone in an orange uniform in front of the terminal." He knew they would have their eyes glued to the windows during the descent. "We're cleared to land on runway three-zero north. That will put you on the southern end of this runway when I let you out. I don't need to tell you that the speed of your departure is paramount. So hurry away and don't fuck up. I don't want the tower to notice you in, or around, the plane."

"Thanks for taking the risk, Captain," Kinsley said. "We're not familiar with this airport. Can you tell us which way we should walk?"

"I'm not exactly sure, but you might head west toward the main highway." Martinez knew that the only highway in the vicinity was due east from their landing point, but couldn't resist sending them in the wrong direction.

The Boeing 747 landed and rolled to the end of the runway before turning toward the tower. It stopped briefly. The passenger door swung open unseen from the tower. The two Britons plunged down the steps and ran like jackrabbits toward the high brush beyond the westward-most hangar. Martinez retracted the steps and taxied to the terminal parking area. The Gulfstream IV landed just behind the 747 and Mary could see Kinsley and Roberts running through the brush, heads hunched into their shoulders, eventually disappearing into the dun and green landscape. She taxied to the Korbel Winery hangar and shut down the engines. As she exited the aircraft, Martinez strolled up with a wide smile.

"I'm beginning to think you're my lucky charm," he

said.

"That's funny. I was thinking the same thing about you."

"Why thanks, Major. Do I get a promotion?"

"To what?"

He wrinkled his brow. "I'll have to think about that. Steal Air Force planes and sell them to the Saudis? Starting our own fleet of floating whorehouses? The possibilities are limitless."

She reached for his hand and pressed it.

"Hey, Jesus, you were something else. Very, very fantastic. Your nerves must be made of steel."

"More like tinsel, I'd say."

She leaned forward and kissed his forehead.

"Let's leave the 747 here for a few days. We'll get Pierre and head back to the hotel. Some April Fool's Day!"

Picard was waiting for them at the terminal.

"Good job, Jesus. I'd have been scared out of my mind. Mary had your call put on the conference key to my phone. I heard it all. They could have killed you."

"I somehow doubt it. They were a couple of sad bastards."

"Well, look at it this way," Mary said. "They didn't have much of an investment to lose, did they? I'm sure that Sadat Haif put up the fifty thousand retainer. So we got four thousand out of them. They conned me into stealing an airplane full of cash and gold to deliver to them without their risking a hair on their heads. And they nearly got away with it. Very clever of them, right? It does make me feel a little better knowing we conned them out of the four thousand and sent them packing into the bushes."

"Where are they headed, by the way?" Martinez asked.

"Toward the hills. Toward the middle of nowhere."

THEY piled into Picard's rental car. Jesus and Mary sat in the back and rode for a moment in silence. Mary stared out the window at the flat, neat rows of vineyards stretching to the horizon under the insistent blue sky.

"Well, we've overcome one hurdle," Martinez said, breaking the silence. "But we still have Al-Jabeer to deal with. It looks like the plane really is his."

"It does look like that."

"Which puts us in hot water."

"Safi says the plane belongs to her."

"I think more objective minds might look at it as a simple case of theft."

Mary turned to him and gave a little shrug.

"You could be right."

"To put it another way, we did not repossess that plane. We out-and-out stole it."

"I don't think that's putting it another way, Jesus. You're saying the exact same thing."

"And if necessary, I'll say it again. I believe we're in deep shit."

"We can plead innocence. Kinsley and Roberts misrepresented themselves."

"But we stole the 747. That's the bottom line. If the two assholes disappear—which I suspect they will, at least 'til the air clears a little—then we're the guilty ones. We're the thieves. We stole the fucking plane, period."

"Don't be a broken record," she said softly. "What can we do?"

"There's only one thing we can do. We have to return the plane. It belongs to Al-Jabeer and we have to find a safe way to return it to him."

"He's not going to be too happy when he goes looking for his money and gold."

"I believe you're right. But at least we can give him his plane back. Any ideas?"

"Right now my mind's a blank. I'm tired, I'm hungry, and I'm numb." She sighed. "I wonder what the General will say when I tell him about Kinsley and Roberts. He almost did business with them once. He thought they were above board."

"We all make mistakes."

"We made a doozy."

"You mean you did."

"All right, *I* did."

"That Sadat character they were talking about, I wonder what role he played in this. Maybe he was cut in for a third. My guess is, he was on board and saw large sums of money being handed out. Maybe he saw some of it doled out as bribes to passengers or payoffs to the girls. But then it's possible he's nothing more than a flight attendant. In that capacity, he would know Al-Jabeer personally. He would also know his London mistress and probably the aircraft's itinerary."

Mary listened intently, twisting a tendril of hair into a tight knot.

"So you figure this Sadat guy recruited Kinsley and Roberts to steal the plane in exchange for a split?"

"Something like that. At least it's a theory until a better one comes along. And while I'm into theories, here's another one. I think they planned to steal the plane in London, not Jeddah. We know it was there a couple of months ago. And then, for some reason, there was a change of plans. Maybe Al-Jabeer had to return to Jeddah suddenly. The British guys ran out of time to steal the plane in London, and the whole picture got more complicated. That's when you came into the picture. They morphed into an aircraft leasing company and offered you a rich deal to do the heavy lifting."

Mary nodded slowly.

"I'm embarrassed. I'm blushing, right?"

"Blushing as red as your hair," he said with a grin.

"How could I have been so stupid? So goddamn gullible?"

"Don't be hard on yourself. People get conned everyday. It's sort of capitalism on the fly, I guess. Here was an airplane worth a couple of fortunes, pretty impressive to military types like you and me. The repossession fee was pretty damn attractive, especially since you were at loose ends."

"They wrote the fee agreement on hotel stationery, and it was because I demanded it." She shook her head. "How stupid can you be?"

"You thought they were legitimate, and why not? They're bright guys, they sound educated, and they advanced fifty thousand. Don't tell me money doesn't scream and yell. And then there was your knowledge of Saudi Arabia. They couldn't go in there themselves to repossess that plane. They needed you desperately and they used every trick in the book."

Mary regarded Martinez with a smile. "Jesus, you're not trying to lift my spirits, are you?"

"Of course I am."

"I guess you have to admire them in a way," she said.

"That was a shrewd plot. If you think about it, they could've gotten their hands on twenty million with almost no risk. Plus, the aircraft itself could have been dismantled for parts—probably another twelve million. That's been done plenty of times in the Eastern Bloc countries. The General has told me how that works. So yeah, they almost pulled off something pretty incredible." She paused. "I wonder what will happen when Al-Jabeer finds out the money is gone."

"I've been thinking about that. The first thing he'll do is interrogate the flight crews, and that might include this Sadat fellow. But no one will know if the money went missing in the maintenance hangar or on the way from London or Paris. So he'll have to look into various friends and high rollers. The options are endless. My guess is the British guys are not done trying to deal. They may go directly to Al-Jabeer, accuse Sadat whatever-his-name-is of stealing it and try to get a piece of the action that way."

"Do you think Kinsley and Roberts are smart enough?"

"I think they're plenty smart. There's also another possibility. Sooner or later they'll connect the dots, figure out you found the money and come back looking for you." Martinez stared out the window. "I've been thinking about that since I landed the plane and sent them on their way. I've been thinking about it a lot, and I don't like it."

Chapter Seventeen

SCOMA'S restaurant was built in the mid-1950s on piers over the bay. It was originally a repair shop for fishing boats and electric devices, and it was off the beaten track from the tourist crowds on Fisherman's Wharf. In order to survive, it had to attract the locals, plus the food had to be better than anything offered on the Wharf. It was very successful on both counts. Over the years the interior had not changed and the menu had remained unchallenged. The taxi driver negotiated the narrow alley to the pier, pulled up to the entrance, and came to a stop.

As they entered, the bar on the left caught Safi's attention. Its walls were covered with celebrity photographs and 49er football memorabilia.

"How nice it is to be here. Look," she said, pointing. "Frank Sinatra ate here. So did Elvis Presley and Marilyn Monroe." She smiled. "Back in America…It's like a dream."

"I keep forgetting this kind of place doesn't exist in Saudi

Arabia," Martinez said to Safi as they were ushered into a small dining room in the rear of the restaurant. "There is nothing that's not great on this menu. Try everything. We are suddenly very, very rich."

They took half an hour to order wine, study the menu and order. Picard had the sand dabs as an appetizer, a house specialty; Martinez, Mary and Safi selected fresh crab salads. The Coney Island red clam chowder arrived just as the Chianti was being served. Mary noticed that Safi was shifting around uneasily in her seat. She leaned toward her.

"Just give it time. You'll get used to being out in public exposed to all the male stares," Mary told her.

Safi's face reddened. "Is my discomfort that obvious?"

"Yeah, pretty obvious."

"You have no idea what it's like, Mary. When I was in Arabia, I read the story about the man in the iron mask. I could feel his agony and I imagined what it would be like to remove that mask after so many years. At times I thought he would be less afraid and more comfortable by keeping the mask on, rather than facing the scrutiny of those who would see him for the first time without it. Unconsciously, I think I'm waiting for a blow from a rubber truncheon, the kind the morals police use when they beat women in the street for revealing a toe or an ankle." She dipped a spoon in the chowder but did not lift it to her lips. "Being a princess was no shield. Not really. I was held to an even higher standard of modesty because I had to set an example. Sitting here in the open with people talking, wine being served—men actually seeing my face and even my cleavage—it sends chills through me. I just can't explain it."

"You have to accept your beauty," Picard said, touching

her hand.

"There's so much to accept. I'm overwhelmed."

"The only thing I ever felt wearing the burqua was anger," Mary said. "Even hatred."

"I felt that too," Safi said.

Martinez moved quickly to change the subject.

"The more I think about it, the bigger the picture gets. There must be hundreds of airplanes out there we could have a go at," he said.

Mary smiled and tapped him lightly on the shoulder.

"You must be drunk."

"Drunk, maybe. But also serious."

Mary turned to Picard. "What are your plans, Pierre?" She lowered her voice dramatically. "Now that you're rich?"

"Well, I can tell you what I don't want to do. I'm never returning to Saudi Arabia to work in construction. I didn't like it all that much, even though the money was good. I want to do something I can build on, and be a part of, not just an employee."

"Weren't you trained to be a naval architect?"

"Yes, but at best that would be a hobby. My expertise might get me a low-paying job designing yachts. The big shipyards build floating behemoths, and I'm not interested in that. What I do see is designing my own yacht some day. I've got some ideas about how to reduce drag up to forty percent on a motor-driven craft. I'll show you on paper sometime what I have in mind. Something maybe sixty-five feet long." His eyes were trained on Safi. "Do you like yachts?"

"I think I would like your yacht," she said with an absolutely straight face.

Mary burst into laughter. “Pierre, my God! I think you’re blushing.”

“If I had a boat,” Martinez said, quickly shifting attention away from Picard. “I’d have myself a three-master. Nothing motor driven.”

“The purist speaks,” Picard said with a slight bow of his head.

As the talk drifted back to the 747 and the events of the past few days, Mary spoke.

“Pierre, you’ve been around Marcel’s circle of friends. They seem to be into everything. What do you know about stolen airplanes?”

“That’s more Peter Jarbon’s department,” Pierre answered. “But I have learned a few things. When the Communists fell, the Eastern Bloc countries substituted one set of gangsters for another. The Russian Mafia moved fast to fill an enormous need for machinery, cars and planes. You name it. They would steal it from the West and send it East. I was in Bulgaria not too long ago. Did you know that there’s not a single car dealership in Sofia? Yet, there were thousands of cars from the West—Mercedes, Jeeps, Cadillacs, the works. All stolen, of course. And, for a few dollars, the thieves could get legitimate paperwork inside the country where they made the delivery. A bureaucrat in auto registration probably makes forty dollars U.S. per month, so a hundred-dollar bribe would do wonders. I know less about what goes on with airplanes, though. I imagine very much the same as with the cars.”

“I’ve got an idea,” Mary said to Martinez. “Let’s have a meeting with Global Aircraft Leasing. My guess is the contract Roberts faxed to me was valid. The U.S. office is in San Francisco on California Street. It can't hurt to do a little nosing around. If it turns out the lease payments were really in arrears and they want their plane back—well, we might just be able to help them for a small fee of, say, the one and a half million we didn't get from Kinsley and Roberts. What do you think?"

"I think we're better off out of the whole thing."

"I don't know. Something tells me we should look into this a little further."

"Something tells you?" Martinez regarded her. "Is this the feminine instinct thing?"

"Don't get smart with me."

"Look, why push this, Mary? We're way ahead of the game."

"If I may be permitted, I think Mary is right," Picard said. "If they are a legitimate company with a real problem on their hands, you two could be useful to them."

Mary winked at Jesus. "See?"

"I just don't know, Mary. It seems like you're asking for trouble."

"I reached them earlier when I tried to verify the cashier's check," Mary said. "Why don't I call for an appointment?"

Martinez broke into a slow grin. "My sainted grand-mother once told me that when you see trouble ahead walk the other way. I hope to hell you're not reversing the process."

WHEN Mary dialed the leasing company the next day, her call was directed to the asset management department.

"This is Matthew Taylor. How can I help you?"

"My name is Mary Jane. I have reason to believe you have a leasing contract for a Boeing 747 with the Al-Jabeer organization in Jeddah, Saudi Arabia. I understand the payments are in arrears and that your efforts to repossess the aircraft are made impossible because of Saudi laws."

An uncomfortable silence ensued until Taylor finally spoke.

"If that were true, what business is it of yours?"

"We, my partner and I, have just moved the aircraft out of Saudi Arabia in spite of the protests of the Al-Jabeer organization. We can deliver it to you within twenty-four hours. If that's of interest to you, maybe we should meet to discuss the details."

There was another silence before Taylor responded. "What authority did you have to move the plane?"

"We can discuss that when we meet."

"This is certainly one of the most unusual telephone calls I've ever received. I'm not sure I shouldn't just hang up and pretend this never happened."

"That's up to you."

"All right," he said. "I'll meet you here in my office. Would two o'clock tomorrow suit you?"

"That's fine. My partner and I will be there."

As Mary hung up, she began to worry that perhaps this was happening way too easily. She was a total stranger who had repossessed an airplane without authority, yet the man had asked her almost no questions. She turned to Martinez.

"Do you think we're sticking our necks out? Suppose we really did steal the aircraft, which you're positive we did. What then? They could have the police waiting for us."

"I know I said it was stolen, but I've been thinking more about that. It is stolen, and yet it isn't. The plane is in Safi's family name, and we can produce Safi, if necessary. I don't think we have anything to lose by seeing this guy."

"Okay, Jesus. Although I have to tell you, you worry me."

"Why is that?"

"All along you've been the pessimist and I've been the optimist. Now we're switching roles all of a sudden. That scares me."

"We're not switching roles. After all, you're the one who suggested this meeting. I had reservations."

"And now your reservations are gone."

"Not really. You've just worn me down, as usual."

HALF an hour before his two o'clock meeting, Matthew Taylor swallowed three indigestion pills and two painkillers. As Jesus and Mary entered his office, he rose to greet them with a practiced smile.

"Matthew Taylor," he said, extending a hand.

"Hi. I'm Mary Jane."

"Is Jane your last name?"

"Yes."

"I see."

"This is my partner, Jesus Martinez. I appreciate this opportunity to meet with you."

"I've ordered coffee and Danish," he said.

"Wonderful," Mary said. Martinez nodded.

Mary produced the Global Aircraft Leasing contract. Taylor looked it over and nodded, but his expression gave nothing away.

"Why don't we sit around the conference table? Perhaps

you can begin by telling me how you managed to get the Boeing 747 out of Jeddah. That must have taken some doing."

Mary gave him a carefully edited version of the facts, omitting any mention of Kinsley and Roberts by name or any mention of the money and gold. When she finished, it was obvious that she had Taylor's complete attention.

"It's really quite an amazing story," he said, as he twisted back and forth in his swivel chair. "Stranger than fiction as they say."

Mary leaned forward and tapped his knee.

"We have the airplane," she said. "Maybe we should discuss terms for its delivery to you."

Taylor crossed his hands over his stomach and gave her a look of distant amusement.

"I'm afraid I haven't been totally forthright with you, Ms. Jane. You see, we did not lease that aircraft to Al-Jabeer. Our rules are extremely stringent about leasing planes to Middle Eastern countries, as you can imagine. Furthermore, the contract you have is a phony. Someone obviously got their hands on one of ours and doctored it to suit this particular aircraft."

Jesus and Mary exchanged a quick glance. The room was suddenly silent. As Martinez started to ask Taylor why he had let them tell the story at all, the man wiggled his fingers as if to silence him.

"Let me tell you a little story," he said. "I am the board chairman of the Aircraft Leasing Association. It's a trade organization for leasing companies that concern themselves with legislation, FAA compliance standards, and more recently, aircraft theft. Did you know that, during the past year alone, seventeen Lear jets, three Falcons and five Gulfstreams have disappeared from America? We think they wound up in Russia, or in some of the old Soviet countries. I'm talking about private luxury aircrafts, but there are also commercial jets missing. I don't need to tell you that some of these aircrafts are stolen and being used in drug trafficking between Latin America and the U.S."

Increasingly uncomfortable and sensing that Taylor might be stalling for time before the police arrived, Martinez interrupted.

"So why did you bother listening to our story?"

"Our company lost five airplanes last year alone. We cannot collect the insurance on them until we prove they've either been stolen or crashed. The insurance companies view our problem as a simple matter of clients who have stopped making their payments, which in some cases is true, of course. At the same time, our firm cannot accept huge losses without doing something about it."

"There must be security firms that can repossess these airplanes for you," Mary said.

"It's not that easy. Eastern Bloc countries take a dim view of bounty hunters. They have no legal standing there. In most cases, the aircrafts are re-registered in a local jurisdiction overseas that cares only for the money it gets under the table. The planes are then flown throughout Russia, China, Eastern Europe, Africa and South America—countries where scrutiny is almost nonexistent. Most won't risk flying into North America or Western Europe, although I have no doubt some do. Often the planes are dismantled for parts, which are sold right here in the States." Taylor pressed a hand to his stomach and concealed a belch with a slight cough. "I'm afraid that's the situation we're faced with."

Martinez made eye contact with Taylor and began to feel that the meeting was not a trap, after all.

"What's your success rate on repossessions under these circumstances?" he asked.

"Middling to awful. Some come back to us trashed, others with missing engines or electronics. We have yet to retrieve a plane from the countries I just named. There is simply no global security organization that can handle the problem."

"What are you suggesting?" Mary said.

"When you telephoned me, I wanted to hear more. Now that I have, I'm wondering if you couldn't create an organization that specializes in aircraft repossessions. Our association has discussed trying to find such a group and our members are willing to pay twenty percent of the leasing contract balances to get their aircrafts back. Spiriting that Boeing 747 out of Jeddah is really impressive. For that one, assuming he'd only made the down payment, you would have made around fifteen million. If you were interested in forming a security company, our firm and the association would provide you with a long list of aircrafts that we want back."

"There's one thing I don't understand," Martinez said. "Why would you trust us? We brought a plane into this country under the impression that we were repossessing it for your company. What does that make us look like? Idiots, right? Either that or out-and-out thieves. I mean what kind of resumé is that?"

Mary shot Martinez a warning glance, but Taylor was nodding his head and looking thoughtful.

"I appreciate the point you're making, Mr. Martinez. Believe me, I don't take chances and I'm a great believer in risk evaluation. The two of you will be subjected to the most thorough due diligence. All of that is a given. But I look at this from a different perspective—one I've developed through necessity. Performance. Performance is the key to everything. You managed to move that 747 under the most difficult of circumstances. Okay, you were stung, and perhaps you were overly naïve. But if you work with us, there will be strict rules of compliance. What intrigues me is your obvious talent for this type of work."

Jesus and Mary said they would think about Taylor's proposal and get back to him within a week. They left his office in a state of wonderment and stopped for a cappuccino on their way back to the hotel.

"You looked pretty pissed at me in there," Martinez said.

"I thought you were painting us in the worst possible light."

"The stuff I said, it had to be put on the table. I wanted to see how the guy would react."

Mary sighed. "You're right," she said. "Why are you always quicker to see things than I am?"

"I'm not," he said. "It's just that I grew up in the streets. You learn to negotiate a certain way, always keeping an eye on your back."

Mary toyed with her cappuccino but did not drink it. Instead she chewed on a wedge of lemon.

"Do you think we can pull something like this off? Luck played a big role in moving the 747. If Safi hadn't shown up, we would have had big problems. Frankly, the idea scares me."

"It is scary," he agreed.

"Do you think we should pursue it?"

"I'm not sure. I have enough money now to sail away

into the sunset. It's great to have an option like that."

"Is that what you want to do?" she asked, her mouth set tight.

"I don't know. Taylor is talking business and what do we know about business? We're pilots, not bean counters."

"It's not too late to learn something new, Martinez."

"I suppose not." He rolled a cigar between his fingers, but then returned it to his pocket. "That is, if you want to learn something new. I'm still officially tied to the Air Force, in case you've forgotten, at least for another month or so. When I get free of that, I'm due for some serious R and R."

"R and R. You and your precious R and R." She reached across the table and covered his hand with hers. "I really wish I knew what was going on inside of your head."

"No, you don't. You don't want to know."

"I get the feeling you're always running. Running and hiding."

"Mary," he said gently. "Don't analyze me. I don't like it. My demons and I will deal with each other in our own way."

She took a sip of her cappuccino, never taking her eyes from him.

"I wish you'd let me inside—at least a little."

He smiled. "Maybe there's nothing inside."

"Bullshit."

"I think it's time to change the subject."

"Okay, let's play a game."

Martinez regarded her, but said nothing.

"Let's just imagine that we do decide to accept Taylor's proposal and form a company. A company has to have a name. So what do we call it?"

Martinez shrugged. “I don’t have the foggiest idea.”

“What about Air Ransom?”

“Ransom? Are you kidding? That sounds kind of criminal to me, like we kidnapped the airplane. If you want to be a repo buccaneer, no one will take you seriously.” He pulled out his cigar again and studied it.

“For Christ’s sake, Jesus, light the damn thing, okay? If you stop smoking stogies because of me, you’ll begin to resent me.”

“Good point, Major.” He lit the cigar, and with the meticulous care of a seasoned smoker he blew a perfect smoke ring toward the ceiling. “So, deep six Air Ransom. Keep trying. You’re good with words.”

“Okay, what about Charter Air Leasing Limited? It gives us a great acronym, CALL. I’d love to have that on my business card. The world’s first call girl who specializes in screwing bad guys out of their planes.” She studied Martinez. “So what do you think?”

“Pretty damn clever. Did you just come up with that?” He snapped his fingers. “Just one, two, three?”

She shook her head. “I have to confess I thought of it a few days ago. What Taylor’s talking about, I’ve given that a lot of thought recently too.’

“I think you think too much.”

“Women tend to do that.”

“And you never told me.”

“Martinez, there are many, many things I don’t tell you.”

“Another woman thing?”

“Another woman thing.”

“I guess I’d better watch my step,” he said.

Chapter Eighteen

MATTHEW Taylor knew that without some kind of plan to recover the company's missing planes, he would soon be out of a job. He also knew that, at fifty-two, it was highly unlikely that he would be able to command the same generous salary from another employer. Consequently, he pulled out all the stops to convince the two newest members of the Global Leasing Board of Directors that they needed him. He covered up the Global name from a copy of Mary's Boeing 747 contract and substituted an obscure German firm. He used the doctored contract as an example of what his department could accomplish. He then told them the dramatic story of how Mary Jane, a former Air Force major, had managed to get out of Jeddah with a Boeing 747 for repossession. He did not tell them that, in fact, the plane may have been stolen and that Mary Jane had been swindled by a couple of con men.

"I received a telephone call from Major Mary Jane today," he told the board. "She and her partner have a company called Charter Aircraft Leasing Ltd., or CALL. I'll be going over our list of airplanes with them tomorrow morning. I've already asked legal to draft an agreement with them, and it will be ready this week."

Among the many problems Taylor did not share with the board was the questionable availability of Jane and Martinez. Global had done a quick and thorough check on them both. They had passed with flying colors, but they had not yet committed themselves to the deal. Taylor was aware that he still had a job of delicate persuasion to perform and that his professional life depended on bringing them around. A week of frantic negotiations followed, and finally, Jesus and Mary agreed to a plane-by-plane one-year contract, with an option to renew for a second year at terms to be mutually agreed upon. At the next board meeting Taylor was expansive and full of himself.

"Their first assignment will be to repossess the French Falcon jet, the one with all the fancy trimmings," he said. "Leonard Lev made two payments, and then cut us off. Big media mogul indeed! He's just another Mafia guy in my book, with a better accent and haircut, and he got to us. You know that it's next to impossible to sue someone in Russia. Forget it! God knows where the plane is now."

"How much have we got in that one, Matt?" asked one of the two new Directors.

"Base price new was fifty-four million. There were some add-ons for electronics, long-range tanks and luxury trim that raised it another eight million. If you count the unpaid interest we're looking at fifty-six million, minus two four million dollar payments."

"That's the one I want back," said the chairman of Global, Luther Gravely. "Let's show these pricks we're not pushovers. Get your people on that one, okay?" His eyeglasses glittered as he stared at Taylor. "Let's hope and pray they really have that magic you're promising us, Matthew."

Taylor sensed the implied threat but it didn't faze him. He was pleased with himself, he was sailing on air. CALL was his personal connection, and because repossession of lost planes was not the kind of activity the company could brag about at shareholders' meetings, he knew that his CALL relationship guaranteed him his job. He struggled to maintain his business-like demeanor when what he wanted to do was leap up on the conference table and dance, dance, dance.

"Gentlemen, leave the matter to me. I don't think any of our financial people expected the kind of losses we've sustained in the past three years. The Russian Mafia got to us as well as many other big leasing companies." He wanted to let the directors feel that they were not at fault; they were simply innocent victims of well-organized criminals, and when it came to solving the problem, he was their guy.

After the meeting broke up, Taylor returned to his office, leaned back in his swivel chair and lit a clove cigarette. He had picked up the clove habit on a business trip to Tokyo. He grinned. That was not all he had picked up in the Far East. What a fantastic three weeks he had had. I'll go down to the Castro tonight and celebrate, he thought. Find myself some beautiful young flesh. I deserve some wildness.

MATTHEW Taylor's self confidence had ratcheted up considerably since his last meeting with Jesus and Mary. It showed in his appearance. His skin was less sallow and his eyes seemed brighter. When they entered his office, he rose to greet them as if they were long-time friends.

They sat at the small pine conference table in Taylor's office. On the table, he had spread out profiles of each of the airplanes he planned to discuss.

"I've talked to our board about priorities," he said as he handed Mary the file on the tri-engine Dassault Falcon 900EX long-range executive jet. "You can look over the specs on range, weight, power and all that later. The main thing is the character that leased it. His name is Leonard Lev. He produces foreign films. We think he's into drug trafficking and he's a strong supporter of the current administration in Moscow. He owns stock in the *Moscow Times* and the *Odessa News*—not the majority owner but he has a voice in policy. He also has a finger in various TV and radio stations. The Falcon was leased to him in 2008 and the financial statement that supported the transaction is in the file. At that time, he was showing a net worth of close to a billion dollars. Here's a picture of him standing next to the aircraft."

"Danny DeVito," Mary said.

"You're right. There is a resemblance. You can see a Mercedes 600SL in the background. He owns a bunch of them. The photo came from the *London Times*. Take a close look at the tail of the aircraft. You can see the initials GI and along the window line you can barely make out Global Industries."

"Why can't you levy against his assets in America?" Martinez said.

"Everything he owns has been transferred to offshore companies in the Bahamas. At this moment, in this country, he has the cash flow of a street corner bum. Nothing to attach. Lev travels with an entourage of very dangerous people and he's been thumbing his nose at us ever since he took delivery."

"Obviously the Falcon doesn't come into U.S. or European airspace," Mary said. "Where does he use it?"

"We assume mainly Eastern Europe, Russia—perhaps some of the Asian countries. He has five aircraft—this is the smallest. We think it's used mainly as an organizational tool to shuttle his hoods around the crime empire. It's also possible it may be chartered to some of the more powerful political hacks. If I were a betting man, I'd probably look at Moscow, maybe even Leningrad."

"I wonder why he decided to stop making payments," Mary said.

"That has us stumped. It makes no sense. He could write a check for it out of petty cash. We think he has a criminal mind and gets his kicks from cheating others. We've heard that he's done this with a container ship and a tanker, so that's what we're dealing with." He smiled. "Tougher than Jeddah?"

"Could be," Mary said.

"So the Falcon is your priority," Martinez said. "Let's not check out the others until we get this one back in America. My mind works on one channel."

Mary laughed, and Taylor joined her uncertainly.

"We have a lot of work to do," Mary said. "Did you get a draft of the proposed agreement ready for us?"

"I have it here."

"What about addresses or phone numbers of people Lev works with or, has contact with?" Martinez said.

"We have a few leads, but I'm not sure they'll do any

good. Those are also in the file."

The meeting adjourned. Mary picked up the Falcon file and the draft agreement. They left for a restaurant on Post Street where they had agreed to meet Safi and Picard for lunch.

Safi had arrived at the restaurant first, but had not been able to bring herself to sit at the bar while waiting for her friends. Being perched on a barstool alone was just too much for her to handle. Instead, she ordered iced tea and waited in a booth as she watched the lunchtime crowd chatting and smiling. So relaxed. So American. She envied their ease and freedom, and she wondered if they had any idea what it was like to live in virtual shackles and chains. She saw Pierre come through the swinging doors first. A few minutes later Jesus and Mary arrived.

"How did the meeting go?" she asked.

"Uneventful," Mary said, grinning. "At least given our lifestyle. We have the Falcon file and draft agreement, and right now that's all we need."

"More than we need," Martinez said with a sigh. He sat down heavily, removed a cigar from his suit jacket, examined it, toyed with it, and then replaced it in his jacket. The others watched him with amusement.

"Have you called Dani yet?" Mary asked. "He must be wondering where you are by now."

"I guess I'm putting it off. I've been doing some thinking."

"About what?"

"Since being around you, I've begun to realize that it doesn't have to be Dani who dictates the next step. It's up to me. I think I should call him on one of those cell phones where he can't trace my call."

"That sounds like a prudent move," Picard said, nodding.

"No, cell calls can be traced," Martinez said. "You can use mine."

"Dani knows I have the 747 somewhere and probably assumes I don't have any real use for it. He's also likely to assume that we haven't found the cash and gold. So he's thinking, I not only have the plane, but I have his treasure too, though I don't know I have it. I know Dani. He's a very greedy person. He would kill all of us to get it back." She sipped her tea and the others waited for her to continue. "So my plan is we offer the plane to him for, say, five million."

"But, for all we know, the plane is his free and clear," Martinez said. "The British guys were crooks; they lied to us and made up a phony contract. And we now know that Global Leasing never leased a plane to your husband. So that looks to me like we actually stole the plane. I know it's listed under your family's name, Safi, but I think Al-Jabeer may have a good case in any court of law."

Safi shook her head. "I would fight in a court to claim that 747. I believe I would have a good chance of winning."

Martinez looked dubious.

"I agree with Safi," Mary said. "He'll jump at the chance to get the plane back. He still thinks there's twenty million on board. He gets his plane and *thinks* he gets his money and gold. If he gives us five million, he's still ahead fifteen million, plus the airplane."

"Strange math," Martinez said. "He gets the plane back, period. There ain't any money and gold."

"But he doesn't *know* that. I guess it all depends on your

point of view. He's done some really dirty things—unconscionable. Factor that into your calculations. And remember, the plane is worth one hundred million."

"Am I the only one who sees an ethical problem here?" Martinez turned to Picard. "I mean if we were really on the up and up, we'd return the gold and money to the plane and let him have his plane back with no charge."

"Safi's told me a lot about him in the last few days." Picard shrugged. "I think he deserves anything he gets."

"In other words, stick it to him."

"Stick it to him. Yes."

"Are you against doing this, Jesus?" Mary's lips were compressed with concern.

"I'm just asking questions."

"Well, I think this is Safi's call. If she wants to return the plane with no conditions, I'm okay with that. But she seems to have something else in mind."

"A measure of revenge perhaps?" Picard said, his dark eyes alive with amusement.

"I want him to pay," Safi said. "For all the suffering he's caused me, he can never make it right."

Martinez nodded and thought, a woman scorned. "We would have to be very careful about how we delivered the plane to him, you know," he said.

"Strategy is not my department," Safi said. "I leave that to you and Mary."

Mary began thinking out loud. "We pick an airport with a series of large hangars. San Francisco's a real possibility. He comes alone at a specific time to meet one of us, not Safi. We give him the keys to the 747 and he hands over the cash."

"He's going to want to be taken to the plane before handing over the money," Martinez said. "I suggest we use two golf carts, one to hold him, his pilot and me. We go to the aircraft and make the exchange. Mary, you follow in another car, pick me up and we scoot. Pierre will be waiting in a car with Safi with the motor running. It will take Al-Jabeer at least five minutes to get into the plane and look inside the hidden safe. By then we'll be driving away."

"He may insist on seeing Safi," Mary said.

"Not negotiable. Not part of our deal anyway. He'll have to arrange that on his own."

"Suppose he insists on inspecting the plane first before handing over the money?" Safi said. "You mustn't underestimate Dani. He is very shrewd."

"That's easy," Martinez replied. "I'll be carrying a pistol. I'll agree to let him inspect the plane and insist on walking step by step with him. I'll demand that the pilot be locked out of the plane during the inspection."

Mary began twisting her hair into tight knots, a sign that she was troubled.

"Won't he think that's peculiar?"

"When you're delivering or receiving such a huge amount of cash, it's not unusual to take precautions that you're not outnumbered. Al-Jabeer, of all people, should understand that."

"I don't know. It sounds risky," Mary said, continuing to twist her hair.

"Of course it's risky. Everything we do these days is risky. But it's a good plan for another reason. He isn't going to want me to see him searching through a secret compartment. And no way in the world would he let me see what he thinks is hidden there. I have a gun and I might try to steal it. So what does he do? He pretends to give a look around but he's not going to really look with me there. So he gets rid of me as fast as possible."

"But what if you're alone with him and he suddenly decides not to pay you the five million?" Safi said. "Dani can be very stubborn."

"He won't do that. There's too much at stake."

"But what if he does, Jesus?" Mary said. "You have to consider the possibility."

"Well, I tell him to get lost. You and I will fly the 747 back to Santa Rosa."

"He may put up a fight," Picard said.

Safi, listening intently to the exchange, broke in.

"He won't get physical—not unless he has a gun in his hand. Dani will do anything he can to get his way, but he's a physical coward. If it comes to a physical confrontation, he'll walk away."

"I hope you're right," Martinez said.

"The San Francisco airport is the best place to make the exchange," Mary said. She glanced at Martinez. "Do you agree?"

"Why not?" he said, and with a wink he added, "It was my original suggestion."

"We'll call and find available dates for hangar space," she said, ignoring the wink. "That will dictate the date of the delivery."

Safi felt a blush of pleasure. She could imagine Dani's expression—astonished, slack-jawed, engorged with rage—when he opened the box to find it empty. He had never shown her proper respect as a woman, as a human being, and the time had come for him to begin to pay. And his debt was not simply money: he owed her all the years he had stolen from her. He owed her for his treatment of their son. He owed her for his many transgressions. She would diminish him sufficiently before casting him from her mind forever.

Chapter Nineteen

SAFI called Jeddah at midnight Pacific Coast time. It was morning in Saudi Arabia.

"This is Princess Safi Al-Jabeer calling," she said. "Please put my husband on the line. I'll hold."

The voice at the other end rose a few notes in surprise. "Yes, your highness. It won't be a minute."

When Dani Al-Jabeer's voice flowed softly through the wire, Safi felt a moment of fear followed quickly by cold anger. She knew his tricks. He was going to be calm. His calmness had always terrified her more than his rage. His moods were never spontaneous, but more like various forms of strategic warfare.

"So you finally decided to call your husband. What a lovely gesture—most appreciated. Where are you?"

"Never mind that. I'm calling to give you a simple message. You can have your Boeing 747, your whorehouse of a plane, in exchange for five million dollars American. In cash.

Have it with you, or your representative, on April 26th at two o'clock in the afternoon at the San Francisco airport's domestic terminal. Bring an extra pilot with you. You will disembark from the plane and the transfer will be made on the tarmac. The pilots will remain in whatever plane you fly to San Francisco until the transfer is made. Is that clear?"

"Very clear, Safi. But it doesn't need to be so cloak and dagger. I need the airplane and that's that." He hesitated. "Five million is a stiff price to pay for a plane that belongs to me and was illegally hijacked. Wouldn't you agree?"

"The plane is registered in my family's name."

"I paid for the plane, my dear."

"Dani, I've stated the terms. You don't have to accept them."

"Your terms or someone else's?"

"Mine."

"I wish you would come back to Jeddah," he said, his voice becoming deeper and even quieter. "This is where you belong. I promise that nothing will happen to you. Things will be as they were before. Everything will be forgotten and I will behave like a proper husband again. We will travel, perhaps consider having another child."

He wants me, she thought, but for other reasons. Not those reasons. He is desperate to have me back so that he can exact revenge. She would not allow herself to speculate on what form that might take.

"I'll speak to you about that after we conclude our business," she said. "But I won't be at the airport. If you create any problems there, you can expect me to file a divorce in California. Is that understood?"

"You've turned into a hard woman, Safi. You've changed. I no longer recognize you. Who is it that's influencing you? The same ones who helped you get out of Saudi Arabia?"

"You will never know," she said, her voice more forceful than she felt. "Now listen to me closely. If no one shows up at the airport, I plan to file the divorce papers immediately. I will sell the airplane. There is a Nevada gambling casino that's interested and would be a good buyer for your airborne whorehouse. But before I sell it, I'll let the press have a tour. Hopefully the *Jeddah Times* will carry the story." She hung up and Mary clapped and then whistled through her teeth.

"That was one hell of a performance for someone who just escaped from the inside of a formless black bag. He must have been in shock."

"I know him, Mary. I know him so well. This call will send him into a fury. He'll do anything for revenge. It's part of the Al-Jabeer code of righteousness and manhood. But until he gets his plane back, he's going to be very nice to me."

DANI slowly hung up the telephone, then dropped the receiver to the floor, and deliberately ground it into pieces under his boot. He then leaned back in his chair and tried to induce self-hypnosis, a technique he had spent thousands of dollars perfecting in a private clinic in New York City. But, for some reason, the eye roll refused to open the door to that secret place deep inside him. He could not create the proper panels in his mind that would release the terrible tension. His mind was consumed with the color red—the red of rage. He needed to destroy something—something animate, living, susceptible of feeling pain. He practiced his breathing exercises: deep breath in, deep breath out, slow inhale, and slow exhale. Slowly, the redness began to fade, replaced by the darkness of gloom. Bitch of an American woman, bitch of an American woman… He lit a cigarette, drew in a lungful of smoke, removed a silver cell phone from his pocket no larger than a matchbox, and dialed a number he had memorized. The phone was answered on the second ring. Al-Jabeer was one of three people who had this number.

"Dani?" said David Sassoon. "Are you all right?"

"I've had better days. She has the plane." He went on to describe the details of the five-million-dollar exchange in San Francisco. "What do you think we should do?"

"Depends on how far you want to go, my friend. Anything is possible. I think we should meet and discuss this in private."

"What's more private than this secure line?"

"I think better when I see your face."

"Okay. Meet me at the palace at eleven o'clock. Something has to be done. If she embarrasses me publicly, she could disgrace the very principles of Islam in the process."

"Eleven then, Dani. But let's cut the bullshit about Islam. This is about a hundred million dollar airplane and nearly half that much in money and gold. People get killed for a lot less. But as an added bonus, if we can figure out a way to get her to Jeddah you can file an accusation of adultery. You only need two witnesses and we can arrange that. Chances are the court will decide she should be stoned to death in the square." Sassoon chuckled softly.

Al-Jabeer hung up feeling invigorated. As he headed to his session of deep massage, thinking of various tortures that could be inflicted on his bitch of an American wife, he grew an immense erection.

Chapter Twenty

"MATT, this is Jesus. We faxed your agreement to our attorney. He's made some modifications and I've just faxed those to you. If they're acceptable, make the changes and call me back at the Hilton. I can be at your office in fifteen minutes for a signing."

"Who will sign on behalf of CALL?" Taylor asked.

"I'll sign as partner. CALL is a limited liability company that we just formed this morning. Mary and I are the co-managers and partners."

Taylor, in high good humor, was full of congratulations. He had enjoyed a lucky time the night before. The Foreign Legion bar on Castro Street had been busier than usual and a young man in vintage-70s bellbottoms, studly with apple cheeks, had spilled his drink on his lap. Taylor had offered to sponge it off for him. Two hours and many drinks later, they had found themselves in bed together. Taylor was still daydreaming about the young man's wiry body, his flat six-pack of a stomach, his insatiable ardor. It took a moment to refocus his thoughts on Martinez's words.

"Okay, I'll be calling you back before noon," he said, after a pause.

Taylor's secretary buzzed to tell him there was a call holding. He picked up the telephone and was thrilled.

"Greco, I really didn't expect to hear from you. If you're free for a few days, I have a great idea. I'm thinking of Aspen…"

WHEN Martinez hung up, he turned to Mary. "You know what I think? I think Matt Taylor is gay."

"Of course he is," Mary said offhandedly.

"What do you mean he is? You mean you knew it and didn't tell me?"

"What difference does it make? It's not exactly news these days."

"Like prostate cancer. The numbers haven't gone up, just the recognition."

"I wouldn't be surprised if we live to see a gay president of the United States."

"If we haven't had one already," Martinez said.

Mary regarded him with a smile.

"Your little mind is whirling away, Martinez. I can almost hear it. What scheme are you hatching?"

"If we're going into this aircraft repo thing in a big way, we'll eventually need someone like Taylor to make personal contact with some of the big leasing firms that need our services. He knows his way around and we can't just cold call ourselves.

I mean, think about it. What do we give as our history or references?"

"But we're contract clients of his firm, Jesus. They're going to give us plenty to do. Why? Are you thinking of hiring or making a deal with Taylor?"

"I'm thinking down the road. A year from now, after we complete our contract with Global. I'd feel more comfortable with more than one client. Global is fine for now, but I had enough of the single client thing in the Air Force."

"You're still not telling me everything, Martinez. I'm getting to know you. You're one devious son of a bitch when you want to be."

"Well, I'm thinking, what if it's a while before we work things out with Al-Jabeer? The 747 is just sitting there doing no one any good. It's a flying whorehouse, right? I especially like the fact that it has cameras in the bedroom ceilings and video screens for the porn films." Martinez paused and closed his eyes, thinking it through. "What I'm tempted to do, when I go to Global to sign the papers, is to let Taylor know that I know he's gay. Then I'm going to suggest that our deal be celebrated on the 747. I'll tell him we have four bedrooms for anyone he wants to invite. We spring for the pilot, the wine, and the food. The plane lands at the Tahoe airport, but we'll fly around so that it takes eight hours to get there. Once on the ground, they can stretch for an hour, and then we'll head back to San Francisco. And we'll make sure the return trip takes another four hours. I know we have at least three weeks—and that's if there are no hitches—before delivering the 747 to Al-Jabeer. Could be much longer." Martinez paused and took a deep breath. "So what do you think, partner?"

"I don't know. What do you hope to accomplish?"

"Well, if nothing else, the event would produce a lot of hype as well as gratitude from Taylor, our benefactor. Also, it might lead to another way to make money."

"Jesus, are you turning greedy on me?"

"Maybe. Money does that to you."

"Do you know you're a devil?"

"If you say so," he said.

"You'll have to be the pilot of course. No women allowed. Pierre might agree to help you out."

"Are you in favor of it or not?"

"If you do it, you'd better keep your ass in the cockpit. You're too cute to mix."

MARTINEZ arrived at Global Leasing late that afternoon. After he signed the documents, he leaned back in his chair and studied Taylor.

"I think I told you, Matt, we'll be delivering the 747 to its owner in about three weeks. It's really some airplane, by the way—totally loaded. I know you guys at Global think you've seen the best in the sky, but this thing has been designed to be a pleasure palace." Martinez went on to describe the plane in detail. "It's a shame to let it sit in the airport idle. Don't you have some friends you'd like to provide with a once-in-a-lifetime experience? Can you imagine what fun it could be—four private bedrooms at 35,000 feet?" Martinez rose as though the meeting was ending, and, after a slight hesitation, Taylor held up a restraining hand.

"I would love to take you up on your offer," he said. "But it could have the potential to compromise me. I'm afraid I'll have to decline."

"Compromise you? I can't imagine why. I'd be the pilot and if you're compromised, so am I."

Taylor hesitated, uncomfortably trying to say yes and no at the same time.

"I, ah, might have a different idea about what an exotic flight might be from yours, Jesus."

Martinez decided to take the plunge. "Why? Because you're gay?"

Taylor felt he should be insulted, and to a certain extent he was, but he was more curious than angry.

"How do you know I'm gay? Are you?"

"No. I'm still giving the straight life a try."

"Then how do you know?"

"Mary told me. She knows things like that. But so what? Who gives a shit?"

"I'm sure my company gives a shit."

"Well, I don't. Mary doesn't. By the way, this is her idea, the celebration in the air. She wants to express her gratitude for creating the kind of business relationship that holds such promise for all of us."

Taylor's first flush of defensive anger quickly changed to confusion. Am I that obvious? What are these people after?

"I don't trust others with my personal life," he said stiffly, eyeing Martinez.

"That's fair enough. You're right. This is personal, it isn't about repossessing airplanes. I guess we've overstepped our bounds, and if we have, I'm sorry, Matt. I can only tell you we meant it in the right spirit."

Taylor managed a smile. "No offense taken."

"And none intended, believe me." Martinez returned his smile and extended his hand. "Listen, if you decide you'd like to discuss this further, give me a call, okay? If you're interested, then figure on a full day in the air, eight hours in one stretch and four hours on the return leg. We'll provide the fuel, pilot, food, drinks, telephones and pornographic material."

Taylor regarded him sharply. "Pornographic material?"

"The 747 has an extensive library of pornographic videos. About a third of them are homosexual," he lied. "You know how it is in Arabia with the men not being able to see the women."

"I've never been there," Taylor said.

"The thing is, the airplane is equipped to give pleasure to all tastes."

Instinctively Martinez knew that Taylor was hooked.

"Matt, I think you're overly concerned about possible scandals. My advice is to lighten up a little. Have some fun." He walked to the door and turned. "Let me know what you want to do."

MATTHEW Taylor returned to his desk after Martinez left and, for five minutes, stared ahead at nothing. Gradually his fears began to subside as he thought about Greco. Then about the bartender at the Foreign Legion Bar and others he could invite, if he decided to accept Martinez's offer. But what if he was caught taking advantage of a client's largesse? What would happen if his sexual orientation became public knowledge? Global was a traditional organization, with traditional values. In Taylor's view, it was sexually repressed and still believed in white shirts, somber neckties, short haircuts, and the wife and children. Still, even with all the risks, the offer was enticing, and it wouldn't cost him a cent. What fun it would be!

I can't do this by telephone, he thought, as he put on his jacket. He told his secretary that he would not be back that day.

THE Foreign Legion bar was never busy in the afternoon, but Taylor knew that George Butterfield, the bartender, lived upstairs and often ate at the café two doors away. When he found that Butterfield was not behind the bar, he tried the buzzer to his apartment.

"It's me, Taylor," he said. "Can I come up?"

"Is it important? I'm a little busy at the moment."

"I understand, sorry." Taylor realized that his friend had someone with him. "Meet me at the café as soon as you can. It is rather important."

Taylor studied Butterfield as he walked through the door, squinting in the sudden darkness. His skin was sallow and there were dark circles under his eyes.

"You look like shit, my friend. I told you to stay away from the young ones. We're getting too old for that."

"Hey, I'm only fifty-four and still very cute."

"Fairly cute. But no longer thirty-year-old cute."

"I've still got the most shapely ass in town." He sat down. "So what gives?"

Taylor ordered breakfast for both of them, even though it was late afternoon. With rising excitement, he told Butterfield about the fabulous airplane and the all-expenses paid sin tour of the sky.

"I love it, I *love* it," Butterfield burst out after hearing the story. "But why the rush? We have to set this up in a about a week."

"The plane goes back to the owner on April 26th. Maybe we should aim for the weekend before that. It's a Saturday. What do you think?"

"Saturday is always best. Everybody's in a major party mood. We could call it a 'Destination Unknown' party. Maybe we can all dress up in Arab costumes."

"Arab costumes—what a great idea! I'll ask if we can request Middle Eastern meals. How exciting this is going to be! I was hoping you could recommend some guys for this trip. Any ideas?"

"You have to be *trés* careful these days; I don't have to tell you that. But with four bedrooms, we'll need at least a party of eight. I know you don't want Harry, but I do have people on my special list. Do you remember that big black-haired guy—you know, the German?"

"Herman the German, you mean?" Taylor gave a comic grimace.

"The very same. Absolutely studly—legendary. Well, he's been away and he just showed up last night with an African-American guy that's to die for. I'll be seeing him tonight. Besides Herman, I've got a list of at least twenty others to choose from. So you needn't worry. I'll pick the best of the best."

"I knew I could count on you, George. I'll work out the details and be in touch by the weekend."

"Last things first, old dear. What about money? I mean it's a grand party and all that, but my friends will want a little gratuity."

Taylor hadn't thought of that and realized that George had a point. He thought for a minute and then offered $6,000.

"A thousand for each of the invitees," Taylor said. "I'll spring for that myself. Why not? This is a weekend we'll never forget. Not only that, but when word gets out afterward, a lot of the young ones are going to be chasing us."

"Yes, I love that!"

As Taylor left the café, he felt energized and chided himself for having been tied to Harry for far too long. I'm going to dress like Laurence of Arabia, he thought as he jumped into his car. If I were younger I'd be a belly dancer.

AT nine o'clock the next morning Martinez received a call from Taylor accepting the offer. Martinez immediately phoned Mary.

"Are you decent?"

"Always."

"I'll be right over."

He arrived at her suite five minutes later.

"Matt Taylor is all for the trip in our pleasure craft. He sounded all a-tremble with excitement."

"Great."

"And you know what's even better? He wants them all dressed as Arabs. I mean, I couldn't have planned it that way if I'd tried." Martinez walked behind her and began rubbing her back. Through his fingertips, he could feel her stiffen slightly before relaxing into the contour of his hands.

"What are you doing?" she said.

"Massaging you."

"I know *what* you're doing. But why are you doing it?"

"I feel like it. I'm in a generous mood."

"There's a little intimacy in the touch, Martinez. A girl

could take it the wrong way."

He dug his fingers in deeper.

"Mary, I told a couple of white lies."

"White lies? Didn't your mother tell you there's no such thing as a white lie? A lie is a lie."

"I said the celebration idea was yours, not mine. I thought the idea would sound better coming from you."

"What made you think that?"

"I don't know. Male intuition."

"That's one big oxymoron, Jesus. Men have no intuition, just appetites. So what was the other lie? You mentioned a couple of lies."

"I said there was a big stash of porno films on board."

"Well, that means we're going to have to go shopping, doesn't it?"

"It looks that way."

"Wait a minute—wrong pronoun. *You'll* do the shopping. We're talking male pornography here. Women don't buy that stuff."

"You could start a trend, Mary."

"No thank you."

"Oh well."

"And while you're making your preferences known in some skuzzy video store, I'll buy a digital camera with a telephoto lens. I want to make sure we have a photo of his friends boarding the 747. Maybe I can get a shot of them in front of the Al-Jabeer tail marking, or near the fuselage lettering. When Dani boy sees them, along with the pictures of the party inside, he'll know they're intended to be seen by the Morals Police in Jeddah if he becomes difficult."

"That's a good angle, Mary. You're thinking around corners."

"I think the phrase is thinking outside of the box."

"I think that's a cliché."

"By the way, Safi came up with a great idea. There are cameras in all the bedrooms. What if the cameras reveal the partygoers discovering the hidden box and the cash? The drawer is left open and the box is unlocked. It wouldn't take long for someone to have a look."

"You've lost me, Mary. The money's gone."

"But the box won't be empty. We photocopy sheaves of hundred dollar bills, cut and stack them in piles with rubber bands. If we do maybe fifty stacks, with some real money on top, it's a great photo opportunity. When Dani looks at the video he'll assume the revelers made off with his fortune."

Martinez frowned for a moment, and then broke out in a wide smile.

"My God, Safi's devious, isn't she? I never would have guessed it."

"A great idea?"

"Not a bad idea at all."

"Jesus?"

"Yes?"

"Keep rubbing me, okay? If you keep rubbing me I'll be your slave forever."

"That's what I'm afraid of," he said.

Chapter Twenty One

MARY set up an appointment with Frank Bailey, a well-known attorney who had handled General Charles Jane's affairs for many years. Bailey was not your ordinary attorney. He was not one to nod agreement with a client and launch into dissertations on the pros and cons of arcane laws that might or might not apply to your case simply to stretch his billing time. He actually read the documents and other materials that were provided to him by his clients. Frank Bailey employed several associates in his Santa Rosa office and was very successful. He could afford a large, elegant corner office, but he had no need for the trappings of tapestries, Oriental rugs, and original art. Instead, his personal office was just large enough to seat two people; any more than that and he used a small conference room, into which he now ushered Mary, Martinez, Picard and Safi.

"Mary," he said, kissing her on both cheeks. "It's been

years. I must say, you look radiant." He waved at chairs and a small oval table. "Please, all of you sit down."

After introductions, Mary outlined Safi's situation and concerns. Bailey rested his prominent jaw on the fist of his right hand. He paused.

"The Al-Jabeer name will not necessarily appear on property, shares, or other assets. I suggest we begin a nationwide investigation of his holdings. While that's ongoing, we should file for a divorce in California, because this is where you were married. Your complaint will be based on your husband's activities with his three mistresses. I'll need any information you have on them—telephone numbers, anything and everything. Our investigators will obtain all the information and photos we can, to prove their relationship to your husband. I don't think we should raise issues of abuse, because in Arabia those things might well be considered normal behavior under Islamic law. And in an American court those issues will obscure the main thrust of our argument, which is that he's an adulterer." He paused and looked from face to face, his small hazel eyes bright and alive with intelligence.

"Make sure that before you deliver the 747 to him, it's photographed inside and out, which should make a telling exhibit for your case. Regarding cash or gold that you have already received, I suggest you invest in a variety of financial products." He turned to Safi. "I would also suggest you consider setting up holding companies under separate names that would protect your anonymity as a famous princess, limit your personal liability, and provide you with the flexibility to pursue a variety of business interests. You understand that these holding companies will make it that much more difficult for your husband to make claims on the assets in your possession."

Safi, who had listened intently, suddenly leaned forward. "My husband might try to create a defense against his abuse of me based on 'Shari,' or Islamic law."

"That's dangerous territory," Bailey replied. "If he took that line he could find himself defending all the strange variants of such a law. In Lebanon, for instance, men are legally allowed to have sex with animals, but the animals must be female. Having sexual relations with a male animal is punishable by death. In Bahrain, a male doctor may legally examine a woman's genitals, but he must use a mirror. He can't look at them directly." Bailey smiled. "It's quite a quagmire, in other words. I don't see an American jury relating to all of that."

"Perhaps not," Safi said. "But if we went to trial, it might just be sensational enough to be newsworthy. And if his lawyers took such a tack, it might hurt his position."

"You could be right," Bailey said. "Let's look at examples of things an American jury would consider offensive or abusive, and that your husband might consider culturally correct in his country." His smile grew wider; he was clearly taken with the soft-spoken princess. "You begin."

"Well, women are not allowed to drive or vote," she said. "Men are in charge of all matters relating to women. A woman can't get an exit visa without her husband's consent. Clothing can't cling to her body. It's forbidden for her to shake hands with a man or imitate one. She must always lower her voice when speaking to any male. A woman's testimony in court is given only half the weight of a man's. She can't become a judge, she can't dance and she can't attend a movie or a concert in public. A woman is forced to wear a burqua." Safi took a deep breath, glanced at Mary for encouragement, and then continued.

"There are numerous acts, all normal here in America, that can be punished with death by stoning, floggings and amputation. Speaking of amputation, girls are subject to having their clitorises amputated. Remember, Mr. Bailey, I'm an American citizen, and while I went to Arabia voluntarily, I was prevented from leaving and have been subjected to some of the cruelties I've just mentioned for the past twelve years. Being held against your will is still a crime all over the world."

Bailey nodded gravely. "I can see your point, Princess Safi, and I can certainly feel your passion. You would make a compelling witness, on your own behalf."

"Thank you."

"I'll take this up with my associates. It seems likely there are grounds to claim your husband violated basic human rights." He smiled as he began to think of the media appeal of such a filing. "You say that the 747 will be delivered on April 26th at the San Francisco airport?"

"If all goes according to schedule," Mary said.

"Perhaps we can have him served at the airport, preferably with a camera available to take some photos. He will be required to appear in an American court. It's a great opportunity, and if we miss it, there's no telling how or where we can serve him otherwise."

"If you get someone to serve him," Mary said, "we'll take care of the photos."

"Very good," Bailey replied. "But before any arrangements can be made, I must discuss this with my associates."

Martinez sat low in his seat, fingering an unwrapped cigar.

"You can light that if you want. We don't observe a smoking ban here," Bailey said.

Martinez slid a quick glance at Mary. "That's all right. I'm trying to cut back."

"I can just see the headlines now," Picard said. "'Sheikh Al-Jabeer Divorced.'" He was about to continue when Bailey interrupted.

"This will not be a circus on my watch. Princess Safi has legitimate complaints, and if we proceed by the book, we'll have a strong case. The press will certainly play up the story and, while it may be sensational, the princess must appear as the underdog in an overmatched contest. Mr. Al-Jabeer, by all accounts, is a billionaire several times over."

"Okay, Mr. Bailey," Mary said, rising. "Thank you so much for giving us your time."

"I'll be back in touch before the end of the week," he said. "Please give my regards to the General. How's his golf game these days?"

"Last I heard, still a ten stroke handicap."

"His biggest handicap is his temper," Bailey said, laughing.

"Tell me about it," Mary said with a smile.

EVERYONE met at the Foreign Legion Bar at seven in the evening on Saturday night April 24th, a mild and windless evening. Greco had agreed to join the party, to Taylor's delight, and Herman the German brought two friends, both black ex-football players. George Butterfield managed to get local radio's most attractive gay talk show host, Bret Hawthorne. He, in turn, invited a star female impersonator whose stage name, Sasha

Butkick, guaranteed notoriety. Sasha invited another impersonator who agreed to perform belly dances on board. The charge of electricity in the bar was beyond anything George had ever felt before.

The Arab costumes were wildly inventive. Herman the German arrived dressed as a Sheikh. His Bish, or robe, was made of white silk decorated with gold trim and rhinestones. His throb, or shirt-dress, was also trimmed in gold. He wore gold slippers, and his Ghutra was made of black and gold silk, instead of red and white cotton. A gold chain hugged his waist. Butterfield, dressed as an Arab slaver with a bullwhip, rushed over to him.

"Herman, you look gorgeous. I just adore your makeup." Then dropping his hand in front between them he said in a low sultry voice as he fondled him, "I see you have brought the Sultan's jewels with you." He laughed and dragged Herman along to join the others as they arrived.

"Sasha!" Butterfield screamed. "I can't wait to see what lurks beneath. C'mon now, open the robe."

Sasha spun around once, stopped, produced a royal bow, rose and opened his robe to reveal an exquisite belly dancing costume.

"A friend of mine at the San Francisco Opera arranged this little number, darling. I have another in my bag." Sasha wiggled his fingers in farewell and swept into the bar.

Greco, Bret and the two ex-football players were dressed a little less flamboyantly, and when everyone was gathered together at the bar, they gawked and touched with abandon. Taylor ordered drinks for everyone, and they toasted the evening they all so keenly anticipated.

"Cheers to our adventure," he shouted above the din, raising his glass. "Let us toast the magic carpet that will take us up into the sky towards an unknown destination." As everyone touched glasses and roared approval, a black stretch limousine pulled up to the curb.

"Girls, drink up, our chariot awaits." Draped in his gold robe, Taylor seemed to float out the door.

The Lincoln limousine could seat twelve, but with added luggage, it was full. Less than an hour later, it deposited them at San Francisco airport's domestic terminal. The guests themselves brought cameras, whose flashes partially obscured Mary's efforts to take pictures of the group. They boarded in a high state of excitement and whooped as they rushed through the aircraft's stunning appointments.

"This is my room," Taylor shouted at Greco as others whirled around.

"Let's not waste a bedroom. The three of us can use this one. We can switch around with the others later," George Butterfield yelled at one of the football players and at Sasha.

Picard rolled his eyes as the guests arrived giggling and gushing. Dressed in an AJ uniform, he looked the part of a most discreet steward. When everyone settled down, and before Martinez began his taxi to the runway, Picard gave the guests instructions on how to use the television sets in each room and how the porn videos were organized. He handed everyone menus and announced that dinner would be served in two hours.

Drink orders were taken. The 747 roared into the purple evening sky. Sasha began belly dancing in the aisles as everyone clapped. Arabic music played through the intercom and Picard could see that for his guests, this was truly a magical night. Between deliveries of drinks and appetizers, he sat with Martinez in the cockpit.

"You know, these guys are all right, really high spirited. Maybe a little flamboyant, but everyone is a gentleman. Well, not exactly, but you know what I mean."

"I was a little nervous about this party, but when they showed up as Arabs, I knew that Allah was on our side."

"Didn't you know they were going to wear Arab costumes?"

"Matt Taylor hinted at it," Martinez said, "and I gave him encouragement. But it was his idea, and it couldn't work better for us."

"You want something to eat, Jesus? I'm the chief cook, after all."

"And French. How can I refuse?"

MARTINEZ and Picard arrived at the hotel after the sin tour, exhausted but pleased with their work. After a nap, they met Safi and Mary at the hotel bar. Pierre described the trip in detail and he saved for last the video clip showing Taylor, Greco and Sasha discovering the cash.

"They squealed like teenage girls," Picard said. "Sasha danced on the bed and Greco threw piles of money at her."

"Him," Martinez corrected.

"Him, her—it's confusing. When the excitement cooled they realized most of the money was play money. I explained it was just a party trick but the real money was theirs and they could keep it and divide it. They were happy with that." He turned to Safi. "What a genius idea that was, the money thing."

She reached for his hand. "Just another way to stick it to

Dani," she said. "You see? I know my American vernacular."

"We cut the sound," Martinez added. "That way the viewer won't be able to tell if the guests spoke Arabic or not. Along with the costumes, what a break that was. I think this is a pretty convincing tape."

"When are we meeting with him again?" Mary asked.

"Right after the swap with Al-Jabeer."

"So everything went really smoothly?" Safi asked.

"To be honest," Picard said, "I expected the worst kind of behavior, but they were really decent and appreciative. Maybe it was because they were away from an audience and could be themselves. I even got propositioned a couple of times myself."

Safi frowned. "No more sin tours for you."

"And were you propositioned?" Mary asked Martinez.

"Never left the cockpit."

They chatted for a while longer before Mary brought up the problem that had been bothering her all evening: the telephone call from David Sassoon.

Chapter Twenty Two

BACKTRACKING to the Jeddah Sheraton for clues that might have been missed, David Sassoon followed a hunch. He demanded, and quickly received, a list of people that had checked out of the hotel on the day the 747 disappeared from Jeddah. He was not surprised to learn that a Captain Jesus Martinez, the man who flew the plane out of Jeddah, and a Major Mary Jane, also a pilot, had had adjoining rooms. Neither checked out on that day, but housekeeping confirmed that there was no one in the rooms after that time. The airport security people counted four people in the escape party and Sassoon felt he knew three—the fourth was of no particular importance. It didn't take long to discover Mary Jane's history in the US Air Force and that her father, Charles Jane, was an Air Force General. Sassoon did his best to obtain photographs of Martinez and Mary Jane, without success. There were news articles in Arabia regarding Jane, but no pictures. Finally, the $1,000,000 check made out to Mary

Jane made sense. Finding out where General Jane was stationed was not difficult, and two days later, Sassoon was in California and dialing a telephone number in San Francisco.

"General Jane," he said after half an hour's wait. "Thank you for taking my call. My name is David Sassoon and I'm a friend of your daughter. We met in Jeddah and I promised to be in touch with her when she arrived in America, but I've lost her phone number. I felt that perhaps you might have it."

Charles Jane had little knowledge of his daughter's recent activities. She had mentioned that she was on a clandestine mission with a Boeing 747 but he knew nothing beyond that. The General was a suspicious man by nature and he was suddenly alert to danger. "How did you get my number, Mr. Sassoon?" he asked. "It's not listed anywhere and I'm very careful about giving it out."

"Mary mentioned that you live in San Francisco. With a little help from U.S. intelligence, it wasn't difficult."

"You seem to be going to a lot of trouble for a social call," Jane said.

"I told Mary I'd be in touch."

"I'll tell you what. Give me your number. If I hear from her, I'll let her know you want to reach her."

General Jane jotted down the telephone number and noticed that it was a Bay Area exchange. Immediately after hanging up, he telephoned the Hilton Hotel and Mary answered.

"Somebody's looking for you, Mary. Oily voice—Middle Eastern. I don't think he wishes you well. Be careful."

"Did he give you his name?"

"David Sassoon. He left his number and it's a local one. Do you know who he is?"

"I think so."

"Dangerous?"

"Yes, I think so."

"Well, let me know if I can be of any help."

"I will, Dad, and thanks."

"I mean it about the help."

"I know you do."

She sensed his hesitation. "Don't take this as a criticism, Mary, but you're very independent."

"I learned that from you," she said.

"Yes, I know, but sometimes we need help. I just want you to know I'm here for you."

She smiled as she said goodbye and slowly, softly hung up the telephone.

MARY said to the others, "I didn't want to alarm my father by telling him too much. This Sassoon guy can present big problems. What do you know about him, Safi?"

"He is Dani's top security guy. Anything that needs to be done, Sassoon is the man. He lives in Lebanon. He's very, very rich and well connected. I believe he and Dani have interlinking businesses, but Dani is clearly the leader of the two."

"Why do you think he gave his real name?" Mary said. "An alias would make more sense."

Safi shook her head. "He wants to scare you."

"Do you know Sassoon?" Martinez asked Safi.

"No, we've never met."

"Do you know what he looks like?"

"I'm afraid I don't," she said.

"I'm also surprised he used his real name."

"Pride, hubris," Safi said. "And as I said, he thinks he'll scare you. That's the way these people are."

"His being here adds an element of risk," Mary said. "Even so, I still think we should move ahead with our plan."

Martinez agreed, but he was worried. It was clear that Al-Jabeer did not intend to let Safi dictate terms to him. His people had been quick to find them, far too quick.

"I'm amazed they've been able to trace us here," he said. "Maybe someone at the Sheraton recognized us leaving. That's not good."

"Mary did make a fuss at the airport in Jeddah," Picard said. "Maybe someone passed the word to Sassoon. So, let's assume they may know what you and Mary look like. Maybe you both need disguises, at least on the day of the exchange."

Martinez took a sip of his drink without speaking. "Let's not treat this as some kind of high school play. These guys are professional and they may be armed. In fact, I'm certain they will be, if for no other reason than to protect the cash they're carrying. But they're also businessmen. We mustn't lose sight of that." He paused, put his glass down and looked at Mary thoughtfully.

"We've discussed disguising ourselves, impersonating cops to intimidate Al-Jabeer if he tries to double-cross us. But the more I think about this stuff, the less it makes sense." He paused and studied the other three.

"Here's what I'm thinking. It's just a suggestion," his eyes fastened on to Mary's, "but hear me out. We can use the same security firm Global uses when they repossess a plane. Taylor has told us about them. Let them arrange for uniformed security guards to be on the tarmac in San Francisco, give them clear instructions about the exchange, and let them handle the cash using Brinks or the same security agency to deliver it to us later. Forget makeovers, hiring a detective, all this cloak and dagger stuff. If it turns out Al-Jabeer tries to screw us, we can simply fly the 747 back to Santa Rosa. But if it turns out he's being straight, then we get the money and he gets the plane. It's as simple as that, the way I see it."

There was a long pause. Mary frowned and twisted her hair.

"I thought our plan had a lot of merit." She turned to Picard. "What's your feeling?"

"I think what Jesus says makes sense. We may be out-smarting ourselves."

"Safi?"

"I know so little about this kind of thing. I'm inclined to go along with the more conservative plan."

"Mary, we don't want to make a circus out of this." Martinez leaned forward and made chopping motions with his right hand, a habit of his when he was agitated. "We need to keep it simple. With the uniforms, makeup, wigs and blue lights we risk being stopped by airport security, especially since it's on a constant yellow alert."

"Part of me wants Dani to screw up." Safi sipped her beer and crossed her legs. "The plane would be a nice asset to have, especially with the remaining BMW, wouldn't it? Dani can contest the legal ownership all he wants but in the meantime, we could travel in style."

"I'm not looking for a screw up," Martinez said. "They have a way of backfiring. Let's hope it's a simple transaction."

"I was only fantasizing, Jesus."

"I figured that."

"But I do want to be at the airport with Pierre," Safi said. "We'll have our cell phone with us. When we see Dani and his pilot, if they appear to be double crossing us in some way, I'll hit the automatic dial button and you can speed off with the 747. In fact, I might even page David Sassoon at the airport, just to see if he is there. I just don't have any trust, Jesus."

"Nobody can blame you for that." Martinez expelled a deep sigh. "It's hard to believe that a couple of months ago, I was moping around in Jeddah wondering if the Saudis would chop off my head or stone me to death. And then along came Mary." He grinned and winked at her.

"I think you were a very lucky man," Picard said.

Mary gave a thumbs-up. "You tell him, Pierre. He's like most men—he needs to be told things again and again before they sink in."

"Jeddah seems like years ago," Martinez went on. "And now look at us. Up to our necks in international intrigue."

"And rich," Mary said. "Don't forget rich."

He nodded. "So I guess all things considered, I'm glad you came along when you did."

Mary smiled at Safi. "He's finally beginning to understand, isn't he?"

"It seems so."

"You know what I think we should do?" Martinez said. "Let's go to North Beach tonight and eat a good Italian meal." He grinned. "And nobody better call it a Last Supper."

Chapter Twenty Three

EARLY spring winds blew through the Golden Gate, and as Martinez looked down from the cockpit over Alcatraz Island, he could see white caps on the bay flowing southwest toward the East Bay. Along the Marina Green in San Francisco, hundreds of kites pirouetted in the sky. The San Francisco airport tower cleared the 747 to land, instructing it south toward San Jose before making a right turn onto the north-bearing glide path and runway. He sang deliberately in an attempt to stifle thoughts of bad things happening in the next few hours. He didn't stop singing until the landing gear lowered. He approached the runway apron with another aircraft on his left wing, an Airbus, making a simultaneous landing. He pulled up to the domestic terminal, a metal staircase rolled up to the fuselage, and he opened the cabin door behind the cockpit. Two of the four security guards boarded, while the others waited on the tarmac with a Brinks armored truck and three armed guards.

The domestic terminal was two stories high with the ground level emptying onto the tarmac. Inside, on the second level, Mary and Safi could see Al-Jabeer enter the terminal from a distance. He was with two men, whom they assumed were his pilots. One of the men pulled a large suitcase on wheels toward the escalator that would lead them to the tarmac.

"Safi, time to put the call through to see if we have company," Mary said.

She did, and within a minute the terminal paging system barked, "Mr. David Sassoon, White Courtesy telephone please." The message was repeated twice and Mary and Safi watched the terminal for signs of attention. A small man in a dark suit lowered his newspaper and scanned the crowd before rising. He exchanged glances with another larger man drinking coffee from a paper cup, then walked casually to the White Courtesy telephone and was put through to the caller.

"Who am I speaking to?" a low voice asked, soft in timbre and clearly Arabic.

There was a moment's silence before Safi spoke. "David Sassoon, I have never met you, but I know who you are and that you're in the terminal with others. I am Safi Al-Jabeer and I'm calling to let you know there's a small package for you at the Continental Airlines luggage storage center. It's a video that you and Dani will find interesting. I'm sure the Saudi authorities will find it interesting, too. Don't bother to make mischief on the tarmac, unless you want that video delivered. As you can see from the window, there are a number of guards greeting the arrival of the 747, so your chances of cheating me are non-existent."

She hung up and watched as Sassoon continued to talk demandingly into the telephone, gesticulating wildly with his free hand. A moment later, he slammed the phone into its cradle, raced toward the terminal's window and stared down at the tarmac. Mary could see his lips forming the word "shit," before he ran down the escalator. They watched as he reached the apron in front of the 747 and was restrained by a guard from approaching the aircraft.

"He is one pissed-off Arab," Mary said. "Keep an eye on the one drinking coffee. I'm going down to the plane. Dial my cell phone number now, so you have it on automatic redial. If that guy approaches you, call me and then start screaming, okay?"

Safi sat alone clutching her cell phone, feeling a mixture of excitement and fear. A woman in a black burqua entered the terminal, looking from side to side as she walked toward the ticket counter. Safi felt instant sympathy for the poor soul trapped in that god-awful bag. She turned to her with a smile, as the woman suddenly veered off and sat down next to her. She was about to say something in Arabic to greet her, but her thoughts froze when a man's voice came from behind the veil.

"Princess Safi, I am David Sassoon. What you are feeling in your ribs is my stiletto, and I have instructions to use it if you refuse to cooperate. I will cut out your heart. Dani has asked me to deliver it to him personally if you cause trouble."

"I thought you just went downstairs. I was just talking to you on the telephone…"

"You are all amateurs. Now listen very carefully. You and I are going for a little walk down toward the 747. But first, you are going to put this burqua on."

He reached under his robe and produced a black burqua. Safi stared at it, not knowing what to do. She glanced around quickly. There was no one to reach out to, even though the terminal was bustling with people, she had never felt more alone.

"Quickly now, Safi, put it on," Sassoon ordered. "Don't make me cut you."

"Where are we going?" she asked, her voice breaking with tension.

"Why, back to Jeddah, of course. Did you believe for a moment that Dani Al-Jabeer would permit you to live in America? Just as soon as the exchange is completed and the guards and Brinks people leave, we will simply board the 747 and fly away."

Safi put the burqua on and flinched when Sassoon gripped her elbow. His small hands were powerful. He took the cane from her and left it on the seat. The cane would make it too easy to identify her. She could feel the knifepoint just below her ribs, as he began to guide her toward the ramp that led down to the gate.

MARTINEZ cut the engines and stepped down from the aircraft. He spotted one of the pilots in an AJ uniform being held at bay by the security guards. He walked toward Al-Jabeer, trying to make eye contact. He could see that the man was uncomfortable.

"Sorry about the reception committee, Mr. Al-Jabeer," Martinez said, as he stood before him. "We were informed that a David Sassoon, and some others, were going to be at this terminal. Our guess is they intended to kidnap your wife and bring her back to Arabia with you on the 747. Maybe true, maybe not. I really hope not. Just looking at you I'd say you're an honorable man."

Al-Jabeer was both subtle and clever. He knew that his

face was being rubbed into it, but he hadn't become a success without a profound understanding of human nature. Dressed in his Armani suit, he looked like a visiting dignitary. Without missing a beat, he responded with a smile.

"Ah, so you must be Captain Martinez. Let me first say that I have to admire your ingenuity and courage. After this is all over, I'd like to think we could do business together."

This guy is fast on his feet, Martinez thought. He never expected to see a small army greeting him at the airport, and he's not showing me a thing—not a trace of nervousness.

"I've heard a good deal about you, Mr. Al-Jabeer, and I'm sure you're a man of your word. As you can see, I've arranged for an armored car to take delivery of the money. I would appreciate it if you'd enter the aircraft with the suitcase, the guards will count the money. Once that's done, I'll turn over the 747 to you or one of your pilots. Whatever you decide."

Martinez watched Al-Jabeer's eyes harden. They burned cobalt blue, a blue so deep, they bordered on black.

"You seem to have thought of everything, Captain. My pilot will take the suitcase aboard and make the transfer. If you don't mind, I'll just wait here until that business is done. I had hoped to see my wife, but she doesn't seem to be here."

He's given up on trying to open that secret compartment to check on his cash and gold, Martinez thought. The security guards make that impossible, so he's grandstanding.

"Unfortunately, your wife is not available," he said. "But she does know that you're here and she sends her regards."

Al-Jabeer's eyebrows rose slightly with that remark. "Yes, well, that is how things are at the moment. Perhaps another time." He motioned to his pilot to take the suitcase into the aircraft.

Nearly an hour passed before the counting was completed and the Brinks guards emerged from the plane. They handed Martinez a receipt for the money. The armored truck door slammed shut and drove off. Of the four security guards, two remained with the aircraft until its doors closed and its engines began to turn. The other two accompanied Martinez as he walked to the airport lounge to pick up Mary.

Picard, who had been shadowing the man he thought was David Sassoon from the moment he took the White Courtesy call, stayed close to him until he left the second floor and headed toward the lower level. He then hurried to the tarmac where the 747 stood idling. A process server placed a divorce complaint into Al-Jabeer's hand, just as he was about to board the plane. Picard watched as the fuselage door closed, and then opened again, which struck him as strange. He turned and saw whom he thought was David Sassoon with two women wearing burquas hurrying toward the plane. Martinez and Mary were back at the gate and Picard decided to join them there, but something was bothering him. Something was not right. He rushed back to the lounge, hoping to find Safi there, but dreading that she would be gone. Her cane was on a chair, but she was no longer there.

Kidnapped, he thought, while I'm stupidly following a decoy!

He grabbed the cane and ran toward the gate. "What's going on?" Martinez yelled.

"I think Safi just boarded the plane," Picard yelled back, fighting for breath. "We've got to stop it from taking off."

The 747 had already backed away from the gate and had been released from the tow car. It began making a turn toward the runway. Martinez reached into the bag, which he had just taken off the 747, pulled out his .45 pistol, and raced onto the tarmac. Mary was running just behind him with Safi's cane in her hand. Without a word between them, they both knew they had to puncture a tire or shoot out an engine.

Maybe a few shots at the intake fan will do it, Martinez thought. When he saw Mary running for the starboard wheels, he knew that was the only rational target. There was not enough time to get in front of an engine air intake.

"Mary!" he yelled. "The cane won't puncture those tires—thread it through the hydraulics. It might stop the wheels from rising."

Mary moved in that direction. Before she could get near enough, Martinez took careful aim at four tires on the right wheel pod and fired nine shots. He prayed to God they would find their mark, but to his dismay the 747 continued to turn. Mary sprinted forward and thrust the ebony cane into the struts, but the slender cane was no match for the landing machinery. She looked desperately at Martinez as the plane began its taxi.

Both stood frozen, out of options and praying for the sound of nitrogen hissing from the tires. The aircraft pulled away. Then, it happened. The right wing dipped slightly and they could see rubber coming away from the wheel pod.

"We got it, goddamn, we got it!" Mary shouted.

"Go back to the gate," Martinez screamed at her over the roar of the engines. "Get those guards up here or anyone else you can find." She nodded and ran off, her hair streaming behind her like a flame.

Martinez stood for a moment, then calmly walked up to the disabled aircraft and began banging on the underside of the lowered wing with his now empty pistol. Meanwhile, Picard, watching from the gate ramp, understood immediately what was going on and reached for a White Courtesy telephone.

"The 747 that is just leaving the private terminal," he said, anxiety thickening his French accent. "There's a kidnap victim on board. Please notify security. I'm at gate 7-A. Domestic terminal. Please hurry!"

Inside the aircraft, Al-Jabeer held Safi's arm in a vice-like grip. "You are now where you properly belong, my dear, with your husband. America was a great mistake. You should never have left Pakistan for America. It corrupted you. It ruined you. Our son would have been born whole if you had remained whole, a true woman in all senses of the word. But no, you had to be the American bitch, didn't you? Spoiled, completely caught up in material things. You began to think that you're better than a man." He spit the words out. "Enjoy this flight on, what did you call it?—this flying whorehouse. When we return, life is going to be very, very different for you."

Safi, still in her burqua, turned to him and touched his sleeve. "Dani, you don't want me. You don't love me, and I'm not sure you ever did. Take the plane and let me go. I'm no good for you. You can have any woman you want—someone who will make you happy, give you sons."

"You will give me sons," he said. "But first, we will fix your mind."

"You know you can't get away with kidnapping me. If something happens to me, the world will know."

He laughed and was about to say something, when he felt the aircraft dip sharply to the right.

"What the fuck was that?" he yelled at the pilot.

"Something's wrong with our landing gear."

"Get it fixed."

"I can't. One set of wheels isn't moving. The instruments say they're blown."

"Forget about your instruments. Get this goddamn thing in the air. I'm ordering you!" Al-Jabeer stopped his raving when he heard a loud metallic banging on the side of the plane.

"What's that?" he demanded, his eyes darting around wildly.

"It seems to be coming from the fuel pump under the wing. I can't be sure," the pilot said.

Al-Jabeer peered through the window at the runway. He could clearly see that the 747 listed to the right. Instinctively, he knew that the problem was more serious than simple mechanical failure. He had to get himself and Safi off the plane. In the distance, he could see the flicker of blue lights speeding in their direction.

"Lower the boarding steps, goddamn it, *lower them*," he screamed at David Sassoon. "We've got to get out of here." Sassoon leaped up and pulled the emergency door lever. Automatically, a yellow evacuation chute deployed downward toward the tarmac.

"Quick, everybody, jump," he yelled over the engine noise rushing through the open door.

Al-Jabeer grabbed Safi and hurtled her out of the aircraft. He then jumped behind her, followed by Sassoon. When they hit the tarmac, Al-Jabeer dragged Safi along toward a different gate, which at the moment was deserted.

Blue flashing lights suddenly created a cordon around them. Police, with guns drawn, approached them on the tarmac.

Safi instantly yanked off her burqua and pulled away from Al-Jabeer. He stood perfectly still and slowly raised his hands.

The police escorted them into the terminal, where they also had Martinez in handcuffs. They had caught him banging on the airplane with his pistol, an act of seemingly senseless vandalism, which needed a better explanation than he had yet been able to provide.

After three hours of questioning, Al-Jabeer and Sassoon were taken into custody and charged with suspicion of kidnapping. Martinez was finally released. The 747 was steered into a hangar, its rightful ownership to be argued in court on another day.

THE van moved slowly north through the traffic along Highway 101 that led back into San Francisco, its occupants quiet and subdued, each wrapped in silence until they had passed the San Bruno exit. Safi was the first to speak.

"What now?" she said, as she stared out of the window, watching the low flying gulls skim the shoreline.

"I think it's time to breathe a long sigh of relief," Mary replied without turning her head to look back at Safi. "I know I need a few days to just gather myself."

"I'm sure we all do," Picard said.

"We took so many risks," Mary said. "And we did a lot of learning on the job. We did some things that were pretty amateurish and got away with them. I feel we were more lucky than smart. What do you think, Jesus?"

"Definitely more lucky than smart," he said. "There are no schools offering graduate degrees in aircraft repossession. We made it up as we went along. All in all, we didn't do badly."

"We all made a hell of a lot of money," Picard said. He turned to Safi and covered her hand with his. "And we made some very good friends."

She smiled and slowly nodded in agreement.

"So to repeat Safi's question, what now?" Mary said. She turned to Martinez. "First of all, we're going to use our newly acquired skills and go after that Falcon 900 for Global."

"Newly acquired skills?"

"Yes, Captain. And what are you thinking in that strange mind of yours?"

"Before I can think two days ahead, I need some serious R and R."

"Anything special in mind?" Picard asked.

"Yes." Martinez turned a solemn face to Mary. "I was thinking of Istanbul."

"Istanbul?" She stared hard at him, trying to read his thoughts. "Are you joking?"

"It's been a while," he said. "I'd like to see how much it's changed since I was there last." He broke into a slow grin. "Would you like to come along, Mary?"

Praise for Plane Jane

Readers will hope this becomes a many-edition series with the redheaded hotty, Air Force Major Mary Jane...compelling story... interesting and detailed preparation...sinks us right into a tale we won't want to leave.

Colleen O'Brien
Columnist and editor

Compelling reading, well described fast moving adventure.

Mary Lou Gallagher
Beyond & Above Corporate Flight Attendant Training Inc.

Extremely well-written...moves at a fast pace all the way to the climatic ending...Fischer...breathes life into each character through detailed description and realistic dialog.

Bettie Corbin Tucker
Independent Professional Reviewer

Fresh addition to aviation-themed literature...suave, jaunty tone... reminiscent of some of my favorite Ian Fleming novels, moving quickly through a chain of twists and turns but remaining intelligent and surprisingly relevant.

Richard Porter
The Atlantic Monthly Flyer newspaper

I have read many aviation themed books and *Plane Jane* is by far the best. This is an adventure tale I won't soon forget.

Jarkko Haarala
Planegrazy, flying news publisher

Fischer's writing is not cookie cutter prose, but instead almost three dimensional. I would recommend this novel to anyone who enjoys a good aviation novel.

Henry Holden
Blackhawk Publishing and Women in Aviation